Mark of Silence and Secrets

Jacyn Gormish

Winnipeg, Canada

Developmental editor: Craig Gibb
Proofreader: Sanford Larson

Published July 2024 by Deep Hearts YA.

Deep Hearts YA
PO Box 51053 Tyndall Park
Winnipeg, Manitoba R2X 3B0
Canada

Visit deepheartsya.com for more great reads.

Mark of Silence
and Secrets

Chapter One

Cassava's feet hit the cobblestone road with tempered impatience. Her current target had been elusive, jumping from island to island, and seemed to have no home base. Cassava had been tracking her down for three miserable days. Monsoon season had hit the islands and everyone was hunkering down. Everyone but Cassava. Her clothes were soaked and hung heavy on her body, stretching from the weight of the water alone. Every time Cassava pulled back her hood to get a better look down a narrow alley she was greeted with a torrent of rain down her back.

Cassava took a moment under a stoop to wring out her long black hair. It was only getting in the way like this, so she took a moment despite the freeze to her fingers to braid it up clumsily. She quickly shoved her fingers back into her pockets for some warmth. She was getting annoyed, and that made her stupid. Her father had always said she needed to slow down and breathe. Perhaps this once he was right.

Her target was untethered, unlike most—no job, no home, no friends. There were plenty of places her target could be that she couldn't go, especially in weather like this.

Everyone with any sense was wrapped up warm at home. So where did the homeless go?

Cassava played out the map in her head. This was much more Arabast's area of expertise. But this was not their job. Cassava tried to remember when they had been searching for a home for Ferran, knowing there had been a few areas they'd considered. It would give her somewhere to start at least, and give Cassava a break from the rain.

She turned on her heel and darted down the street, her soft breeches hanging slightly. It was always hard to find good clothes. She knew she could order them from any tailor in the isles, but Cassava disliked the upturn of the face, the fright in the eyes, and the wretched obedience of the shopkeeper. A life of paying for things had made her quite uncomfortable expecting people simply to do for her what she willed, but it wasn't as if Cassava made money. She was exacting her price for her service: to ensure all the dark pieces of the world were hidden away from innocent, clean citizens. Cassava had once been one of them: blissfully ignorant, content with shadowed beings occasionally passing through her life—a fearsome nightmare that kept the rest at bay. Now, Cassava was every child's boogeyman.

Cassava turned down another street, running into the wind. She put her hand to her face to shield it, and felt the raised bumps of her brand across her temple The new marks had mellowed now, a soft pink instead of a raging red. Cassava still knew she would never be pretty again. But Sins didn't need beauty, no matter what Cassava's lingering vanity said.

Cassava tried the old warehouse door. Locked. She

opened her pack of tools against the rain and slipped out her kit. This wasn't a fancy lock, and a simple nudge in the right spot slipped the door open. Just another skill Cassava had picked up since her life had completely turned over.

Despite the howl of the wind, Cassava took care to edge it open gently. She held it firmly as she stepped inside and immediately her senses were assaulted by the permeable smell of malting liquor.

The relief of being out of the rough weather was immediate. Cassava threw back her hood and shook the water from her cloak with a quiet joy. Her head pounded down on her already; she didn't need the weather to do it too.

Cassava looked around the large warehouse. Huge casks of soon-to-be-ale were sitting upright in rows, a few stacked precariously on top of one another. Cassava shook her cloak from her shoulders and threw it over one of the barrels. It wasn't the best hideout, but it was quiet and barren and didn't have many people coming through on a regular basis. It wasn't too far from the markets and foot traffic was frequent enough it wasn't strange for someone to be walking down this street. Perfectly unremarkable

Her shoes squelched slightly, the worn leather pressing in against the heel of her sock. Cassava took a slow, deep, silent breath and pressed on. Nothing particularly seemed awry, but if she was going to stay a while, she should at least have a proper look.

As she passed the second-to-last row, Cassava spotted a splash of red between the dark brown barrels and the off-white stone floor. Red, an uncommon color on the Islands, was almost certainly a foreigner. Her target. Cassava put her hand to her side where her knife was. Cassava was still far from a pro with blades, but usually brandishing one was enough to make someone do something stupid like try to run. Everyone was already afraid of her; she didn't need to carry weapons for protection. No one dared touch a Sin.

Cassava approached silently, with only the occasional drip from her spoiled clothing giving her away. Cassava heard each little plink as it hit the stone, but she doubted her quarry would notice. She slowed further as the red began to clarify into an abandoned garment. Cassava crept farther forward. In the space between the barrels was a small pile of clothing, an assortment of foods, and a candlestick. She bent forward and pawed through the clothes, looking for some other hint of the owner. Whoever this belonged to was either extremely stupid to be out in this weather, or had been driven by some greater need. Cassava went to straighten up when suddenly a weight dropped onto her back.

Cassava had her dagger in hand in an instant, turning and swiping. Cassava didn't fight hard, she fought smart, and she knew all she had to do was make contact.

The weight jumped back, and Cassava spun on her heel, searching. There in the dim light was an enigma. The girl was likely Cassava's age. Her hair was cut short and stringy, but most notably it was a shocking yellow color. Her skin was pale; not the pure white of the Chajian traders, but still pale and nearly pink. Silver hung from her ear and nose, a simple but effective marking. There was no doubt this was her target—how many young Belish Trikingese were wandering warehouses during monsoon season? Any trader worth their salt was in a safer harbor.

Cassava never spoke to her victims. It made things easier. But something in the piercing green of her eyes made Cassava stop. They stood facing each other silently for several seconds. Without meaning to, Cassava noted the gentle crest of her breast, the lick of her collar bone that poked out from her tattered clothing. Exotic. Beautiful. And, Cassava reminded herself sternly, soon to be dead.

"You're a fucking child," the girl said.

Cassava steeled her gaze and adjusted her grip on her knife. "Do you know who I am?"

"I'd heard about the Black Sins but, falls, fucking children? You're part of a corrupt system."

Cassava stared, uncomprehending.

The girl continued prattling, apparently severely unaware of her impending doom. "It's not your fault I suppose, but, really, how do people fall for this shit? It's laughable, really."

"You know I'm here to kill you."

"And I was all prepared to kill *you*, but you're so fucking young."

"And how old are you?" Cassava demanded, smarting.

"Sixteen."

Cassava stared at her again. She was tall, and built a little like a stalk of wheat. Cassava had more substance to her, despite being her junior by a year.

"My name's Nimmory, but my friends call me Nim."

This was more familiar territory to Cassava, but she usually didn't let them get this far. And she usually knew names already. "You're not going to convince me not to kill you, so if you want to speed through the saga to the begging for your life part, that's fine. I don't need a life story."

Nimmory put her hands up. "I'm not begging for my life. Unnecessary. I'm just trying to get a sense of *you*. Usually when someone introduces themselves, it's reciprocated. At least where I'm from."

Cassava's patience at this curiosity was waning. No one was supposed to want to know about her. "You're clearly not from around here. Everyone knows not to talk to Sins."

"Yeah, that just seems rude to me, but, if you insist, we can dispense with the pleasantries."

Cassava inclined her head. "Best of luck in the next life," she said, a blessing she did not usually bestow on her victims. Most of them were much easier to hate. What had this young, bright, friendly girl done that had sentenced her to die? But Cassava didn't pass judgment. She just delivered it.

Cassava lunged forward, but as she did so a great force seemed to bellow up from the space between the barrels. Somewhere, Cassava heard the bang of a door pressed in against a lively wind.

She tried to move again, but the air between her and Nimmory was now thick and heavy and it felt like she was moving through molasses.

Cassava stared at Nimmory who was still standing a scant few feet away. As Cassava watched, she saw Nimmory holding her hand out.

Cassava couldn't understand the sudden pressure she was under. She moved sideways, finding it less difficult, as though she had turned away from the eye of the storm. But as she moved, she saw Nimmory's hand quake, and the force surrounded her again.

"I'd love to stay and chat, but, unfortunately, I can't do this all day," Nimmory said. Her hand moved in an arc, and as it did so Cassava felt a rush of wind stronger than she had ever felt crash into her body. She was blown sideways, up a couple feet, and sailed into a double-stacked barrel. Cassava tried to move her hands to brace against the collision, but it was nearly impossible to move. Her head knocked hard against the wood and everything went black.

Chapter Two

Her head was throbbing. Cassava opened her eyes and blinked gingerly into the light, or the dark rather. The storm outside had eased some; Cassava heard the gentle patter of rain rather than the slap of each drop vicious on the pavement. Cassava groaned. She had been hurt before but the throbbing inside her head was new. She had previously sustained damage to her head, but only surface level. She felt the raised scars on her face as she sat up slowly, regaining her bearings.

The warehouse was deserted. While before items had lain scattered across the ground, now the stonework was bare—all except for a small mango that sat mere feet away from Cassava. She felt like the mellow, cheery yellow skin was mocking her. Cassava groaned again, resting her throbbing head on her knees. Cassava muttered a curse under her breath.

Cassava had never been defeated before. She'd always completed her mission. She had worked carefully with her blades, she knew how to throw them, how to skim the surface. She was used to watching people writhe and waste away before her. She didn't get beat. She didn't let her victims get away. She was a Black Sin.

People had tried to fight her before; most did not do well. The girl had caught her off guard and could have pressed the advantage—she might have even succeeded. Cassava was too used to being the hunter. She didn't know how to handle having it turned around on her.

But she hadn't—not really. Cassava hadn't seen that she had a weapon of any kind. She had jumped her, but without a weapon she was really doomed. Cassava had been in that situation in training before. It was really best to just run. But the girl hadn't run, and Cassava had ended up on the ground alone in some warehouse. How?

Cassava's mind was rejecting her memories. The wind had been strong—it had blown the door off its hinge. She stood up now and saw that was still the case. Dirt too had flown in, fast and furious, and a new coating of mud covered much of the stone. Had she gotten caught in some kind of wind tunnel? Had she been standing in just the wrong spot? Was such a thing even possible?

But it seemed more probable than the alternative. Cassava had seen the look in Nimmory's eye, the way her hand had seemed to move in time, her full confidence that she would make it out of the situation unscathed.

Cassava felt sick. She just needed to lie down, rest a little, and then maybe things would make sense. She gathered her cloak and threw it over her shoulders. There was nothing to do about the door; the hinges had been pulled out as though torn by a hammer from wood. Well, if the owner complained, the Priests would make amends. Cassava wasn't responsible for the damage of her tasks.

She felt uneasy walking back and kept her hood down just to watch the look in people's eyes as they saw her face, registered fear, and turned away, scampering head down. Cassava was the predator and them the prey. Everything was just as it should be.

Except Nimmory was out there somewhere, wandering free. What should she do? Admit to the Priests that their carefully chosen tool had failed? Or lie, let her go, and risk being caught a liar? Cassava's head hurt too much to think about this now. Abruptly, she decided she didn't want to deal with the Priests. She turned down toward the outskirts of town, walking quickly and still feeling somewhat ill.

It had been a while since she'd visited Ferran. When she had the time to feel guilty about it, she did, but the Priesthood kept her busy and would notice if she spent too much time away. After a mission was her favorite time to visit. Ferran always had such a gentle, tender nature that made her relax even after she'd been amped up by a mission.

Ferran lived in an apparently abandoned house with a private wharf several miles outside the city proper. Henequen had arranged with one of his many contacts for the property; they thought it was a lease to the Asylum, but Henequen hadn't mentioned the acquisition to the Priests. It was a neat little trick which meant Ferran could live undisturbed, with Cassava or Henequen delivering food periodically. It wasn't a perfect system, but it was far preferable to Ferran being dead. For all intents and purposes, to the world he was. He had died shortly before his execution. His crime? Being born to those like Cassava—a Sin.

Cassava settled into a run once she had reached the outskirts. The mud made it difficult to go too quickly on the road, and she found herself trampling over the grasses where the roots held the ground together through the saturation. Cassava hated monsoon season for this reason. Any time she couldn't run, she felt pieces of her brain slipping. And if they slipped too far, she didn't know how to bring it back.

It was nearing full dark by the time Cassava reached Ferran's homestead. The worn-down cottage was tucked away behind banana trees and large green bushes with leaves taller than Cassava. She checked behind her out of habit as she approached, but with the rain still coming down and being so far out it was highly unlikely anyone would be around. Still, Cassava was a character that garnered significant attention when she didn't disguise herself.

Cassava knocked on the door—the brief one-two they had developed just in case some wanderer came through. It wasn't long before the door opened to reveal a slightly shorter teenage boy with long black hair. He was paler than Cassava by a few shades, but still distinctly Meinish. He was getting darker, now that he was actually able to spend time in the sun.

His face broke into a broad unguarded smile. Most things about Ferran were just the way they seemed; he didn't have a deceptive bone in his body unless it involved saving someone's life. "Barli!" He waved her in. "You look terrible."

Cassava normally found his lack of social skills somewhat endearing, but at the moment it beat down onto her already injured pride. "That's not how you're supposed to greet a guest," she said snappishly. "Try, 'oh, Cassava, what a lovely shirt.'" Cassava, not Barli. Barli was the name she'd left behind when she'd made her first kill. There had been many since then, and she no longer always felt comfortable with the relative innocence and purposelessness she'd had at that time.

"It's not though."

"That's not the point."

"So what—"

"Ferran, I didn't come here to argue with you."

Ferran closed the door gently. "I don't want to argue."

"Then maybe you should just stop talking!" Cassava exclaimed. Her headache had built steadily on the way here and the nausea was worse.

Ferran collected Magi, the small black cat they had rescued together, and disappeared into another room without a word. Cassava sighed heavily and sank onto the threadbare couch, head pounding. She threw her arm over her eyes and sank into the darkness. She just needed to sleep, then everything would be better.

Cassava's mind did not want to settle. She felt her body start to relax, and then suddenly she felt as though a great force was constricting her, keeping her from moving, and all the tension came rushing back. Her eyes were heavy and she reveled in the darkness, but it wouldn't stay put. Cassava kept having vivid images of Nimmory, her strange yellow hair, her bright green eyes, and her hand above her breast, turning slowly. The image felt frozen in her mind, and when she stopped trying to deny it and really looked, she became more and more convinced that there had been concentration and purpose in Nimmory's eyes, and coordinated movement from her hand.

Deeply rattled, Cassava took a breath and waited an appropriate amount of time before calling out to her host. "Ferran!"

She heard a small shuffling. "Cooled down a bit? Going to tell me what you're actually mad about?"

Cassava's face flushed and she was glad her arm was mostly covering her face and she didn't need to look at him. "Sorry."

Ferran settled on the couch by her feet, and she curled slightly to give him room. Small paws wandered out onto her lower leg, seeking a new perch. "What's going on?"

"Do you—do you think magic might be real?" she asked in a rush.

There was only a moment of silence before Ferran replied. "Of course," he said, with confidence Cassava rarely heard from him. "Magic is one of the historically worst manifestations of the demon."

"What?" Cassava said, utterly floored.

"Didn't you ever go to school? Magic is the seeping of the demon's evil powers into the hands of mortals. They can't contain it. Anyone with magic is extremely dangerous and must be killed."

Cassava thought back to her schooling in the Priests' hot room where they had learned letters and sums and about the demon. She recalled now that they taught long ago the demon was stronger and more concentrated, there were people who communed with the demon and tried to gain enough of the demon to tap into magical powers. Cassava had always discounted it as fantastic fiction, and as such had forgotten all about it. Ferran, who had grown up with no other matters to consume himself with, clearly remembered. "But that was supposed to be ages ago, wasn't it?" Cassava couldn't remember the details.

Ferran took Magi back into his arms, and she heard a soft purr as the cat relaxed. "Yes. The priest Henon communed with the Angel and discovered a way to silence the demon. And since that day, the demon has not spoken but continues to express itself through breaking people." Ferran spoke as though reciting from a book, and Cassava had no doubt he was.

Cassava took this information in and spun it around her mind. Her head was still hurting and the whole topic, the endorsement of this possibility, was staggering. "I think the demon might be speaking again," she said uneasily.

"What makes you say that?" Ferran asked.

Cassava recounted as best she could the experience she had with Nimmory. Ferran listened silently, and when she was done got up and made her something to drink.

"This is bad," he said.

Cassava shook her head, sitting up and sipping water. "It doesn't seem terrible. She was...odd, but I don't think she was evil. Communicating with the demon sounds...well, she could have hurt me a lot worse. Once I was out, she definitely could have killed me."

Ferran had picked up Magi and was pacing with her in

his arms. "I don't know, Cassava. These people were deranged, the way the Priests tell it."

"Yes, but so are we. You're supposed to be dead. We decided that wasn't necessary."

Ferran swallowed hard and would not meet her eye. "Maybe that's wrong," Ferran said lowly. "Maybe that's why this is happening."

"Oh, so this is somehow your fault?" Cassava asked. "Ferran, for being a nobody you're remarkably self-obsessed."

"The Priests were going to kill me, they didn't, and now this happens. What am I supposed to think?"

"We have no idea how long she's had magic for. It might have been for ages."

"Maybe since I was born." Ferran said. "Maybe they should have killed me in the beginning."

Cassava's headache was bad enough she could not entertain Ferran's ridiculous self-delusions anymore. "Ferran. You are not dangerous! You have never hurt anyone! The Priests are wrong!" she exclaimed loudly, wanting to shake him.

Ferran stood quietly while she shouted, and when she was finished he hunched down on the ground, his body curled over.

Cassava groaned. "I'm sorry, Ferran, my head is killing me. I just don't know how many times I have to convince you not everything the Priests say is ironclad."

"They told me," Ferran said quietly. "They always told me."

"I know," Cassava said with a sigh. "Come here. Touch me. Touch Magi. We're both fine, just fine."

Ferran came together mutely and curled up beside her. She put her arm around him and gave him a gentle squeeze. "You're not hurting anyone," she told him, "in fact I think my headache's improving." Magi, black, lithe little thing that she was, came and lay on her lap. Cassava brought her hand up and stroked her gently.

Cassava and Ferran lay together for a long time, and eventually Cassava drifted off.

She awoke to the smell of chicken and rice. Ferran had cooked in the Asylum, and his skills had only improved since he had come to the cottage.

Ferran greeted her with a plate. "Feeling better?" he asked.

Cassava nodded. "I'm sorry. I get so aggressive sometimes," she said.

Ferran shrugged. "You're better than Henequen."

Cassava groaned. "If I'm ever as bad as Henequen, throw me out."

"I do throw him out sometimes."

"Good."

"But he seems better to me. More...put together."

Cassava spat out a chicken bone. "Really? I swear he's getting worse. The only time I can talk sense into him is when we're running."

Ferran shrugged. "I don't know. He's sweet. But he makes me feel...I feel like he makes me sick."

Cassava frowned. "Is he visiting you when he's ill? I didn't think whatever's going on with him was contagious."

"No, not like that. My brain is fine. I think. I don't know. It's…I feel very warm, and my stomach hurts, and then…"

"And then what?"

Ferran gestured generally to his crotch. "I get large and heavy."

Cassava burst out laughing.

"Barli—"

"I'm-I'm sorry, Ferran," she said through a chord of laughter. The peaks kept running into each other and she couldn't seem to make it stop.

"Barli, it's not funny. Something's wrong, isn't it?"

That sent her into yet another tizzy, and it took a good ten minutes for her to collect herself. "Ferran, that means you like him."

"Of course, I like him. I like you too but—"

"No, Ferran. Demon's blood, you never got the sex talk, did you?"

Ferran shook his head dumbly. "I'm not supposed to touch anyone."

Cassava was glad her headache was gone because this felt like a traumatic experience in itself. "Ferran, I'm going to get you a book on this, but basically…you know how in normal families you have two parents and then kids? Well, the two parents have special feelings for each other. Normally people call it romantic feelings. Now, you don't have to be parents to have romantic feelings."

"Like you and Visea?" Ferran asked.

Cassava's mouth formed a thin line. "Not the example I would have chosen, but yes. Romantic feelings mean you want to be close to that person and share everything with them, and usually do some physical things with them."

"Like what?"

"Like kissing. And...stuff. I will get you a book on it," Cassava said, not really wanting to entertain thoughts of Ferran and Henequen getting together. Cassava wasn't even sure if Henequen was attracted to men.

"Is it bad?" Ferran asked.

"Not necessarily," Cassava said. "Being together made my parents very happy."

"But you tried to kill yourself," Ferran said.

Cassava bit her lip. "I've got to go, Ferran. I need to talk with the other Black Sins."

"You need to talk to the Priests."

Cassava hesitated. She knew he was right, but she didn't like dealing with the Priests any more than strictly necessary. She was always a little afraid if she came to their attention they would decide to kill her. Unfortunately, discussing the matter with the Priests was necessary. "See you soon, Ferran."

She bid him goodbye before he could backtrack to their earlier conversation and headed out. It was pleasant to divert her attention to the blooming affections of Ferran, but even that would be far more complicated than Cassava looked forward to dealing with. If Kazini found out...but that was a problem for another day, or maybe never. Ferran was so wrapped up in himself he'd probably decide not to risk spreading the demon.

Cassava turned over in her head who she would discuss what to do with Nimmory first. Henequen was an obvious choice, but he was erratic and unpredictable and Cassava feared he would hunt down Nimmory just to get the puzzle out of his head. And Henequen was much more proficient than Cassava.

She briefly considered one of the other Sins, but she couldn't trust them not to take action on their own. They might want to track Nimmory down and kill her just to prove they could. And they probably could, at least the ones who didn't let their victims get close.

That left the Priests. Cassava hated to be in this position, but if she had to pick a Priest, she knew which one it would be. Cassava only knew one Priest remotely well. It was time to pay him a visit.

Cassava finished her run back into town. The battering from the storm had lifted now and people were beginning to hang out their shingles. Cassava pulled her hood back up as she approached more people. She always did so when she was in a crowded area. It tended to cause fewer traffic jams when everyone wasn't clearing the street for her. And Cassava hated the looks. Once, Cassava had reveled in attention. But fear was an ugly emotion and Cassava hated to see people turn that way toward her. Disgust was still worse.

Cassava kept her eyes ahead, focused on her destination. She had learned from Henequen not to look at anything, but not to look down. Watching your feet only made you look suspect.

Arriving at the docks, Cassava searched for a small

dinghy that looked like it would take to the water soon. Cassava disliked imposing most days, but today, knowing what wildness was going on and fearful of what more might follow, Cassava had no qualms about approaching an eager fisherman and commandeering his ship to take her to Neesi.

Neesi was about an hour by boat, and Cassava used the silence to puzzle over her words. The Priests were tricky to talk to, and Cassava couldn't afford to make any missteps. She knew her line of thinking was not the same as her masters', but Cassava had never studied in school enough to know what the right thing to say was. Sometimes she wished she had a pocket Ferran.

The fisherman made no attempt to converse with her, and resolutely rowed as though this duty would save him from certain doom. Cassava watched the water lap against the boat and the pull of the oar into the ocean. She was grateful at times that she was left so unbothered, but at other times the silence grated on her and she tried to engage her escort in some small communication. It never went well.

That was what had struck her most about Nimmory. Not only had Nimmory looked at her, Cassava realized, but she had seen without flinching, had engaged her like a human. And Cassava was so single-minded in her directive she had squandered that shot at normalcy. There was so much more Cassava wanted to know, so much that would likely die with this girl, a gift Cassava hadn't been ready to receive.

But what if it was the demon? After all, what other possible explanation could there be? If the Priests had worked it away before, perhaps they could again. Perhaps then Nimmory could go on living, sanctified.

Cassava thanked the fisherman as they pulled onto the dock, still fighting with the words in her head and heart. The more she thought about Nimmory, the more convinced she became that Nimmory was only acting to defend herself, and she had just as much right to existence as Cassava. Of course, according to the Priests, Cassava herself would need to be dealt with—if they knew her true heart, they wouldn't dare to keep her around.

It was a short walk from the docks to the Asylum, and Cassava felt it too short for her liking. All too soon she had arrived at the great iron doors. The Asylum on Neesi was the largest one, made of thick stone cut from the dark green quarries on Peln. When cut properly, the stone gleamed like a ghostly prison, and pieces of the front temple were so fixed. The majority was rough, uncut, and hewn so that every so often it gave off a sparkle, but mostly it was tall and foreboding. It was a fortress, but it had not been built to keep people out, rather its task had always been to keep them in. The top raises were spiked, the windows narrow and barred, and the whole place raised a sinister energy. This was home.

Cassava sorted through her pockets and found the jangling string of keys. Most people could only get in and out by invitation of the Priests, but being a Black Sin had its privileges. The gate whined as Cassava made its hinges work, alerting the residents to her presence. Cassava allowed her hood to fall back as she swept through the atrium and unlocked the door to the courtyard.

Several children were playing with a ball in the center of the courtyard, all five of them hopelessly muddy. With the general lack of bathing allotted to residents, it would take some time to come off. There were few adults out today, most were probably in their rooms still, letting the wash of the enormous storm fade a little further before venturing out.

As Cassava entered, one of the children pointed and shouted. They altogether abandoned their game and crowded around Cassava, calling out greetings and questions.

Arru, one of the newest members of the Asylum, tugged desperately on Cassava's sleeve. His face was still red and puffy from the branding. "Did you see my da?" he asked plaintively.

Cassava shook her head, setting him back a step. "Arru, the outside world doesn't matter anymore."

"*You* go outside," Arru muttered.

It was hard to know what to say to someone ripped from their family. Cassava had been too, but at a less tender age. "I don't talk to anyone," she said. "No one will talk to you anymore, even if you left. Your parents would pretend you didn't want to exist."

Arru folded his arms. "My da loves me."

Cassava knew the proper response was to tell him that people could love from a distance and Arru was better off here. But she couldn't bring herself to do it. "Maybe he does, Arru. But barring a total reversal of hundreds of years of tradition, you're not going to see him again."

Cassava did not want to see him cry, and so she pried

herself away from the children and stepped through yet another door. This would bring her to the Priest's inner sanctum, a place no one went without invitation.

Cassava stood just inside. The waiting area had two simple wooden chairs and a small library of books on theology. Cassava was sure Ferran had read them all.

Cassava knocked on the door and waited patiently. Before too long, a young Priest arrived. She took in Cassava's get-up. "What can we help you with?" she asked.

"I need to speak with Veran," Cassava replied.

"One moment, please."

Cassava did not utilize the chairs, but kept moving in the small atrium. Before long the door opened again.

Veran was in his late twenties. He was clean shaven and fresh looking, like most Priests. Cassava preferred him to the older Priests who tended to be stodgy and suspicious of anything to do with Sins. Veran had at least escorted her with grace, treated her with respect.

"Cassava. This is a surprise. What can I do for you?"

"It's about my mission."

"Ah." Veran paused, his face reassembling from mildly intrigued to serious. "Perhaps this should be brought up with Iskor."

Cassava did not want to talk to Iskor. "Something happened on my mission today, something that's supposed to be dead and gone."

Veran, who had been moving away from her, stopped abruptly. "What, exactly?"

"Magic," Cassava said. "My target used magic."

Veran's eyes widened slightly, and then he bowed his head. "So, it has come to us."

Cassava's mind twisted. "What-what do you mean? Did you know about this?" she asked.

Veran took a deep breath. "Maybe we should sit down." He gestured to the chairs and sat stiffly. "Where to begin…" he said, drumming his fingers on his leg. He took another deep breath, and then launched into a truly remarkable ramble of words. "We've been trying to keep this quiet, but on the mainland magic has been popping up all over the place."

"Magic is...back?"

"It appears so. This is all heard from sailors, of course. We haven't had any tale of it on the islands. Until now."

Cassava's mind was racing. "So, what are you doing about it?" she asked. "Didn't the Priests get rid of it last time?"

"Our policy has always been to limit our meddling to our own island. Of course, we hope that without our direction, people steer clear of the demon, but we simply don't have the ability to impose our guidance on all of them."

"So, you're just...letting it grow?" Cassava asked.

"The Priesthood has not been completely lax," Veran explained patiently. "We have been combing our texts for answers. But the wider world has been in chaos from this magic, and we are reluctant to descend into the madness. Now, perhaps, it is time to act."

"Why isn't anyone here having magic?" Cassava asked.

"My colleagues will tell you it is because we have

carefully pruned away the demon and not allowed it a foothold."

"But you think differently?" Cassava asked.

Veran tilted his head. "When Henon silenced the demon, he communed with the Angel, who exerted her influence over the whole world. But I believe she was most strongly connected to the Islands, and therefore here her protection was greatest."

Cassava let out a longer breath. "My target was a foreigner," she said. "Trikingese."

Veran leaned forward. "What happened?"

"She put her hand out, and suddenly it was like the wind from the storm had all been diverted to me, and it followed her lead, moving where she willed it."

"This is troubling indeed. Did you deal with her?" Veran asked.

Cassava shook her head. "She was too powerful. She knocked me out. I...I don't know how we can deal with this."

Veran wet his lips. "It's something to take under advisement. We can't have magic walking our shores."

"She could do...anything," Cassava said after another pause, realizing the insane unbalance that magic brought to the world. "How are they handling it elsewhere?" she asked.

"Not well," Veran said. "There was a huge war, I've heard tales of undead soldiers."

Cassava's eyes widened. Wind was one thing—but what Veran was talking about was something else entirely. "*Kitadu.*"

"A man visited our libraries several years ago. He too

was searching for answers. Although he was not a Priest, we allowed him access to our books. They say he found a way to silence the demon."

Cassava's head was spinning. "Well, can't we just go get that, then?"

Veran inclined his head slightly. "Perhaps. It would require us to do something we have not done in a lifetime."

"So? Foreigners are going to keep coming, and who knows what will happen here?" Cassava exclaimed.

"I agree," Veran said. He paused for a moment. "The Priests won't go by themselves. We aren't popular outside of the islands. No nations treaty with us, and we're vilified by many."

Cassava frowned. "Why do they hate you so much?"

"We're a threat to the demon, which has made its home in the world. We are the one stronghold. Of course, they see us as a threat."

"It sounds like you need a bodyguard or two."

Veran inclined his head. "Perhaps you are right," he said. "Yes, perhaps that is the solution. We'll take a team and bring back the cure. And someday we will discover how it was done and everyone will be silenced again."

Cassava thought silence probably involved death. It usually did with the Priests. "What do we do about my target?" she asked.

Veran's eyes narrowed. "Let me talk with the others."

"She could help," Cassava said in a rush. "She knows the Trikingdom. If we were to go, we'd need a guide, and she likely knows something of this cure."

Veran frowned. "Do you think she could be trusted not

to kill us all? Anyone who speaks with the demon is incredibly dangerous."

Cassava swallowed. "She seems...earnest. She could have killed me, but she didn't. I think if it was a mutual promise, she'd keep her word."

Veran's eyebrows drew together. "Perhaps if we extracted a promise she never return to these isles."

Cassava wasn't sure how she felt about that, but she supposed it was better than Nimmory having her head on the chopping block.

Veran lifted his head. "I'll speak to the Priests. Perhaps now they will feel moved where they had not before. Thank you for bringing this to my attention, Cassava."

Cassava nodded, still not entirely sure she had done the right thing.

"How are you settling in? I know expanding your duties can be...difficult."

Cassava blinked in surprise; this was the first time a Priest had truly seemed concerned about how she was doing. "It's...different. It's harder to be in the world than I thought it would be. For so many years, I was treated one way, and now...it's entirely different."

Veran nodded solemnly. "It's hardly the same, but the way I am viewed with these robes on has set a tone with people as well. They always assume I'm on serious business, and none know how to talk with me."

Cassava rejected this attempt at companionship out of hand. "You chose to be a Priest though."

He shrugged slightly. "In a way, I did, but I find it to

be more of a calling. And you did choose to venture out into the world again. You didn't have to be a Black Sin."

Cassava got up abruptly. "Let me know what they decide."

Veran stood as well. "You will know shortly. Have a good day, Cassava."

She left without another word. The children ignored her this time, but Cassava thought she saw Arru watching her with cold jaded eyes. It was hard dealing with some of the other Sins now. Her status as a Black Sin made many resent her.

Cassava wound her way up the stairs to her bedroom. Cassava had few belongings, and she hopped around the islands so much that even here, when she wasn't in a spare bedroom, there was hardly anything on the shelves or walls. Cassava kept a few changes of clothes and a sole picture of the sunset Ferran had made for her, but beyond that Cassava didn't have things. She hadn't been allowed to take anything with her entering the Asylum, and she hadn't picked up much since.

She slipped off her clothes and lay naked in her bed, staring at the plain wood ceiling. This was her life now, days of running down targets and bringing them back or leaving them in the streets, coming back to a cold room and getting up the next morning to do it all over again.

It was not often anymore that Cassava's mind wandered to Visea, but tonight it did, and with it a wild wanting to know. She had told herself she didn't need to—that Visea had made her opinion clear and it would hardly have changed now that Cassava was a Black Sin. But what if...Cassava stopped herself. Going back to Visea would only lead to pain. She had Ferran now, and Henequen, and while her feelings for them were not the same, they amounted to more support than Visea had ever been. Dooming Visea to this life beyond bars on the off chance she had changed her mind was a terrible, vicious idea. And yet Cassava had it. Frequently. Well, she was a Sin after all, perhaps it shouldn't be surprising.

Cassava tried to throw Visea out of her mind. She had needed to practice it, but now it went smoothly. But now, for the first time, something besides her and Ferran's promise on the bank came to her. Images of a shock of blonde hair and sparkling green eyes.

Chapter Three

Cassava spent the next day mostly in bed, feeling somewhat hungover from the ordeal. She briefly considered actually cracking a book open and learning some of the things Ferran did, but Cassava had never liked school and the idea of learning math or reading voluntarily irritated her. Instead, she spent the afternoon working on her dagger skills with Anelace. The practical was her preference.

Anelace was a relatively short, squat sort of person—not what your first instinct was for grace and poise. But Cassava had seen Anelace work, and they blended seamlessly into crowds, and their knife work was a marvel. Anelace could, within fifty yards, hit just about any target they were presented with. Cassava, on the other hand, was still working on a seamless pull from her sleeve, belt, and boot. Anelace was profoundly deaf, but had gone deaf at a later age and spoke without too much trouble. They lip read well, and it was only occasionally they and Cassava reached an impasse.

Now was one of those moments, and Anelace, trying to make themselves understood, took Cassava's arms in their own and moved her arm in the motion Cassava could not seem to make on her own. With Anelace's assistance, Cassava's dagger flew straight.

"Again," Anelace said, making motions as well so that their intention could not possibly be misunderstood.

Cassava tried to remember the feeling. Muscle memory had always taken her longer than most people. Playing with the other children, Cassava had frequently found herself scrambling to keep up. Maybe that was why she had never gotten into sports. She didn't like looking like a fool, and running she could do on her own, with no one to tell her she was wrong.

She loosed her knife and it spun through the air. Cassava thought for once it looked straight. There was a satisfying thud as the metal sunk into the splintered board—a good foot short of the bullseye. But it was progress. Cassava let out an excited yell, but Anelace either did not see or did not care and signaled her to throw again.

"I'm getting better," Cassava said, after regaining Anelace's eyes. She took another knife and threw it. It sailed past the target and chipped on stone. "Sometimes," she amended bitterly.

"You have the technique," Anelace said, "you just aren't careful enough to use it. You must *think* your throw."

Cassava grit her teeth. Paying attention wasn't exactly her strong suit. She liked things that just came to her. School hadn't been one of them and neither, it seemed, was knife throwing. "Let's go back to hand-to-hand," she suggested. "That's more my style."

"Someday you'll end up in a situation where hand-to-hand won't cut it, and then you'll be sorry you were lazy."

"I'm not lazy!" Cassava exclaimed.

Anelace didn't respond.

Cassava scowled. She had worked to get here—yes, she had taken an easier way, but Cassava hadn't had the luxury of years of practice leading up to her test. She'd only had all of a few months. Anelace had spent years honing their skills before becoming a Black Sin. Cassava knew she never would have gotten to where she was without Ferran's help, but Cassava was different from the other members of the Black Sins. Most of them had been inside an Asylum from a very young age, if not from birth. Cassava didn't even have a year under her belt yet. She knew the other Black Sins judged her. The others trained with each other, but with an air of excellence. Cassava was still in training stages. Still, she was successful with her missions—at least until the last one.

Cassava resolved to practice on her own until she could school Anelace, or at least make a fair showing that wouldn't disgrace her. Cassava picked up another knife and threw it moodily. It landed just shy of the target.

"You're letting your emotions get involved."

"Yeah, that's kind of how I function," Cassava replied bitterly. "I'm not a brick. I have feelings, unlike some people."

Anelace's response was interrupted by Henequen arriving, waving his hands wildly to get both of their attention. Cassava put her knife down. Henequen could be unpredictable, and it was best not to have anything sharp in her hand when he was around just in case. Henequen was tall, with short hair that stood up at all times.

"Henequen," Anelace said tautly. "Another emotional disgrace."

Cassava rolled her eyes. "At least we're human."

"Teenagers." Anelace said succinctly. "Human teenagers." Anelace was in their late twenties.

Henequen jumped down in front of them. Today he was wearing a too-small shirt over baggy pants. Henequen was the most erratic of the Black Sins. Something was a little twisted in his head. Cassava knew a little something about that. But Henequen? That was something else entirely. "There's a meeting. All the Black Sins and some Priests," he announced.

"When?"

"Tonight," Henequen said. His hand tapped out over his thigh. "It's something big."

Anelace folded their arms. "What about?"

Henequen tilted his head. "A long trip," he said. "Be there!" he demanded, pointing his finger at each of them in turn. He tapped his head. "It's gonna be loud." He tapped his head again, growing more and more aggressive about it.

Cassava moved forward and took his hand. "Hey. Let's go running, okay?"

Henequen nodded. "Run to run to run to run," he said.

Anelace shook their head. "Good luck, Cassava."

Henequen took Cassava's hand and pulled her away aggressively. Cassava and Anelace locked eyes, and for a moment they were in agreement with each other. The Black Sins were cliquey, but they took care of each other. It was a joint project taking care of Henequen, and the others had their moments as well, where they just weren't right.

Henequen was hands down the most complex mission, and they took turns babysitting him.

Cassava and Henequen hurried out of the Asylum. Cassava could tell something was bothering him—something more than usual. His words to her were jumbled and Cassava could only half guess at what he was attempting to say. Cassava led the way. Henequen used to best her every time, but now when he was distracted she had the lead on him.

They took their normal path up the island. Their path was well traveled, even if just by the two of them. It led up the mountain path toward the peak of the volcano. Perhaps someday it would explode again, but it had been quiet for over two hundred years, so they felt fairly safe. Henequen was always calmer up here—Cassava wasn't sure if it was because of the exertion, or the atmosphere just calmed him, but it was always easier to talk with him up in the mountain air.

They collapsed together at the top of the hill. Sometimes Henequen would spar her too, but today he sat down and folded his knees into his chest. Cassava sat down quietly beside him. "Hey, Quen."

Henequen dug his hands into the earth, his fingers flexing and stretching. "Don't go away," he said quietly. "I can't do this without you."

"Quen, what are you talking about?"

"I know," he said. "I know. I know. I know."

"Quen, take a deep breath. I'm not going away."

"Bye bye on a ship. Sail on the blue, blue. Yes, she says it will go."

Henequen always seemed to know more things than he should. Cassava had frequently found that he was highly perceptive, but the way he talked sometimes made people think he was absolutely insane. Cassava knew all of it didn't make sense, but more of it did than some of the other Sins believed. "Are you talking about the Priests going away? Sailing across the ocean?"

Henequen took her hand and pressed it to his head. "You go away, everything goes away. Shut up. Kacheck. No more." He squeezed her hand.

Cassava pulled her hand away. "What about Kazini? Ferran? Anelace?"

"It hurts. Kazini hurts. I don't want."

Cassava sighed. It would be unconscionable to leave Henequen to Kazini's whims. The other Black Sins didn't understand how Henequen felt, or they didn't care, and were just glad that they didn't have to deal with Henequen themselves. "I want to be out on the sea again, for real, Quen. I grew up on it. And can you imagine going somewhere else? Seeing another place? All those different people?" Cassava let out a breath. "Can you imagine? People just staring because you're different, and not because you're a poison?"

Henequen dug his fingers deeper into the ground, pulling up grass by its roots. "Ship slip. New mess, run right."

Cassava sighed. Apparently, the run had not taken care of the problem. "Look, Quen, I don't know what's going to happen. But someone has to stay here and take care of Ferran." Honestly, Cassava wasn't sure if she could trust

Henequen to remember to deliver food to Ferran on a regular basis. Kitadu. When had she become responsible for so many people? She used to be the kid, getting taken care of. Things had changed rapidly, and Cassava was suddenly not sure she liked it.

Cassava spent their run back puzzling over what she should do. If she didn't take the reins at this meeting tonight, Nimmory might get moved to the target list again—and Cassava believed Anelace could take care of Nimmory without her being aware enough to use her special powers. Cassava had always wanted to travel the world. She had liked being out on the sea, but with her father a deep-sea fisherman, Cassava had never been anywhere but the Islands. She had always wanted to see other shores, but there had never been a need. Now, having experienced the way Nimmory's eyes had slid over her face, how she hadn't flinched away from the severe branding that marred her, Cassava was curious to see whether other places might be different. Maybe Nimmory was a singular human, but what if she wasn't? What if there existed a place where Cassava wasn't cursed? How could she not try to experience that? This was a fate that she had never accepted, had never fully given herself over to—unlike Ferran, unlike Henequen, unlike Anelace. She remembered being treated differently, and somewhere she believed she could be treated better again.

But Ferran needed her—Henequen was unreliable, and no one else could help him. Henequen was a problem himself—one Cassava hadn't considered before. Henequen had struggled before Cassava, but when he was doing better, he had told Cassava how much he preferred her assistance. How could Cassava abandon them? Her friends, people she would give her life for, had risked everything for. Unfortunately, that wasn't a one-time thing. It was a commitment Cassava was just beginning to understand.

Friends before Ferran and Henequen had been plentiful, but they had never been deep. Cassava had played with them, and lied about what boys she found attractive, and listened to their stories. It had been companionship, but it wasn't until Visea that Cassava had felt something truly strong. And that had been infatuation more than anything. After all, when Cassava had laid it all out on the line, she had been rejected. Ferran and Henequen knew who she was, and they accepted her. That was more than anyone else had ever done. So how could she abandon them now?

These thoughts consumed her even as she readied herself for a meeting with the Priests. She found herself walking beside Arbalest, the pint-sized archer assassin. "What do you think this is about then?" Arablest asked conversationally.

Cassava shifted uncomfortably, not sure what to say. "I'm sure we'll find out soon enough."

Arablest spared a glance at her. "No thoughts at all?" Arablest asked. "The last time we had a meeting like this, it was because Mace had passed."

"Oh." Cassava said softly. She had heard tales about Mace, a strong burly man who had been successfully bludgeoning people to death for twenty years before he fell sick. He had gone downhill quickly and Cassava felt some of the uncertainty about her was the Black Sins still missing their long-time member. Henequen had even referred to him as father before. "I don't think anything like that's happened," she tried to reassure Arablest.

Arablest shook her head bitterly. "I hope not. But any crisis big enough to call us all in is bound to be no good at all."

They entered the temple classroom, which had been rearranged so that a bunch of benches were in a row facing a spread of Priests seated in padded chairs. Henequen was already seated with Kazini on his lap. Cassava guessed from the dark spot on Henequen's neck it hadn't been long since Kazini was otherwise occupied. It was only being before the Priests that was taming her now; if it had just been the Sins, she would have been all over him. Anelace was speaking with Dani, and Celurit was of course sitting with his paramour Jin. The Black Sins were all dressed in their formal uniform: black pants with a black sailor's shirt and long black cloak. Cassava didn't know the Priests, except for Veran, who was not seated but standing just to the side. They were in Priest finery, a deep sea-blue robe tied with a sandy beige cord and beige accents.

Cassava sat down between Arablest and Jin. It was strange seeing all the Black Sins assembled together. The marked assassins all together under one roof. It was powerful and awesome, and yet here they were, sitting silently, waiting for someone else to take the reins. It felt like a waste.

Priest Feyru started the meeting. "Welcome, all of you. Our faithful servants, who serve our Islands so well. We have gathered you together to ask your assistance—a special mission for one particular Sin. The rest of you will need to step it up while your fellow is otherwise engaged."

None of the Sins asked questions. They knew better than to interrupt a Priest.

"We are not certain how long this special mission will take, but it will involve accompanying our gracious volunteer Veran Assidu to the Trikingdom. You will serve as bodyguard and assistant. I know it will be a struggle to be among people who do not respect your authority, to be among so many Sins and without license to do anything about it. So, I want you to consider this opportunity carefully."

Cassava waited for him to say something about magic, to mention her or Nimmory, or anything about the purpose of the mission. But he didn't. He didn't trust the Black Sins it seemed—didn't trust them with anything but murder.

Cassava glanced carefully at the others. It was hard to gauge what they were thinking. Kazini was playing with Henequen's hand. Jin and Celurit were giving each other silent glances, and Cassava felt their expressions might have been full conversations. Arablest had her arms crossed and a heavy frown on her face. Anelace was leaning forward, their eyes intent on the Priests.

"Now, if all things were equal, we would devise some method for determining who should go," Feyru continued. "No doubt a contest to determine who would act as the best bodyguard. I know you are all well-tested assassins, but protecting a body is a somewhat different skillset, though I have no doubts you would all be up to the task. However, we have to consider how best to keep this mission secret.

Cassava is the only one among you who has experience with long distance sailing."

Cassava blinked, and then frowned. That might have been true, but she had her own thoughts about why they might have singled her out—she already knew the true nature of Veran's task. She had contact with Nimmory, and she was less attached to the others as far as the Priests knew.

Cassava wasn't the only one a little surprised by this blunt announcement. "Her?" Kazini exclaimed. "She's fresh. She hardly knows anything."

"It's true," Anelace said. "She barely handles a knife competently."

Cassava flushed. It might be true, but it didn't mean she liked it. "I still get my targets," she said hotly. "And I have more experience on the sea and dealing with normal people than any of you."

Kazini scowled. "I protest."

"Your protest is noted, Kazini, but irrelevant."

"Wait—" Cassava said, "they're not completely wrong. I have street smarts, but there are more experienced killers. And one of us is particularly talented at discovering and investigating unsavory characters."

"What are you suggesting, Cassava?"

"Henequen should come too. He knows people, and he gets them to like him and trust him. He's the kind of face you want."

Feyru's brow furrowed. "Two Sins? Perhaps…"

"Hold on," Anelace said, "if someone else is going, it should be me. Henequen's not exactly subtle. Neither is Arablest or Kazini," they added with a glance at both of them. "I know how to slit someone's throat and get out, without it being traced back to me."

Cassava couldn't let that sit. "Henequen doesn't leave a blood trail, and I'm the hardest to trace of all of you," she replied. "Besides, Henequen just gets senses about people. You've all seen it."

Feyru looked at his fellow Priests and signaled them together. They talked for a brief moment. "We will allow a second companion for Veran. It has been decided a nonlethal contest will decide who will join Cassava. Anyone who wishes to attempt, come up here." The other Priests began moving the chairs back so there was a small circle within which the soon to be fighters could tussle.

Cassava's pulse quickened as she watched Anelace, Kazini, and Henequen stand up. Kazini said something to Henequen that made him shake. Cassava hoped Henequen didn't throw the fight; it looked like she wasn't getting much of a choice in whether she was going or not and she wanted him by her side. If Henequen came, Ferran would still be a problem but at least they could deal with it together. Cassava really didn't want to end up on a trip with Kazini. Of all the Black Sins, Kazini was the one that got on her nerves the most, probably because she was a pathological liar, but also because her solution to Henequen's demon was to fuck him and leave him. Cassava didn't understand his and Kazini's relationship, but the word "abusive" definitely came to mind. Talking to Henequen about it was like talking to an obstinate, less-intelligible toddler.

"Any weapons you have on you are fine—but no

permanent damage," Feyru decreed. "We can't have any of our Black Sins out of commission, especially if we're going to be down two. Three of you—simultaneous—last one standing wins."

Anelace palmed their dagger quickly to their hand and twirled it quickly. Kazini flexed her fingers and began circling. "Don't think I'll go easy on you, Quen."

Henequen didn't respond, but took a thin lace from his sleeve. He moved at the same time as Anelace, their forearms meeting in a fight which neither won. Kazini took the opportunity to kick Anelace's legs out from under them. Anelace collapsed with a thud but quickly swiped at Kazini's exposed leg. It wasn't deadly, but it was surely painful as red immediately bubbled up and began to flow down Kazini's leg. Kazini responded by kicking at Anelace's head. Henequen caught Kazini's extended foot and twisted it till she screamed and collapsed to her knees. Anelace bounced back to their feet and began circling Henequen, their knife shining with blood.

Henequen responded by circling as well. Kazini suddenly snagged her hand out to grab Henequen, but he jumped back. At that moment, Anelace lunged forward, catching one of his arms. He kicked up into their stomach and they released their grasp, momentarily doubled over.

Kazini took the opportunity to cartwheel back to her feet, kicking Henequen in the face as she did so. Henequen ducked down and spun, sweeping at Kazini with a kick of his own. Kazini blocked with her arm, grinning wildly. "Maybe we should try this in the bedroom, huh Quenny?"

Anelace suddenly caught Kazini from behind in a

headlock. "If I had my knife, you'd be done already," they said. Kazini fought to free herself, but Anelace was strong. Henequen stepped back to catch his breath, watching the struggle, his eyes moving between the two of them rapidly.

Kazini managed a good elbow to Anelace's head and finally wriggled free, launching herself at Henequen. Henequen sidestepped, caught her off-balance, and grabbed her neck in one hand, pressing. Cassava swallowed at the intense look in his eye. She had never seen that from Henequen before, but now that she was witnessing him in a real fight, she could see how he made such a deadly name for himself.

Kazini's eyes narrowed and she tried to kick forward at Henequen, but he held firm, his legs moving quickly in a dance to avoid any kicks from her. Anelace double-teamed, catching Kazini's arms behind her back and holding them so she wasn't able to punch out at Henequen. Kazini struggled for several more seconds later, before falling limp, seeming to accept her fate. "Tap out, Quenny."

Henequen did not release her. He held her up, arm straight and true. Cassava marveled at the muscles he hid behind the folds of his cloak and his stammering demeanor. His eyes were locked on Kazini, and there was almost no movement there. Cassava wondered what he was thinking.

"Tap out," she said again, her voice a little hoarse now, a whisper as she headed for unconsciousness. Still, Henequen did not move.

"Tap out, Henequen," Anelace said softly, touching his shoulder.

Finally, Henequen's grip loosened, and Kazini fell to

the floor, coughing. Anelace stepped back a moment. "You okay, Henequen?"

He closed his eyes and breathed deeply, muttering something Cassava couldn't make up under his breath. Kazini was still coughing, and only Anelace would have had a hope of hearing Henequen's words. Whatever it was, they straightened up and took a step back. "I concede. Henequen is the best suited to this mission," they said.

Cassava breathed out a breath she hadn't realized she'd been holding. That took care of one problem. Now there was just the matter of Ferran.

"Very well," Feyru said. He looked around at them. "Cassava, Henequen, you will leave with Veran tomorrow morning. The rest of you will need to step it up. With two Sins gone, it'll mean a lot more work. Especially without Henequen. You'll need to do your own investigations, instead of relying on him."

"Priest," Arablest injected hesitantly, "just what is it that Veran is doing in the Trikingdom? Why associate with those sinners?"

"It's a diplomatic mission," Feyru said smoothly, "meant to ensure that we keep our Islands out of the troubles of the rest of the world. Encroachment is, sadly, always an issue we must be aware of. It is not often we venture forth from our homeland, but there are serious concerns afoot in the rest of the world that cannot be ignored."

"War?" Celurit asked.

"Something worse than that, I'm afraid. But it's not for you to worry about; we're sending a Priest and two Black

Sins to deal with it; what more could it possibly require?" Feyru raised his eyebrow, as though challenging the Black Sins to ask more. But they knew their place. It was rare enough to be granted any information at all. Cassava sat uncomfortably, wondering if perhaps she should tell the others the true nature of her quest. But if word got out that she had leaked, her head would swiftly be on the chopping block. No, best to stay quiet and let Veran handle matters as he saw fit; Henequen would no doubt discover the truth through his crazed wanderings, but it was wild enough Cassava doubted anyone but her would believe him.

Feyru dismissed them with a gesture, and the gathering broke. Kazini got off the floor and slunk away, but there was a dark glimmer in her eye and Cassava was glad they were leaving tomorrow. She feared retribution for Henequen if they dallied.

Cassava went to her bedroom as the rest had done, but sat there awake, puzzling over the problem of Ferran. It was still troubling her in the hours before dawn when she slipped from her bedroom and commandeered an early morning fishing boat to take her back to Briov.

Cassava arrived at Ferran's cottage out of breath just as the sun was rising. She knocked riotously on the door, banging loudly to be sure to wake Ferran from any stupor. Cassava waited impatiently for Ferran before she remembered she hadn't used the specific knock she was supposed to, and Ferran probably thought some wild person was outside and possibly he was in danger. Cassava sighed in frustration and called out. "Ferran, it's me. Get out here right now!"

It still took a little while, but it wasn't too long before he was opening the door. "I thought we weren't shouting things," he said, yawning slightly. "Couldn't you come by after the sun rose?"

"No. We've got to go right away. Like, now."

Ferran shook his head wearily. "What's happening?" he asked.

"Henequen and I got roped into a mission. And you're coming too. Oh, and bring all your poisons."

Chapter Four

"Where are we going?" Ferran asked as they ran down the street toward an empty warehouse.

"We're hoping that magic user is stupid, predictable and a bit overconfident," Cassava replied.

She stepped carefully into the warehouse, Ferran a few steps behind her. "Hello?" she offered, holding her hands up. "I'm here to talk."

There was a rustling nearby and Nimmory popped up from behind a barrel, staring at Cassava and Ferran. Ferran's hands immediately went up in a don't hurt me motion. Her eyes flitted between the two of them before settling on Cassava. "What do you want?"

"I want a bargain. Do they trade in the Trikingdom?"

"Not the way they do here. But I've been here often enough," she allowed. "Who's your friend?"

"He's insurance. I didn't think you'd want to kill a kid who hasn't done anything."

"He's not one of you?"

"No."

Nimmory narrowed her eyes. "Okay. I'll bite. What do you want?"

"You get us oriented to Triking society, get our foot in the door."

"No. No way. I'm not going back there."

Cassava took a step back. "You want to stay here? Where you're going to be hunted down and killed?" she asked.

Nimmory waved her hand, and Cassava felt a little breeze. "Well, not really, no, but I only had money to make it to here, and now trade season is over anyway so I'm stuck until the season turns."

Cassava wondered what was so bad about the Trikingdom that Nimmory had fled it to come here. Perhaps it truly was a parasitic land of evil no one could come back from, with terrible wars and famines all the time. Cassava had always heard tales of the Trikingdom being the worst of the worst, and the Islands a mecca. Perhaps it shouldn't be surprising that Nimmory was looking for a way out.

But she wouldn't find a home here. She was far too distinctive to blend in, and her powers made her a target. Someday a Black Sin would succeed—if Cassava had to guess, Anelace. "I'll make a deal with you. If you do this for us, I'll send you on a ship to wherever you want to go."

Nimmory put her hand down and tucked a strand of yellow hair behind her ear. "Anywhere?" she asked.

Cassava nodded.

"How do I know you won't just kill me once I do what you want?" Nimmory asked.

Cassava turned to Ferran. "Do I keep my promises?"

Ferran had spent the entire conversation with his hands

raised in the air, and even now he did not lower them. "Barli, are you sure about this? What if she kills *you*?"

"She's not going to kill me. She wouldn't get free passage if she did that. Besides, she didn't kill me before; it'd be a waste to do it now."

"I'm still waiting for a reason to trust you, and assurances from your boyfriend aren't enough."

"How about this? Ferran here is a Sin. He was marked for death by the Priests, but I didn't feel like that was right."

"So, you, what, convinced them child murder is wrong?" Nimmory said disbelievingly.

Cassava shook her head. "They think Ferran is dead. And I'm trusting you here—the Priests can't know."

Nimmory's eyebrow arched. "So, you're a Sin with at least some moral compass. Good to know, Barli."

"It's Cassava, actually. Do we have a deal?"

Nimmory took a deep breath, looked at the both of them, and stuck her hand out.

Cassava waited to feel the force of air push against her, and she screwed her eyes up, but nothing happened. Cassava glanced uncertainly at Ferran, who still had his hands raised.

"What—oh. Have you never shaken hands before?" Nimmory asked. She let it fall. "I promise to get you through to the doors of the Trikingdom if you grant me passage anywhere I wish in return."

"Good," Cassava said. She could feel the strings of all her discordant plans coming together. It felt like her soul was singing. She was *good* at plotting. She'd manufactured everything to suit her. Now it just had to stay that way.

"Now come with me, quickly, and I'll explain what we do next."

Cassava, Ferran and Nimmory reached Neesi as dawn was truly reaching morning. Cassava cursed bitterly, hoping she could still set her haphazardly created plan in motion. She also hoped Henequen didn't ruin everything—she hadn't had a moment to tell him what she was planning, and Henequen didn't always do well with surprises.

She fixed Ferran with a standard fishing hat in addition to his hooded cloak. Ferran had been extremely quiet since she had taken him from the house, and Cassava wasn't sure whether it was fright or something else, but she frankly did not have the time to worry about it. If he didn't want to starve, they had to venture out on a dangerous journey.

They arrived at the docks out of breath and disheveled. Ferran was taking huge breaths, not used to running like Cassava was, and his hood had fallen back in their haste. Cassava quickly pulled it up and over his head, and then rearranged his hair so that it fell in front of his face so the worst of the scarring was covered. She was glad the day was dour—it explained the presence of a hood much better.

Cassava had not been wandering long before she saw Veran standing with a packed bag and a smile. He waved when he saw her. Cassava nodded to Nimmory. "If you mess this up, all bets are off," she said.

"Don't worry. Acting is in my blood," Nimmory replied.

Cassava walked a few steps ahead of Nimmory and Ferran, who was in the back, face carefully concealed. "Hello, Veran."

"Cassava. I see you brought...company. This is supposed to be a discreet mission," he said pointedly.

"And what better way to be discrete than having a crew all under control? This is Nimmory, she'll help us get into the Trikingdom. We wouldn't want to have to make a splash."

"I see," Veran said. His posture was stiff and uncompromising. "And who is this?"

"Well, we need another hand to crew the ship. I assume you don't want just any hand. They might talk."

"And this one won't?" Veran asked.

"Oh no. He's a mute," Cassava said, "took him right out of Briov Asylum."

Veran frowned. "Another Sin?"

"Did you want someone who can talk?" Cassava replied.

Veran sighed heavily. "I'll admit I don't know much about ships, and frankly I never feel quite right on them. I know it's a travesty."

"Everyone has something," Cassava replied. If she were allowed to touch him, she would have patted his shoulder. "But I need someone to run crew for a voyage like this."

"Very well," Veran replied. "I'm trusting you on this."

Cassava nodded. Now she just had to make sure Henequen didn't mess it up. Veran might not know Ferran by face or name, but if he had a reason to get a better look at his brand, he would know this was no mere mute.

They waited some time before Henequen finally appeared. His hair was even more disheveled than usual, and he bore a black eye. Cassava bit her lip, trying to figure out how to tell him to keep his mouth shut.

"Veran. We riding the waves?" he asked. He hadn't noticed Ferran yet, and seemed distracted as he took them in, not commenting on Nimmory at all.

"Yes, we should be off. Ah—Nimmory was it? How long to reach the Trikingdom?"

"Depends on where you want to go," Nimmory replied. "And my friends all call me Nim."

"I would not presume to be your friend," Veran said shortly. "But I plan to reach Triking City."

Nimmory sighed. "Of course, you do," she muttered. "It's about a four-day trip with good winds, and when I'm around, there tends to be good wind."

Veran nodded. "The ship is stocked for a voyage longer than that. Cassava, take the reins."

Cassava blinked and studied the ship Veran had pointed to. It wasn't so different from one she'd sailed before. "I've got the helm, Henequen on the sail, and—" Cassava just remembered to hold back on Ferran's name. "—you on the ropes. Let's get moving."

It was exciting to be on a ship again. Cassava had always liked the hustle and bustle, and the promise of a new adventure on the horizon made her insides tingle. She felt buzzed, as though she'd been drinking good feelings, and she rode high on it, ordering her friends about and secretly laughing as Veran headed below decks looking a little queasy.

It wasn't long before Cassava felt everything was in a synchronized rhythm. They were all playing the parts

Cassava had assigned to them. She felt like the Priests must always feel: powerful and wise, strong and beautiful.

The ship was called *Farlight*. Cassava spent her time at the helm, occasionally wandering around the rest of the ship making corrections to the many errors her inexperienced crew made. Ferran had been very quiet since they had gotten on board, and Cassava wasn't sure how much of it was his fear of being discovered by Veran and how much was his unease at being near someone who supposedly spoke with the demon.

They hadn't been at sea more than a day when Nimmory approached her. Cassava had just finished making sure the sail was catching maximum air when the girl appeared. She moved like a cat, slinky and silent, but with a brightness about her that Cassava found mystifying.

"So. Cassava or Barli?" she asked, coming forward and leaning on the wheel. Cassava could see a good bit of her breast from that position and quickly focused on Nimmory's face.

"Cassava."

"Is Bari what your friends call you? Or is it a name for a paramour?" Nimmory asked.

Cassava blushed. Paramour sounded so...outlandish. In high fashion. Exotic. Just like Nimmory. "No, Ferran calls me that because he knew me when I went by another name. He calls Henequen something different too. Black Sins take on new names."

"Of course! No one would actually name their kid Strangler. At least, I hope not. It's pretty fucking morbid. What's Cassava mean?"

"It's a poisonous plant," she said. "So, I'm sure you can guess what my specialty is."

"Not what I would have expected from you," Nimmory said.

"Oh? What do I look like?"

"I think you'd look fucking hot with a sword."

Cassava's eyes widened and she stared at Nimmory for several seconds, but the girl seemed completely nonchalant, her fingers flexing on the steering wheel. Finally, she looked up as the silence progressed. "Oh. Am I not allowed to say that? I forgot all you islanders don't believe in same-sex affairs."

Cassava couldn't stop staring at the dangle of her breast. "We know it exists," she said. "Everyone who feels that way is just kept in the Asylum." Cassava reached her hand out for the wheel as if she was making an adjustment, but brushed her fingers unnecessarily by Nimmory. "Like me."

Nimmory's head came up, her eyes shining green like grass. Lush. Healthy. "Is that why you're there then?" Nimmory asked.

Cassava felt a twinge about her wrists where the still pink scars ran. "Yes," she said.

"Good to know," Nimmory said. Her eyes traveled up and down Cassava's body in an instant.

It had been some time since Cassava had felt this way, but here was a beautiful girl staring her up and down, telling her she was hot, and meeting her gaze, meeting her eyes, and not flinching away in fear and disgust. Cassava felt herself moving closer to Nimmory, drawn in by this foreigner's fearlessness and unique posturing. Her chin stretched out just a little until they were inches away.

"Cassava!"

She pulled away and looked up just in time to see the mizzenmast coming toward them. They both ducked as it swung around, unmoored.

Cassava spared a wistful glance at Nimmory before hurrying down the length of the ship to figure out which of the boys was responsible for this latest fiasco.

Dinner aboard *Farlight* was an awkward affair. No one was supposed to spend this much time with a Priest. Ferran had cooked, and the food was decent, but below decks everyone ate in a tense silence. Veran eventually took his plate and sat down a ways away, pulling out a book as he did so. Cassava wondered what he was reading about; didn't he know everything there was to know about the demon?

Cassava looked at the others. Veran was still in earshot, so Ferran couldn't speak, and Henequen was strangely quiet, no murmuring or half-intelligible sentences. It was Nimmory who broke their silence; she had not the respect for the Priests that the Sins did, but she knew he was on the outs and seemed smart enough to know the pecking order.

"So, tell me about the islands—I haven't been on them long. There must be hundreds of interesting things."

Ferran stared resolutely at his plate. Henequen, however, brightened. "There's the bakery on Hevoni that is simply heavenly, and the woman who runs it is beautiful. She's been a single mother for seven years, ever since her husband got sick. And Lulav, well, she sings part time to make a living but—"

"I think Nimmory meant places and sights, Quen," Cassava interrupted.

"Oh, please, just Nim. And I suppose, yes, that's what I meant."

"People are beautiful," Henequen said. "Some of them."

"Why don't you tell us about the Trikingdom?" Cassava asked Nimmory—Nim—impatiently.

Nim got a strange look in her eye. "It's very loud and boisterous in the city. Something is always happening, unlike on the islands. You have to keep a sharp eye while you're out otherwise something is bound to happen to you. But it's vibrant and alive, full of people of all kinds. It's colorful and runs at high speed. It's addicting."

Cassava listened attentively. Glancing at the boys, they seemed significantly less interested. Henequen was staring at Nimmory's ear. Ferran's eyes were fixed on the table.

"It sounds amazing," Cassava said into the silence. "Why would you ever leave?"

Nim pulled at the rice on her plate, tugging it from one side to the other. "That," she said, "is a long tale I wouldn't want to bore you with tonight."

Cassava found herself leading the conversation again, talking about her past aboard a ship and the sea travels she had made with her father. She hadn't thought about him in some time, and wondered now how he was faring. Did he miss her? He had always seemed a little embarrassed when she was too bright eyed and eager. Perhaps the quiet suited him better. Cassava had her moods, though they had only gotten worse as she aged.

Cassava lay alone in her bunk that night thinking about her old life. The tales that had once seemed normal to her now were outlandish. Drinking in a pub against her father's advice? Stealing into the street with a long-haired boy and pretending he was a girl for a little while? Dancing on tabletops and spinning until she couldn't walk straight. Cassava wanted to feel that again. She wanted to be young and wild and taken in by all the pleasures of the night. She imagined drinking until Henequen's word salad made sense to her, getting Ferran to loosen up and move his body, sidling up on the dance floor to a girl who looked like Nim. She imagined it with colors and music that she couldn't even quite capture: a night of bliss in the city. A fantasy. Cassava knew she'd never get more than cold stares and unease for the marks on her face, surely, they were infamous enough that they would be recognized. Even if they weren't, Cassava knew the marks ruined any beauty she had once had.

Cassava fell asleep dreaming of a different world.

Chapter Five

The next few days were a trial by water. The seas were unruly, and the sky opened up again to a downpour on their heads. The raindrops seemed like they were the size of lemons, and everyone sheltered below decks when they weren't seeing to the many necessities of the ship. Cassava spent the most time above deck, and found herself giving orders to Nim to control the wind in one direction or another. It became clear then the limits of Nimmory's powers. While she could control the air in her immediate vicinity, the vessel was too large for her control. When she did manage it, she couldn't hold it for long. It turned out magic had its limits, which Cassava was grateful for.

Below decks, Ferran was always drawing. She had seen some of his work and it was really coming along. When Ferran wasn't drawing, he was cooking up satisfactory meals for all of them. Henequen was surprisingly quiet and still. He had ceased talking in a word salad for the most part; Cassava understood 75% of what he said.

Cassava, when she wasn't ordering everyone around, was practicing with her knife. She had painted some targets on the mast and was slowly working her way through the wood. The *Farlight*'s owner was sure to be displeased. But that was Veran's problem. The Priests had built Cassava to be an implement of destruction. She was good at her job.

Nimmory spent the good days up in the crow's nest. Cassava had tried to find another moment with the foreigner, but she had been a little short and stiff since their dinner conversation and Cassava felt as though she must have offended Nim somehow.

Despite the quiet frictions, there was a peace about the ship that Cassava had not felt in some time: there were no jobs to do, no hit list. There were no people getting in her way. Cassava was in charge of her life again. Veran sat down in the hold or occasionally out on the deck reading, but he made no attempt to command them. Another Priest would have behaved differently, but no doubt Veran had been selected because he had a pleasant temperament.

Cassava felt good, better than she had in a long time. If only she could make things right with Nim, everything would be perfect.

On the fourth night she woke up to Henequen shaking her gently. Cassava woke with a start to see Henequen staring intently at her. It was strange to see him so focused.

"What's going on?" she asked. "Is it something to do with the ship?"

Henequen shook his head. "You know about people, right?"

"I mean I'd like to think so," she said. "But, honestly, Quen, oftentimes it seems like you know much more than me. I know you do all that scouting for the Priests."

He tilted his head. "I don't know what to do," he said.

"Well, I'm going to need a bit more than that to advise you. What's this about?"

"Ferran likes me," he said as though someone was dying.

"Did he tell you that?" Cassava asked, sitting up. That would be bold for Ferran.

"No. I just...know."

"Well how do you feel about him?" Cassava asked.

Henequen wet his lips. "It doesn't matter."

"Of course, it does. That's the whole point of having a relationship. If you like someone, you see if it works. Otherwise, what's the point?"

"I've never had feelings for anyone," Henequen said. "I barely have feelings. Except now."

"Quen, you have feelings overflowing. You want one thing, then something else. You spend your energy trying to fight me, and the next you're in bed with Kazini."

"Those aren't *my* feelings," Henequen said in a frustrated voice. "Everyone else makes me act that way. I know you're happy, and it kind of makes me happy, and Ferran's nervous and all butterflies and Nim's all angsty about going home—"

"Not about me?" Cassava asked.

"What?"

"Nim's not mad at me?"

"Are you even listening to me, Cassava?"

She shook her head. "I'm sorry, Quen. So, you don't know whether you like Ferran or not?"

Henequen gave his shoulders a little shrug. "I feel the

freest I've ever been. Things are getting quieter. But it's not going to last, is it?"

"I don't know, Quen," Cassava said softly. She could see the pain in his face, his fear that this change of events was temporary. And it scared Cassava, who had also been feeling good, to think maybe there was an end for her as well. "Maybe it's the fucking islands. Maybe something about them just makes our heads spin."

Henequen frowned. "If that's true, maybe this really is some paradise Nim is leading us to. But…so what? We're going back."

Cassava knew arguing with Quen on this point at this moment would be unwise. It was better to hold her cards close to her chest and figure things out when she got a better lay of the land. "Well, enjoy it for now and focus on what *you* want. I know you didn't want Kazini here. You've got some bone in this. You just have to figure out where to place it."

Henequen sat back on his heels. "How do you do that?" he asked.

Cassava studied Henequen, hair askew, brown eyes awake and cautious, face open and wondering. "Take some time and just think about it. Think about what's important, what makes your life worth living. I had to do that when I woke up in the Asylum. Had to shift all my priorities around."

"What did you want before you came here?"

"To travel, see the world, and have a secret girlfriend to share it with. Visea didn't share my vision and that…was hard to swallow. I always saw it with her. But I've got something better now."

Henequen swallowed. "All I know how to do is stay alive."

"That's not true," Cassava said. "You chose to become a Black Sin, didn't you? Why did you do that?"

Henequen got a dark look on his face. "I was staying alive," he said. "The Priests told me if I was a Black Sin I could kill anyone who was a threat."

"But you were in the Asylum, Quen. Who was going to hurt you?"

Henequen stood up abruptly. "Good night, Cassava." He rolled into his own bunk.

Cassava stayed awake a while longer. She tried to think about Henequen and his problems, but her mind kept floating back to Nimmory and how she might make everything alright.

The next day land came into sight. Nimmory spotted it from the crow's nest and alerted the rest of the ship. She had spoken less and less as the days wore on, and now that Cassava had encountered Henequen and she had some guess at what was bothering her, Cassava felt now was the time to intervene.

Cassava climbed up to the crow's nest with ease. She had constructed a rigging in the Asylum so long ago for practice, but it had been inspired by this moment.

She took a deep breath as she squeezed herself into the space. You could see so much ocean from up here; a beautiful deep blue mottled with white. Cassava could see a spike of land in the distance. They'd be there before nightfall.

"I used to love it up here. It's so free and empty. Everything stretches beyond you like limitless possibility."

Nimmory let out a sigh. "Not so limitless anymore," she said, her hand stretching out. Cassava felt a light wind dance before them, blowing away from the land as though an omen against them.

"You never told us why you left," Cassava said. "I understand if you don't want to talk in front of Veran. But I know about hard stuff, being cut off from family, being hunted...I tell all these stories about how my life used to be because I'm still bitter about the way it is now. Henequen and Ferran grew up in the Asylum. They don't know another way. They don't remember the before. I've had a whole life taken from me. They don't understand that. But maybe you do."

Nimmory stared at her for several seconds in silence, her green eyes dark and focused. Finally, she looked away from Cassava and opened her mouth. "I don't know how much you know about magic," she began.

Cassava shook her head. "Not much. The Priests don't talk about it. I didn't even know it existed until I met you. I thought I was crazy."

"Well, magic has been around again for a few years now. Kids get it, not adults. But if you grow up, you keep it. At least so far."

"So, you just...have it? You weren't part of some insane

ceremony where you asked to be bestowed powers from the darkness?"

Nim laughed a little. "That would be far more exciting. No. I just woke up one day and was able to do things I didn't understand. Maybe it didn't happen all at once, but I didn't notice it. So, the wind didn't blow in my face for a while. It wasn't till I was running around with my friends and I tripped that anything truly inexplicable happened. I stuck my hand out to brace my fall and I didn't fall. The wind caught me and set me back on my feet."

Cassava frowned. That was hardly sinister. The Priests and Ferran had made magic sound as though it were through some dark communication with some deep evil visage of the demon. "What does it feel like?" Cassava asked.

"Like an extension of myself—like a third arm I was always supposed to have. It feels like a hug. And it's enjoyable to use, sweeping things through the air, giving myself the perfect breeze."

"What does this have to do with you leaving home?" Cassava asked. "If it just happens like that...well it sounds like anything else the Priests lock people up for. But they don't do that in other places."

"Yes, they do," Nimmory said. "It's called jail."

Cassava frowned. "I thought everyone hated us because we locked people up, but you're doing it too?"

"Different people. People who are dangerous. People who can't be left out on the streets."

"Yes, exactly," Cassava said.

"It's not the same. I'll explain some other time."

Cassava didn't really want to let this go, but it sounded like a point she could debate later. "So, what's the problem?" she asked. "It sounds great."

"Well, the Triking doesn't think so. They've decided that you either have to join the army or get 'cured.'"

"So, there is a cure."

"Sure, I guess you could call it that," Nimmory said with an angry tinge to her voice Cassava did not understand. "Except it's not that simple. People can get messed up after getting cured—blanks in their memory, phantom pain, dizziness and passing out. The cure makes you sick half the time. Plus, I'd lose my magic, which I don't want. It's a part of me. It's part of who I am it makes up my essence. I don't want to give that up. I wouldn't be me anymore."

Cassava frowned. A cure that made people sick definitely sounded unappealing. "So, join the army then," Cassava replied. It seemed straightforward enough.

"Of course, *you'd* say that. You basically did. But think about it Cassava, if you'd had the choice, to leave and pick up and move to a new land, or be imprisoned and sent to murder people, which would you choose?"

Cassava was quiet. She had wanted to run away with Visea. She had wanted to do exactly what Nimmory had. They were two sides of the same coin. "You're coming back with us, Nim. I promised you that, didn't I?"

Nimmory swallowed. "Cassava, they might come for me. They might try to take me."

"I'm a trained assassin; just let them try."

Nim took Cassava's hand in hers and sandwiched it between her warm soft skin. "You'd do that?"

"Of course. I know you haven't known me a long time, but I just have this feeling that we've got a long way to go still. I want to see that through."

At that moment, a call from below echoed out. "Cassava! Nimmory! It's about time we talk plans."

"I got you. I promise," Cassava said, squeezing Nimmory's hand. "Now show me the promised land."

Chapter Six

The dock was like any other dock Cassava had been on, but larger. Even the largest dock on Neesi was a fraction of the size. The ships were different too—there were fewer fishing dinghies and it appeared as though everyone worked for larger fishing companies. There were also massive liners and cargo ships, the kind of which only a few ever landed each year on the Islands. Here Cassava saw the ships in their many berths, and could not count the number.

The ships were mostly painted in bright colors, leaning heavily toward bright red and yellow. Cassava saw workers moving briskly among the ships. The sky seemed clearer here and Cassava felt the weight of the sun on her back, but thankfully not in the air around her. The workers spoke quickly in a language Cassava had never heard. It sounded harsh and grating to her ears, but with an amount of emotional expression that would have been severely criticized in the Islands.

Ferran was staring with wide eyes, and he backed slightly into Cassava. "There are so many people," he whispered, in awe or horror or perhaps both.

Cassava realized Ferran had never even been to a

market day, let alone a street fair, and here were throngs of people as dense as any good day at market, and then some. Cassava gripped his hand subtly so that Veran would not see. "And most of them sinners," she said.

Ferran paled, which considering his general pallor was impressive. "Demon's bane," he said.

Cassava laughed a little. "You're already touched by the demon, Ferran. What's it going to do?"

Ferran did not reply, but his expression remained grim.

Cassava guided the ship in, relieved to find the deck hands all spoke Trade and not just Belish. Nimmory helped, while the whole time Veran stood nearby, dressed in his finest Priestly garb.

Nimmory sighed deeply. "You promise you've got my back?" She asked.

Cassava nodded. "I promise."

Ferran looked between the two of them silently.

Without another word, Nimmory led the way off the gangplank. "I know a guy. He should get you a meeting with someone important, but Veran's in charge after that. I have no idea what they'll do with you."

Heading into the chaos was daunting even for Cassava, and Ferran stuck to her like a burr. Henequen was in his own head, but he at least seemed to be following them, so Cassava decided not to worry too much. He would have his own adjustment pains.

The streets were full of people talking, carts on wheels that would have never survived the mud in the Islands, hawkers selling wares off their bodies, and children ducking in between the legs of adults.

Cassava had expected to be one of the only darker-skinned people, but there was a variety on the streets. Meinish individuals mixed with Belish and even whiter—the occasional Chajian that appeared so rarely on the Island. There were even some people with skin darker than Cassava had ever seen.

But it wasn't just the skin colors that gave Cassava reason to stare. Colorful birds sat on shoulders, animals Cassava didn't even have a name for that walked on four legs like a cat, but had a longer face and ears that dropped down. The people were dressed in longer tunics rather than pants and shirt, with colorful and distinctive belts tied around their waists. Their ears dangled with jewelry, most with a silver stud in addition to larger more colorful pieces. Their hair was strange too—many of them were shocking blonde and red, but Cassava saw other colors too that seemed still more eccentric—blue and green and pink. It was incredible.

It was difficult to focus on anything, there was so much going on. Cassava was glad to have Nimmory leading the way. Cassava kept refocusing on her bright hair as a beacon among the madness.

Eventually they made it to quieter streets, though even here people hung out in the stone alleyways. Cassava saw a child with one arm holding out a cup. She was thin and in rags, filthy.

"Something to feed me, bissa" her voice called out, stronger and yet more desperate than Cassava could have anticipated. Cassava wondered what she was doing there. Ferran, who had been stuck to Cassava, detached himself momentarily and placed a mango on the ground in front of her.

"Ta," she said, giving him a chipped smile.

"Come on," Nimmory said, "you can't stop at each one, there are thousands."

Cassava felt bewildered. "What are they doing? Why aren't they being taken care of?" she asked.

Nimmory shrugged her shoulders. "That's not how it works here. Everyone for themselves."

They passed several other beggars, and Cassava's stomach turned each time. How heartless these people must be to leave these nonfunctional people to their own devices! Cassava thought it an ugly blight on what seemed a beautifully vibrant city.

Nimmory took them to a large silver gate with several people standing in front of it. They were dressed differently—a solid bright red with yellow accents, jackets and pants rather than tunics, and swords hung on their sides. Cassava wondered if this was the answer to the Black Sins.

Nimmory approached them and talked in Belish for a short while. The woman in the front looked over their party and said a few more things before stepping aside. The large gates swung open silently, held by some of the other red-dressed individuals.

Cassava walked quickly to catch up with Nim as they passed the gates. She could tell already the character of this neighborhood was significantly different from the rest of the city. The houses were larger and stately, made of white walls with orange tile. They had second and third stories, with large windows and gardens spread out before their gaudy doors. There was little wood in the architecture here; the homes, Cassava guessed, were made mostly of dressed up earth.

Cassava could see three tall towers in close proximity to each other rising before them. They were great spires the height of which Cassava had never seen, seeming to stretch at least seven stories into a vivid blue sky. The sun was high and beat on their backs as they made their way through these much quieter streets. Cassava felt the weight of her cloak on her back and pulled back her hood for a breath of fresh air. Henequen had his hood down as well, and was looking around as though searching for something. Ferran's was still pulled low, a necessary burden when they were around Veran. Cassava doubted if any of the people in the Trikingdom would know the difference between the marking on their faces. No doubt they would assume Ferran was just as dangerous as her and Henequen, an idea that was frankly laughable. Cassava didn't think Ferran had ever hurt anyone.

"Where are we?" she asked Nimmory.

"The Heart" Nimmory replied. "The city is laid out like a wheel and this is its center. This is where the wealthy and important people live. The guards only let some people through. Normally you have to have a pass if you don't live here."

Cassava frowned. "You mean the rich people wall themselves off from everyone else?"

"Pretty much, yeah."

It seemed so backward. "Why would they trap themselves like that?"

"Because they'd prefer to live their pretty lives pretending the rest of the world doesn't exist."

Cassava didn't understand, but she doubted Nimmory could explain it to her satisfaction. Perhaps if they stayed here, it would become clear.

Nimmory led them toward one of the towers. Outside the tower was a wealth of plants, flowers in full bloom of a dozen different colors, and hedges the like Cassava had never seen. A pathway with a pagoda overhead led up to the tower, granting a smattering of shade.

Cassava saw two more redcoats standing outside the tower's entrance. Now that they were at the tower, Cassava could see truly how large it was. It stretched up higher than any tree into the sky, and its width was the length of at least two huge cargo ships. It was an off-white color that Cassava guessed had once been pure, but time and weather had taken its toll. Cassava wondered how old it was, and whether the Asylums were older.

"This is the State's Tower," Nimmory said. "Each tower has its own King and accompanying staff. Normally, ambassadors stay here, which I suppose you are."

"I am," Veran said. "Thank you for taking us here."

Nimmory glanced at Cassava again, then back at the soldiers. "Time to see what you're worth," she said, and stepped forward.

The guards greeted her in the Belish tongue, reaching forward and pulling her into a hug. Nimmory seemed to resist, from Cassava's point of view. Nimmory replied in

Trade and they followed suit. "This is Priest Veran from the Filoli Islands."

"Filoli?"

"Neesi," Veran said. "Hello," he added politely. "I am looking to speak to your master."

"I am Zoal and this is Aravan. Please, come in. We will speak to the Secretary. We were not expecting you."

"I'm afraid the matter came quite urgently, and we frankly weren't sure who to contact," Veran replied.

The two guards led them inside into a large room with a plush rug underfoot. Cassava wanted to take her shoes off and feel it between her toes. Instead, she took Henequen's lead and stood just to one side of Veran, Henequen on the other. Ferran trailed behind, and Nimmory's hands were fidgeting and she kept looking back at Zoal and Aravan.

"Wait here," Zoal said before disappearing down a hallway. Aravan stayed with them.

Cassava looked around the room. There were paintings of several stately looking men and women, dressed in rich tunics with decadent embroidery. There were pictures too of places that looked utterly incredible—a fortress of red rock with a sheer wall, a desertscape with a single tree and the brilliant blue pool of water glimmering out hopefully, a rocky land with shafts of rock sticking up like posts through a thick dark jungle. Cassava wondered if someone had really been to all these places to bring such beauty back.

There were chairs in this room too, and couches that looked plusher than anything Cassava had ever seen. She imagined one would simply sink in and disappear in all this finery.

"Who lives like this?" Cassava breathed in awe. Her family had never owned a painting or a cushioned seat, let alone had a room the size of her house to put them in.

Nimmory let out a breath. "The best and the brightest," she said.

There was class on the Islands, but it was smaller than this. A rich person might have a two-story house, a ship of his own, but nothing as grandiose as this. Everyone wore essentially the same clothes, ate the same foods, and lived in the same places.

Zoal returned with a small woman dressed in a crisp yellow gown. "I understand you've come a long way," she said politely. "Why don't I take you to another room and we can talk?"

They followed her through the hallway to a still-nicer room that had Cassava staring. A large portrait of a naked woman hung on the wall, stretching her hand out for a fruit on a tree.

"My name is Dillian," she said. "I am the King's secretary. He is understandably very busy, but would love to meet you at dinner tonight. What business there is to discuss can be done at a later time. I'm sure you all must be weary from your travels." She looked around and said something in Belish to Aravan, who vanished and then promptly reappeared with a plate of refreshments, which were set on the table.

"I am Veran, and these are my traveling companions," Veran said.

Dillian smiled at them. "You must be Black Sins. I've heard a lot about you, but I've never met one." She put her arm out as Nim had done, but Cassava still had no idea what to do in response. In another moment she put her hand away. "I'm so sorry, it's been ever so long since I studied Filoli manners," she said apologetically. "What are your names?"

"Ca—"

"This is Cassava and Henequen. They are indeed Black Sins, and as such should not be addressed directly for official business. They are more like bodyguards. If they need something, they will tell you. Otherwise, forget they are there. I am who you will be working with." Veran replied tightly.

"Oh, alright." She looked at Ferran too, no doubt aware he hadn't been introduced, but moved on. "Welcome to you all. Veran, I'm afraid we have no knowledge of this visit. It's been a very long time since we've had visitors from Filoli."

"As you know, we prefer to keep our own counsel," Veran said stiffly. He had not reached for any of the delicacies, and although Cassava was highly intrigued, she felt she had best remain professional behind him. "However, times come when one must wander from home for answers."

Dillian nodded. "Well, it might be some time before you can be seen, but it would be an honor to host representatives from the lovely islands. We can, of course, provide rooms for all of you."

"That would be appreciated," Veran said. "We find this city very strange and overwhelming. We wouldn't have made it this far without our guide." He nodded to Nimmory, who squirmed under Dillian's graze.

"You look familiar," Dillian said. "What's your name?"

"Barli," Nimmory said. She shrugged her shoulders. "I just wanted to make sure these good folks got to the right place. I can go now."

Dillian stared at her a moment longer before waving her hand. "You're missing an earring, Barli. You'd better take care. Zoal, see her out." She added something in Belish.

Cassava watched Nimmory walk away, wondering about her lie and if she was in as much trouble as she seemed to think. Hopefully, they would find each other again.

Dillian refocused on Veran and began to ask him about his trip. Cassava began to tune the conversation out, knowing Veran would be furious if she were to say anything anyway, it seemed like the best solution was to use this time pondering over other matters.

Nimmory had used her name when she left. Was there a reason? Was it just because it was the first name she could think of? Had she been thinking about Cassava? She had remembered what Ferran had called her. Did it mean something?

Some time later, Zoal returned to the room, and Cassava's focus shifted to the guard, whose gender she could not quite place, as the last person to encounter Nimmory. Cassava looked at Zoal and saw with surprise that their face was not unaltered. Jewelry stuck out from their nose and eyebrow. But even more shockingly, they had a mark on their face. It was not a scar like Cassava's, but looked as though someone had taken a black pen to their face and drawn on it. There was what looked like a plant of some sort coming up the side of Zoal's neck and rising up to their cheek from their ear. Cassava found herself staring and quickly looked away, changing her focus to the ground. She was doing just what she hated when others did to her!

Abruptly, at least it seemed to Cassava, Veran was rising from his chair. He and Dillian bowed slightly to one another. "I'll have Zoal show you to your rooms."

"Please, follow me." Zoal led them again down the hall to yet another great room that was full of tables spaced at length from each other, with a wide empty floor in the middle and a little stage to the side. Several people were sitting at the tables, talking quietly. One appeared to be doing so over some sort of game. A grand staircase ascended and curled into some unknown space. They did not ascend that stair, but passed through yet another hallway and finally to a more practical stair. Even this stair was carpeted, something Cassava had certainly never seen. Ladders were far more common than stairs on the islands.

They went up and up and up. Henequen and Cassava felt no trouble, given their usual workout. Ferran and Veran on the other hand were both breathing hard as they reached the fourth floor.

A curved hallway greeted them, with a peppering of doorways with different numerals. Zoal led them halfway down and pointed to the room with a 3 emblazoned on the door. "This suite is yours. You'll find the necessities for work and sleep here. Dinner is served in the dining room at six. Of course, you are free to eat anywhere you like in the city; there is no end of delicious restaurants we can show you to. The baths are on the first floor, out past the red door.

There are signs, but I don't think you'll be able to read them. Ask anyone in red for assistance; they should be more than happy to help."

"Thank you, I'm sure we'll find what we need," Veran said.

Zoal pointed to several other doors in turn. "There are a few other guests here now, a family from Mysri and a young woman from the Quakes. And, of course, the Belish ambassador."

Veran nodded as though he understood, but Cassava had her doubts he did. Cassava barely recognized the place names—pressed to put them down on a map, Cassava would have no hope.

Zoal bowed again but took their leave quickly.

Veran pushed open the door and Cassava gasped.

Before them was a full sitting room, with couches as plush as the one downstairs, and a beautiful hardwood desk polished to a shine. Cassava saw four doors off the main room and moved to investigate. Each was its own masterpiece, with a themed color and beautiful landscapes of the plains and fields on their walls. A huge bed with mesh curtains pulled down around it centered in the room. A wardrobe stood in the corner by a dressing table with a large mirror—larger than Cassava had ever seen. A washbasin stood on the table, and there was a plush chair, side table, and elegant lamp in one corner to make the quintessential reading nook.

Cassava felt sorely out of place with her tattered traveling clothes and messy hair. She smelled of dirt, mud, and fish. Cassava sniffed the air to find the room turned down with the scent of lavender. Cassava discarded her cloak, hanging it carefully in the closet, where she found a fine red robe and simple tunic that was made of a shimmery material that felt as smooth as water.

Cassava returned to the main room. Veran had put his belongings down and was placing his books on the desk in organized piles. Veran had been the only one who needed a sizable bag for his things; Cassava and Henequen had brought a single change of clothes each. Ferran was sitting on the bed in his room, staring at the mesh curtains.

Cassava walked over to him. "I can't believe they have this kind of wealth here. I've never seen anything like it."

Ferran fell back into the pillows—there were five on each bed. "I didn't think the demon would be like this," he said, stroking the soft fabric.

There was a knock on the door and a girl stood there with a pile of clothes over her head. "Mas Dillian said these were for you to wear to dinner."

Henequen took the garments from her gently and passed them out. Veran refused; his Priest garb was a part of his identity and one he was putting forward. But he told the Sins to wear them. "I don't want to highlight the fact that I've brought killers with me. It will make them more comfortable if you are dressed like the locals."

Cassava didn't really get the logic: their skin and faces marked them as others. But perhaps there was more enmity here than she had guessed; if other people had marks on their faces, perhaps the uneducated would not realize what they were.

Either way, Cassava was happy to put on the fresh

clothes. They were a bright red like a berry, with yellow-gold accents. The tunic fit Cassava comfortably, and the material felt amazing against her skin. Cassava, feeling nice, did her best to tame her hair and tied it off into a neat bun at the back of her head. Then she helped Ferran with his mess of black hair. She arranged it artfully in front of his face so the markings would still be obscured from Veran. Cassava wasn't sure what would happen if Veran realized Ferran was not only alive, but two Black Sins had orchestrated a trip to the Trikingdom for Ferran.

Cassava realized with a start that this place might be the best life for Ferran. If his face markings would not doom him here, he would have the ability to talk and interact with people as though he were a normal person.

Well, they would see what happened tonight. There was time before they had to make real decisions; Ferran may well not be able to stomach it. Besides, he was wholly unprepared for the real world. Cassava wasn't sure she could leave him in good conscience. What would he do? How would he survive?

Readied for dinner, their queer party departed. The hall with tables was much fuller now, with a good two dozen people talking and chatting over food, which was set up in the middle of the hall on long tables.

Cassava had never seen such foods before, and there were pastries and breads that looked like they had been made by a doll. Long strings were twirled in with a dark red sauce and pieces of meat poked out along with some cooked down green vegetable.

Veran found them a more secluded table, but before long they were joined by a few other Meinish individuals.

"Hello, may we join you?" a teenaged boy asked politely. He directed his question to Henequen rather than Veran. At his side was a younger girl Cassava assumed was his sister.

Henequen glanced at Veran, seeking his approval, but the man was already stuck with his head in a book. Finally, he nodded.

"I am Faita Sinju and this is my little sister Beiru. It's nice to see other Meinish people at the table. My father is negotiating a contract, and my mother is trying to set me up with one of the princesses here," he said with a trite smile.

"I'm Cassava, and this is Henequen and, uh, another Sin. We're accompanying Priest Veran," Cassava said, pointing to them in turn.

Faita nodded warmly. "You're Islanders, then? Ah, my father will be furious. He's never forgiven Filoli for breaking off from the mainland. Believes you should belong to Meinweit."

Henequen lifted his head at that, staring at Faita. "We don't belong to anyone," he said.

Faita made an awkward laugh. "I'll be sure to tell my father that," he said. "Are you enjoying your time in the city? It doesn't appear you get out much."

Cassava frowned, sure he was picking on their choice of clothing and general roughness of their appearance. "We haven't been here long," Cassava said, "but everything seems...ornate."

"The Triking can be a little heavy handed in their

decorations. I frankly find them a bit overstated. You should visit Meinweit; our decor may be more to your liking."

Cassava decided she did not like Faita, but she wasn't sure how to get out of the conversation. Faita began talking about the best parts of the city, and his tone grated Cassava more and more until the moment was broken by the little girl.

"What's wrong with your faces?" the girl asked.

Faita immediately put his hand over his sister's face. "I'm so sorry," he apologized. "So rude."

Cassava smiled thinly. "It's alright," Cassava said. She fixed her eyes on the little girl, who was staring defiantly at Cassava's face. "We got these marks because we were touched by demon. We're unstable. Henequen hears voices in his head. I get total rage and go wild. And this one? He looks so innocent, but he's killed thousands of people, including little girls like you."

Immediately Beiru began to cry and collapsed into her brother's side. Faita gave Cassava a dirty look before hurrying his sister away, attempting to console the sobbing child.

"Why did you do that?" Ferran asked quietly. "They were talking. To *us*."

Cassava shook her head. "I'm gonna take you somewhere with real people. Those two were snakes. It's not your fault you can't tell the difference yet."

Henequen was staring at the space where Faita had been. "Snake," he agreed. "Slither slither bite bite."

"Exactly."

Dillian saw them briefly at dinner and asked how they

were settling in. She told Veran the King would meet with him tomorrow, and, unfortunately, he had other business to attend to tonight. She passed them all out little medallions she said would allow them to get back into the Heart if they left.

After dinner, Cassava did her due diligence scanning the room for danger, but nothing stood out to her. "I don't think Veran has to worry," she said to Henequen. "It didn't seem like anyone cares that we're here."

Henequen shook his head. "That boy knew who we were. He was talking to us for a reason."

"That kid? We'd demolish him in a second," she said.

Henequen did not reply.

Cassava sighed. It was hard to get anything out of Henequen, but his sixth sense about people was not something that should be entirely ignored. "Well, *I'm* going out tonight," she said. "If we're in the pits of sin, I'd like to explore it a little bit."

Henequen stood outside Veran's closed door with resolute shoulders.

Cassava regarded him a moment longer before wandering over to Ferran's room. "Ferran, you want to come with me? I'll show you what normal people are like."

Ferran glanced at Veran's closed door. "Do you think he'll notice?" he asked.

"If he does, I'll just say I was patrolling. We've got to get a sense of this place if we're going to be any good to him at all."

She and Ferran changed back into their road clothes and headed out of the tower. Cassava hoped she could find her way back. The city was quite large and there were three towers. But that would be drunk Cassava's problem.

Cassava kept her eyes open for Nimmory, but she was hard-pressed to make her out amidst so many Belish individuals. There was blonde hair everywhere.

The streets were quieter at night, but still with more life than the Islands. Everyone was early to bed, early to rise there. Here, Cassava got the sense that things were only beginning.

Outside the Heart, the streets were dressed with occasional clusters, having a drink or smoke out in the night. Smoking was strictly disallowed on the Islands, and Cassava considered approaching one of them for a drag, but Ferran coughed and took her hand and dragged her past them.

"I've heard that stuff makes you deadly ill," he said.

"Probably not if you only do it once," Cassava replied, but Ferran's expression brooked no argument. "You'll have a drink with me, won't you? It makes everything fuzzy and sweet."

Ferran shrugged. "I guess," he allowed.

"Excellent!" Cassava exclaimed. She found them a bar near the docks that she judged to be appropriately loud and rowdy: not out of control, but full of life and energy. It was when Cassava got to the counter she remembered that money existed for normal people, and her status as a Black Sin would not provide her free sustenance like it normally did.

She took a seat at the bar and winked at the bartender, a girl with pink hair and painted nails.

"What can I get you?"

Cassava glanced around the bar, looking for someone to play. "Anyone here buying?" she asked sweetly.

The bartender appraised her. "Foreigners? Well, that one likes to buy for little things. Your friend might have some luck with Hershel. He plays with all sorts."

Cassava thanked her, and drifted off into the crowd, dragging Ferran behind her. She flitted up to the man named Hershel and shoved an unsuspecting Ferran into him.

"Hey, watch your—"

"Sorry! Sorry!" Ferran said, glaring at Cassava for a second before he fixed his quivering attention on Hershel.

"It was my fault," Cassava said. She wasn't used to the idea that Ferran would be the one of interest. She used to do this with her girlfriends. It felt strange for the attraction to a man to be played out in the open. Cassava felt as though she was committing an unholy act. Which, she supposed, she was. But everything was unholy here. "I'm Cassava, and this is my friend Ferran."

"Friend?" the man said. He was not unattractive. He had a wide face and sharp jaw and cheekbones. His hair was ruby red and pulled up into a bun on the top of his head.

"Friend," Cassava confirmed. "We're new to town."

He looked Cassava up and down quickly, but his gaze lingered on Ferran. "Travelers, hmm? So, what's your story, fliay?" he asked Ferran.

Ferran swallowed and leaned slightly into Cassava.

Cassava gave his shoulder a little squeeze. "We've been on a boat for a week. We had a harrowing time escaping the

Asylum," she said, gesturing to her face. It was odd. The people here stared at them, but it was not with the same crushing fear that Cassava felt coming off the Islanders, but instead a gentler curiosity. They were odd, not dangerous.

"Really?" The man appraised them both again. "And you've come here for a taste of the real world?"

"Hopefully. We're finding ourselves a little low on cash," Cassava said.

He grinned. "I think I can help you out with that," he said. "Brit, two talos for my Meinish friends."

Cassava put her hand gratefully around the beverage. It was hardier and had more taste than she was used to in her alcohol, but she found it enjoyable enough. Ferran tasted it curiously and recoiled.

"Takes a little getting used to," the man said with a laugh. He put his hand out and gave Ferran a little squeeze. "Do they have liquor on the Islands?"

Ferran took another sip, looking determined. "Yes, but I've never had."

"Oh, a virgin? I should have gotten you the good stuff."

Cassava took another big swig and tasted the honeyed, earthy talo. She felt the warmth building in her cheeks and stomach. "You have friends?" Cassava asked pointedly.

Hershel winked at her, "What's your pleasure?" he asked.

Cassava wet her lips. She had never been in this position before. Hershel was asking, not because Cassava should fear the consequences, but to give her what she wanted. "I like girls," she said.

Hershel nodded and called over a woman with light

brown hair. She was clearly several years older than Cassava, but Cassava didn't care. Her drink was starting to hit her and it had been a long time since Cassava had gotten the opportunity to just have a good time.

Cassava was self-conscious at first—she was young and ugly—but Hershel's friend didn't seem to mind. She looked at Cassava's face and did not flinch away, and eventually Cassava forgot about it. She was flirting. With a girl. In public. Cassava found herself laughing at the absurdity of it.

She glanced over at Ferran, who seemed to be doing okay with Hershel. Cassava thought him an opportunist, but not dangerous. It would have been nice to have Henequen along to be sure, but Cassava wasn't overly worried. Besides, she had more immediate gratification in front of her.

Flirting with a girl was largely the same as with men, only it was much much easier. Cassava didn't have to struggle to come up with compliments, and it felt good when her hand came to rest on Cassava's thigh.

It wasn't all that long before Cassava was touching her back, feeling the build of her shoulder and the curve of her spine. Cassava brought her hand up and gently touched the woman's lips with her fingertips. She leaned in slowly and suddenly they were kissing.

Cassava had not kissed anyone since Visea. She had hardly thought about it. Now she was being assaulted by this glorious sensation of soft gentle lips on hers, the flick of a tongue, the suggestion of more.

With her eyes closed, Cassava found herself imagining someone else. But it wasn't Visea. Cassava broke away from the kiss abruptly, her cheeks flaring. She turned away from the woman and grabbed Ferran. "Let's dance," she demanded, leading him despite his feeble protests to the dance floor.

Cassava didn't recognize all the sounds—they were brassy and full of a different kind of life. It took her a little while to find her rhythm, but before long she had the best of the music in her bones and was leading Ferran into the experience.

At some point, Ferran disappeared, but Cassava kept dancing for a long time, until much of the crowd had drifted out to other pursuits. Finally, the musicians began to pack up, and Cassava collapsed onto a stool, drenched in sweat and thoroughly satisfied.

Ferran was sitting at a corner table with a deck of cards, along with Hershel and two other people. Cassava wandered over and watched for a while, but she didn't understand the game. Ferran at least seemed to and won at least once while Cassava was watching.

Finally, she tapped him on the shoulder. "Ready to go?"

He nodded and thanked his opponents. Hershel leaned forward and gave him a little kiss on his cheek. Ferran blushed and walked quickly to the door.

Outside in the cool night air, Cassava enjoyed the feeling of moonlight on her face.

"That was incredible," Ferran said.

Cassava smiled. "If nothing else, I'm glad you got a glimpse at a normal life," she said.

Ferran nodded, but was very quiet the rest of the walk back.

Cassava went to bed after checking with Henequen that no one had come by. Cassava tossed and turned on the delightfully soft sheets. She knew it was only natural to move on, she knew that was best, and yet...and yet Cassava didn't want to give up on her first love. It felt sacred. How could she be falling for someone else?

Chapter Seven

The next morning they were undisturbed at breakfast. Ferran stayed behind in the rooms while Cassava and Henequen accompanied Veran to a meeting. Cassava hadn't been paying attention when it was announced, but it seemed to be some general meeting between the various emissaries. Veran had decided, as he was in the country, he should do the most he could to demonstrate Island presence in these sinful lands.

They returned to the ornate room Dillian had first met them in. Today, a large man with hair slicked back sat in a well-cushioned chair. He wore a thin circlet on his head. Cassava could only assume this blue-eyed man with a distinguished beard was one of the Trikingdom's three kings. A dark-haired woman who looked to be in her late twenties took a seat at the table as they entered. She had a silver stud in her ear, shoulder-length dark brown hair, and a stack of papers nearly up to her chin. As Cassava watched, she cracked her neck. Shortly after Veran sat down, a middle aged Meinish man with similar features to the brother and sister they had met the other day entered. He did a double-take when he saw Veran flanked by the Black Sins.

The Meinish man turned to the King. "I wasn't aware the delegation from Filoli was partial to this matter," he said tightly.

The King waved his hand. "Sit down, Dasun. Veran here has kindly graced us with his presence, as this is a meeting open to all foreign delegations. The matters of our world concern the Islands as well, I am sure. Now, for introductions. I, as I'm sure you are well aware, am Beziah Pinion, Stateking of the Trikingdom."

The woman inclined her head. "My name is Novenza Altan. I am Queen Ryanna's emissary and personal messenger."

"I am Priest Veran, from Filoli."

"As the Beziah said, I am Dasun Felong, an emissary from Meinweit." He glared at Cassava and Henequen. "Surely, Priest Veran, you do not need your bodyguards in this room?"

Veran folded his hands into his lap, patient as the dawn. "The Black Sins stay with me."

"Perhaps you cannot leash your dogs," Dasun said.

Veran smiled thinly. "My companions are far more competent than the average soldier. A dog may learn to kill, but it will not know why. The Black Sins ferret out the cracks in our system better than anyone; I trust they will do the same here."

"Perhaps we should get to business," Beziah said curtly, "as I have already made it clear Veran and his companions are to be welcomed."

Business, it turned out, was a series of trade negotiations that Cassava had no interest in. Veran, for his part, made occasional comments about Filoli and what they were looking for. Cassava could tell from these exchanges that Veran was at a disadvantage. He was not used to negotiation, nor did he have a particularly powerful position. The islands were small and insignificant compared to the might, size, and wealth of the other three countries present.

Cassava often glanced at Henequen during the exchanges, but he seemed focused and unbothered by the long hours of standing and not doing anything. The worst part was when they brought in trays of delicious-smelling food and Cassava had to still stand behind Veran like a soldier. She could have been doing something so much more enjoyable with her time—there was a huge city to explore, not to mention Nim to catch up with. Where had she spent the night? Surely, if she was so afraid, she wouldn't go back to her family? Cassava wasn't sure and it made her uncomfortable and anxious.

Cassava's mind played out a dozen different scenarios, and the next few hours led to Cassava's head growing more and more plagued by its own fantasies.

Finally, they broke for dinner. Henequen pulled Cassava aside as they walked. "I don't trust him."

"Which one?" Cassava asked.

"Both," Henequen said.

Cassava wet her lips. "What's wrong with them?" Cassava asked, though she barely cared. So what if these people were shady? They would be out of here in another few days. "Are you sure, Quen? Or are you just paranoid?"

Henequen pinched her arm roughly. "This is the mission," he said. "Don't you even care?"

Cassava rolled her eyes. "No one's out to kill Veran. Nobody cares that we're here. Ferran and I went out last night and we're treated like normal humans. They don't care."

Henequen squared his shoulders. "We have a duty, Cassava. We're supposed to protect Veran. And I'm telling you, something's going on."

"Something *is* going on," Cassava said. "But I think you're looking in the wrong place."

Henequen frowned. "So, what do *you* think is happening?"

They fell into lines filling up their plates. Cassava tried to figure how to put this so Henequen would care about something besides his sacred duty. Cassava was no genius tracker, but Henequen could find just about anyone. "The ones with magic are the real threat. They're out here in numbers. You think they want Veran around? We're supposed to kill anyone with magic; that's bound to be unpopular."

Henequen sat down and began shoveling food into his mouth. It hardly seemed like he was appreciating the unique flavors of the Triking repertoire. "You could be right. Magic is dangerous. It could be very difficult to stop that kind of attack," he said thoughtfully.

"Exactly!" Cassava said. "So, I think we need to find out what's going on in that community. They have to exist somewhere in the city; like finds like."

"So where do we start?"

"I think we start with Nimmory. She's our key."

"So where is she?" Henequen asked.

"I don't know."

Henequen sat quietly for several minutes. "Okay," he said. "We need to talk to the guard."

Cassava blinked. "The guard?"

"They were the last one to see her. Then we follow the trail from there."

"Of course," she said.

"But we can't leave Veran unattended. Anything could happen."

"I'll go," Cassava said quickly. She didn't want Henequen interfering anyway. She just hoped his initial insight would be enough to get her where she needed to go.

Henequen did not chat with Cassava over lunch, but instead murmured softly to himself in that way he had. Cassava listened for a while, but the words didn't form a pattern for her and eventually she tuned it out. Veran was sitting some distance away, scribbling fiercely. He may have gotten in a little over his head, Cassava thought with no small amount of satisfaction. It was nice to see this harried side of a Priest—they were always so calm and dignified. Now he was not the top of the food chain, and while Cassava too had felt insulted at today's meeting, her stake in matters was much smaller. She did not run the government after, all.

"Hello. I'm afraid I didn't catch your names earlier."

Cassava looked up in surprise to see Novenza standing in front of them, plate in hand. It took her a moment to remember her manners before she nodded politely and gestured for the woman to have a seat. "I'm Cassava," she said, "and that's Henequen."

"Oh. You're the newest Sin then, aren't you?"

Cassava nodded, feeling disturbed. Even her own countrymen didn't know that. They only knew to fear her.

"Terrible for that girl to go missing like that," Novenza said with a shake of her head.

Cassava frowned. Was she talking about Nim? Her heart sped up and her hands twitched. "What are you talking about?" she asked breathlessly.

"Your predecessor," the woman said. Novenza's eyes were sharp and there was something in the intelligence of her gaze that made Cassava afraid. These were island secrets. More than that, this was something even the Black Sins did not discuss.

Cassava had picked up from bits and pieces that she had replaced a Black Sin known only as Gesid, or the Girl. What had happened to her, no one had ever told Cassava.

The conversation had caught Henequen's attention too. He pulled himself away from his muttering long enough to give her a cold, hard stare. "We don't speak about it," he said. "How do you know of such things?"

Novenza's expression stiffened for a moment and then relaxed. "All countries keep tabs on one another, Henequen. Did you think a such a substantial shift in law enforcement would go unnoticed?"

Cassava had never in a million years heard herself referred to as law enforcement. That was a concept they kept well away from their shores. That was for the demon-fueled, a sad pathetic attempt to bring some order to their disorderly populace. "Our spiritual matters," Cassava said carefully, "are none of your concern."

Novenza fiddled with her food for a moment before lifting it. "The spiritual concerns us all, though in vastly different ways. A wise ruler needs to be kept abreast of all kinds of matters within and without her country."

"I'm sorry who do you work for again?" Cassava asked bluntly.

"I'm here at the Queen's request. But I, like all ambassadors, have objectives of my own."

Cassava knew the only Queen with any power was the ruler of Belin. "And what might those objectives be?"

Novenza smiled at her. "You remind me of myself, Cassava. A hot head without a thought of the consequences I was. It wasn't till I joined with Aravan I began to think beyond now."

Cassava's nostrils flared slightly. She wasn't stupid. Novenza might be kinder, but clearly she still didn't think much of the Black Sins. "I hold my thoughts in better than some," she remarked hotly, thinking about the rude way they had been treated all afternoon.

"But it's not strategic," Novenza said. "You're honest and protective, I think."

Cassava didn't understand how this conversation had become about her, and how it had gotten so far out of hand. "You didn't answer my question," she said.

"We have certain agreements with the Triking, and I'm here to ensure there's follow through." Novenza said.

She was incredibly evasive, Cassava thought. If it hadn't been for their earlier conversation, she would have dismissed it as nothing more than the dull contracts they had been arguing over most of the day. No, this was something different.

Henequen apparently thought so too, because his gaze, which had been focused on her, slipped back to his lap and he began muttering words under his breath. The occupancy of the dining hall was only picking up, and Cassava didn't want to draw attention. They were assassins, after all.

"Perhaps we can talk more another day," she said firmly. "I'm afraid my friend isn't feeling well."

Novenza's gaze turned to Henequen and there was a look of surprise there before she schooled her features. "Of course. Just know I'm here to lend a hand to the marginalized. Of all stripes and colors. I hope you feel better tomorrow," she added politely to Henequen as she left.

Cassava leaned closer to Henequen. "Do you get a bad sense off her too?" She asked.

Henequen shook his head slightly. "She reminds me of Nimmory," he said.

Cassava looked back at the woman and shook her head. "I don't see it."

"Inside," Henequen said. "They run the same."

Cassava shook her head. No. Henequen was wrong this time. That slimy older woman was nothing like Nim. Nim was funny and vibrant and insightful. Novenza was just full of herself. Marginalized? Was she trying to get to them? Make them feel as though they were on the wrong path? Cassava was as powerful as she could be, given her position. She had maneuvered herself and her friends here and, so far, the only thing that had gone remotely off line was Nimmory—a problem Cassava would swiftly remedy.

Henequen started drawing lines in his food with his fork; some purple mashed substance became more and more mangled, dragged between beans and onion. "Sting. Strings. Running. Hide. Harrow."

Cassava glanced at Veran, whose nose was buried in a book. She tapped the table in front of him. "Hey. We should go back to the room," she said, looking pointedly at Henequen. Veran blinked and nodded, gathering up his things in a disheveled pile and pulling them to his chest.

Once they were safely back in the room, Henequen perked up a bit, walking around the room in a circle over and over again, muttering to himself. It made Cassava feel crazy just looking at him, but she knew the only way to stop him was to get in a fight and Cassava didn't feel like doing that, especially not in front of Veran. It just highlighted Henequen's instability. Cassava didn't think Henequen was in jeopardy given his substantial talents, but there was always the chance the Priests would pull the plug on him if his brand of crazy got just a little more out of control. This was Henequen doing well. This was Henequen coping.

Ferran sat watching Henequen pace. He was sitting in one of the cushioned chairs with his sketchpad. When Veran had absconded to his room, he pulled his hood back. Cassava came over to him and took a look at what he was doing. He had sketched out a picture of the night before— some of the players at the table sharking cards. Cassava was impressed. She knew he hadn't practiced people very much, but he had a natural gift. The anatomy was a bit off, but details on parts of people Ferran had experienced personally were crisp—fine hands, the bends of the fingers, the join of an elbow. But the faces were unclear and disproportionate. Ferran just hadn't seen them very often.

"Cooking, drawing, planting, card playing, what can't you do?" Cassava said with a smile. She was glad to see Ferran blooming. She took pride in this point since it was all thanks to her.

Ferran smiled shyly. "Are you going out again tonight?"

Cassava nodded, "but I can't take you with me. I don't know what's going to happen."

"Shouldn't I come with you then?" Ferran asked. "You shouldn't be in this busy place all by yourself, should you?"

Cassava hesitated. It would be nice to have someone to watch her back, but Ferran was really more of a liability than anything else. He couldn't defend himself and in streets like this would need constant watching—though it helped that he didn't have anything thieves would want. Just looking at his poor attire was a pretty good incentive for people to stay away. But Cassava wanted to find Nim, and she had no idea what that would entail, where she might have to go, or what she might have to do—and having the conscious monster attached to her wrist could definitely slow her down. "It'll be easier by myself. And I'm out on the streets by myself all the time," Cassava said. She palmed one of her knives, examining the edge which was still laced with poison.

Ferran dug his hand into his pocket and pulled out a fistful of something that jangled. As he opened his fingers, Cassava saw the glint of mental circles knocking gently against each other.

"Where did you get that?" Cassava asked.

"I won it," Ferran said.

"You won it?" Cassava asked, completely floored for a second. "You were gambling?"

"What's gambling?" Ferran asked.

"It's...it's how people lose a lot of money." Cassava said, remembering her dad's own issues. "Look, just be careful."

Ferran nodded. "Do you want it? It seemed like it was a problem yesterday."

"Thanks," Cassava said, taking the coins and discovering that she didn't have any purse for them. She retrieved her rucksack from her room and tucked the coins into the bottom. She wasn't sure how much it was—Cassava wasn't used to this type of coin and had no idea what any of it was called or worth—but she hoped it would help if she needed to grease any palms. Cassava knew her father used to do things like that. Cassava hadn't experienced it herself. Cassava was a Black Sin. She didn't need to grease palms. Her presence was threatening enough. Her presence was commanding. But she didn't have that effect on people here; they didn't know who she was, why she had marks on her face, and she wasn't seen as any sort of shadowy demon. For the first time, Cassava considered that that might be a downside.

She glanced over at Henequen, who was still making rounds. He would keep Veran safe, even in a state like this. He would attack someone who approached without a careful touch—and Cassava doubted any would-be assassins would try to placate Henequen. "Keep an eye on him, would you?"

"How long has he been like that?" Ferran asked.

Cassava frowned. "He held it together pretty well during the meetings—he can stand still as a statute, as you know, but he's been agitated since we had lunch. I'm not sure what set it off."

Ferran nodded and pulled out a fresh page. "What are you up to anyway? Black Sin stuff?"

"No. It's Nimmory. I think she might be in trouble."

"You like her, don't you?"

Cassava brought her lips together and pursed them, and it felt like so much weight was dangling at the edge of those lips. "I don't know. I just know I don't want anything to happen to her."

"Is it Visea?"

Cassava took a deep breath and let it out. "No. No it's not. I don't think so...I just...it feels kind of wrong to get over her," Cassava said.

Ferran took his pen to paper and began to sketch out gentle lines, forming up a little face. "Why?"

"I...I was so *consumed* by Visea. I mean I...I did this—" Cassava gestured to the scars on her arms. "—and now I'm...moving on? How could I, when she was so utterly important to me?"

Ferran kept drawing, but Cassava knew he was trying to formulate a response. Ferran spoke rarely, and did so with purpose. "Things can change their importance, and it's okay. It doesn't mean they weren't important at one time. We all used to need our mother's milk—we would have died without it—but now it wouldn't give us everything we need."

Cassava nodded. Ferran made a good point. Maybe it wasn't such a bad thing to move on. "Thanks."

"Here," Ferran handed her his sketch—a rough likeness of Nimmory. "In case you need some help."

Cassava gave him a kiss on the cheek, which Ferran tensed for, but did not move away. He was making progress. Maybe he wouldn't be hopeless forever. Maybe one day he'd learn to accept those kind of touches in a new way. It was a work in progress.

Cassava didn't bother to say goodbye to Veran—he likely didn't want to be disturbed anyway—and hurried down the stairs to the tower's main level. Some people were still eating at the tables, and she spotted Dasun and his family eating at one of the far tables. As Cassava moved past them, she saw the son look up and eye her, and she felt the weight of his gaze until she left the hall. Was he scared? Or was there some other reason he was keeping tabs on her? Or perhaps Henequen's paranoia was getting to her. She tried to push it aside. There were more important things to focus on.

Cassava headed outside of the tower. Outside stood Zoal and someone Cassava didn't recognize. "Hi—Zoal, right?"

"Yes, miss. They/them—you can tell by the earring placement."

"Ah." Cassava hadn't known that, had only noticed that some people had the singular silver earring in their lobe, some on the upper ear, and some about halfway up. Zoal's was in the middle. "That's handy. We should do that in the Asylum."

"Oh. I didn't know the Islands had more than two genders," Zoal said.

Cassava stiffened a little at the raw shock mixed with disdain in Zoal's voice. "In the Asylum, what's normally not allowed happens a little different," she said. "We know it exists—it's just not something we allow in healthy society."

"So, I'm diseased?" Zoal asked coolly. "You gonna take out your knife and stab me? Isn't that why you're all here? To cause trouble for the 'uncivilized world'?"

Cassava scowled. "You have to know it's not natural. It's not healthy; there's no reproductive organs to go with it. It's a problem. How will you have heirs?"

"I still have organs that work, I just chose to present different. What is wrong with that?"

Cassava shook her head. This wasn't a fight she wanted to get into now. "Look, I'm looking for Nim—Barli—and you're the last one who I know saw her."

"And why the hell should I help you? You think I belong in jail—what are you going to do to Nim? And I know Barli's not her name. I know her."

"I don't know what jail is, but I made a promise to Nimmory. I said I would take care of her. She was afraid to come back here. And I want to help."

"I don't think you do," Zoal said.

Cassava shook her head. "Why do you hate me? You don't know me."

"I could say the same to you."

"I don't hate you! I understand things are different here—everyone's demon-touched so of course it hardly seems like it matters to you, but we try to keep things... nicer."

"I don't get it. You got ousted from your own society. You know there's nothing wrong with you. You're just you—being a person!"

"No." Cassava shook her head. "You don't know me at all. I am dark and dangerous, and if you don't tell me what I want to know I will murder you. I'm not some poor thing that got shunted out of society. I needed to go. I wasn't healthy. I'm not healthy. I'm demon-touched, just like you. Doesn't mean I don't wish life was better in the Asylum, but there's a reason I'm kept away from good people."

Zoal stared her down with hard eyes. They were blue and icy. Cassava had never seen eyes like that before—not that she'd looked so closely. "I don't know where she went."

Cassava wasn't sure whether they were lying or not. "You must know something. You said you knew her."

Zoal shook their head stiffly. "I'm going to have to ask you to leave now. I have duties to attend to."

"I thought I could ask one of you for assistance. You told us that, didn't you?"

Zoal took in a tight, short breath. "Of course. But, as I said, I don't know where she's gone."

Now Cassava was sure Zoal was lying. Cassava saw their eyes flick away down the street, the unease in their stance. They were nervous, like so many of Cassava's victims. There was something Zoal wasn't saying.

Cassava brought her knife out and waved it in front of Zoal's face, not in a threatening manner, but a manner that definitely said *look, pay attention to this.* "Do you see this?"

she said, aware that the other guard was standing only a few paces away and if she were to actually do anything in this moment she would be in a heap of trouble. "On this blade is a thin coating of apinine. Do you know what that is?"

Zoal shook their head.

"It is the extract from Fetava roots, a plant native to the Islands. Just a bite of the root can kill a horse. If this were to somehow enter your bloodstream, you would have about thirty minutes of intense intestinal pain, vomiting, as your insides tear themselves apart," Cassava said, staring Zoal down. "Now, this knife stays with me, but sometimes it takes adventures when I need it to. I think you know my line of work. I think you know that it would look like if you ate some bad food, and suffered a serious misfortune. I think you know there's nothing you could do to protect yourself from my friend here. So, I'm going to ask you again, where did Nimmory go?"

Zoal's hand was on their sword, but they didn't move to draw it. They stood there for several seconds, and then finally their mouth opened. "I gave her over to the Yegada."

"What's that?" Cassava asked.

Zoal looked at Cassava's knife and back to her eyes. Cassava didn't look away once. "It's the organization that oversees magic users. She's on the registry. She had to go."

The Yegada. "What did they do to her?" Cassava demanded, her voice shaking a little. These must have been the people she was running from. And Cassava had led her straight into their den.

"I don't know. That's above my pay grade. If she'd just

accepted the consequences, she wouldn't be in this situation now."

"She didn't want to follow your rules so you're absconding with her?"

"I'm not. I'm just doing my job. And as if you're any different. Don't you kill people for a living?"

"I kill people, yes, but not to make a living. I do it to make the world a better place."

"Whatever you tell yourself to sleep at night. The sooner you get out of here, the better."

Cassava slid her knife into the sheath around her wrist. She could twist her hand and grab it in a single subtle motion if needed. But Cassava rarely needed to be sly. Approaching the target was one matter, but cutting them down once she was in front of them had almost always been easy. "Where are they? This Yagada?"

Zoal jerked their head slightly. "I don't know exactly. Somewhere in the north city. I see them there sometimes, hanging out by the gate. They wear uniforms like us sometimes, or plainclothes to blend in. It's the Interior's matter, not the State's." They pointed to a symbol on their chest—a silver insignia that Cassava hadn't noticed before of two hands shaking. "They have a wheel. The Yagada carry an additional weapon on their person—you'd like it. It's a type of poison for those with magic. They keep it on their side in a case."

Cassava did not thank Zoal for the information, but swept away with a quick pace. Cassava knew her directions from the draw of the sun, but it was rapidly setting and before long she might well be lost in this monstrous city.

But the three towers loomed above it all, and Cassava believed she could wind her way back in any case.

Nimmory had been afraid—afraid enough to run to another country where her life was in danger. Cassava only hoped she would not be too late.

Running through the streets felt good. They were full of hawkers and people traveling home from a day's work. Cassava saw children in large groups playing some sort of game with a large ball, calling to each other in Belish. In many ways it was no different from any town in Filoli. People were here, making a living, just getting by. Couples were fighting in the streets and the rich passed disdainfully in carriages. The streets were bathed in the smell of refuse, much worse than any town in Filoli however, and Cassava passed several more beggars as she went. The state they were in was terrible—and everywhere she saw starving children in ragged clothes the likes of which were simply nonexistent in the Islands. At one point Cassava sank so deep into manure it threatened to pull her boot from her foot, at another she nearly tripped over a small child with golden hair and pale, sightless eyes who responded by yelling Belish curses at her at the top of their lungs. It was not something Cassava hoped to ever grow accustomed to.

Cassava saw guards every so often, but they seemed more preoccupied with their own matters than in aiding their citizens. Cassava watched one break up a fight and then demand the merchant ply him with free wares for the trouble. Black Sins never made such demands; they never insisted on anything for their aide, but then they wouldn't have stepped into a fight either. It simply wasn't their place.

The north gate was huge. Through it could have rolled two large ships abreast. It was guarded by two guards with wheel pins, but Cassava saw no sign of a pack on their side. She wasn't sure how her questions would be taken outside the State's Tower; from what she had seen, her privileges didn't exist in the wider world. They would not bother to ask for a token before bearing down on her.

Cassava leaned into the doorway of a nearby building. She could hear murmurs of conversation from within, all in a language she did not understand. Perhaps a family lived here by the gates.

The sun sank as she watched the guards—men who did not clock her, or perhaps simply did not care about a straggler in a cloak hunched in a doorway. Cassava would have drawn notice in Filoli even if she were not a Black Sin. People simply did not stand about watching...well, she couldn't think of an equivalent. An entry to the Asylum, perhaps? Yes, someone standing outside the Asylum would be quite conspicuous.

Other red jackets came occasionally in and out of a building built into the city's wall. Cassava saw them occasionally stop and chat with the guards. She didn't see any with additional weaponry, but it continued to baffle her that so many people in the city could carry weapons openly. She realized now that she had passed through some of the less pleasant streets where men without red jackets had been carrying swords. Had they been plainclothes guards? Or was someone else in this city authorized? The thought troubled Cassava. She was used to being one of the top dogs, the only one in the room with a deadly weapon. Here she was out of her depths.

At what must have been approaching midnight, Cassava saw a woman leave the outpost in plainclothes. She wore a light skirt that helped to obscure the bugle at her hip, but Cassava clocked it after watching her walk for a few paces. Cassava pulled her hood up and slipped out into the street.

This was familiar territory: a quiet road, removed from the rough and tumble of town, an unsuspecting target taking a familiar path to them—so familiar that their mind turned to other matters and never looked close to home. Cassava took a deep breath. The air here was not as humid as the Islands, and Cassava felt less stifled under the cloak than she normally did. Summers were no doubt sweltering here; but summer had yet to come. It was not completely out of fashion to be dressed as Cassava was—though the color was dark and the style far plainer than anything Cassava had seen. Even the rags children wore bore bright colors or beadwork.

Cassava clung to the shadows—and she had a good number to choose from. Banners and shop signs blinked out from the sides of the street, though as the woman continued on the streets grew darker and less robust. Still, barrels collecting rainwater stood outside of houses, linked to gutters. The occasional cart was wheel-locked outside on the street, a metal anklet keeping anyone from running away with it. Places crowded with people too were occasional spaces that Cassava used to keep her distance. No one in the islands stayed up this late—it was early to bed, early to rise, except for a few sailor's taverns. Here, however, the landscape was dotted with the sheer mass of the city—occasionally one or two seemed camped out for the night, but others stood in small circles smoking and laughing with each other. Triking City was not so different at night than it was during the day. It was only darker and ranker, and Cassava found herself grasping at her knife when she passed two men running the opposite way. There was something about the taste of the city in her mouth that made her afraid.

Cassava did not like to be afraid. Cassava's father had taught her how to ward off men at a young age, but she wondered now if those methods would mean anything here. There were no rules—a woman could be just as predatory, just as violent, just as driven. Cassava reminded herself sternly that she was a Black Sin—an elite assassin—and she had nothing to fear.

Finally, the woman came to rest outside a tall windowless building. Well, there appeared to have been windows once, but some were boarded and most cemented over so that the appearance was quite like a child's drawing. The woman knocked briskly on the door, which was opened by a person with an eyepatch and a shiny shaved head. Cassava pushed closer, trying to hear the conversation, ducking down beside one of the water barrels.

"—another one. But I'm not sure. I followed him most of the afternoon," the woman was saying.

"We can't be making mistakes. Put that in the press and the King'll hang. Best to keep a close eye."

The woman nodded. "How're the new arrivals?"

"Mostly pliant. There's a girl though, stirring up a bit of trouble."

Cassava leaned forward, straining to catch all of their conversation. As she did so, she felt suddenly the weight of the barrel give way. A loud crash of barrel and water issued up from Cassava's hiding spot.

She darted backward quickly, glad she had practiced such maneuvers with Anelace. She hurried around the corner, hearing a spark of suspicion in the cries that followed. They had been speaking Trade before but switched to another tongue. There was a snap of the door and quick footsteps on the pavement.

Cassava surveyed the street for somewhere to hide herself and saw nothing of note beside yet another barrel. But she knew it wouldn't do to duck down behind one now; they were wise to it. Furious at herself for getting into this position, Cassava shook her head regretfully before plunging feet first into the barrel.

The water rushed up around her, displaced by her body weight, but it did not overflow as she had feared. She kept her head just above the waterline, her eyes tracking the corner of the building from which her pursuers would no doubt appear.

It wasn't but a few seconds longer before the woman appeared from around the corner. Cassava knew they wouldn't be able to see her yet in this dim light. The woman was joined by the other person before long, each taking one side of the street. They talked occasionally to each other as they moved forward, but Cassava did not understand it.

Cassava lowered her head slowly as the woman

approached, dipping her head back in the barrel until only her nose was above the waterline.

She felt slight vibrations through the barrel—the water shifted slightly around her, but Cassava had no idea what was happening. She breathed quietly through her nose for some time, and eventually all seemed still and quiet.

Cassava picked her head up just out of the water. The muffled dullness of sound was replaced by the sound of gentle droplets plinking into the barrel. Cassava tried to make out the street. It appeared deserted. She waited several minutes longer before standing up. The displaced water sloshed around the barrel, but did not spill over. Cassava did her best to delicately extract herself from the barrel, but this proved a difficult task in a fully-soaked wool cloak. Scads of water sloughed off Cassava's clothes and the weight nearly pulled her back into the water.

Cursing under her breath, Cassava unhooked her cloak and let it drop in a wet puddle. Hopefully no one would come along and steal it while she was gone. Cassava wouldn't have been concerned on the Islands, but here she knew crime was far more rampant, and people seemed to be missing such basic necessities as a cloak. Cassava hardly felt she could take it back from someone as destitute as some she'd seen. But Veran would be greatly displeased with her if she returned underdressed. Decorum was the name of the game now and the Islanders were sorely lacking.

Irritated, Cassava plunked the cloak back into the barrel of water. It was probably best to leave minimal evidence behind anyway. She glanced at the side of the building. This side was the same as the front—a mixture of boarded-up and brick-laid windows at regular points along the wall. It looked as though it had once housed rooms for many people. Perhaps, Cassava thought, it still did.

There was no getting around it, Cassava decided after minimal consideration; she would have to climb. The wall here was good for it—not made of steely long pieces worn like glass so that the sides were smooth and unforgiving as the Asylum walls were. No, this had not been erected with the purpose of keeping people inside; that purpose had been brought to it. It looked by all rights like an abandoned building, and Cassava would have passed it right by unless she was looking for squatters. But something was definitely going on here, though Cassava couldn't be sure if this was a hideout for the Yegada or not. Either way, she was getting to the bottom of this.

Climbing had always been one of Cassava's strong suits. She had been a crawler as a baby, making life difficult for her parents as a toddler, and gotten completely out of control as a child. Cassava would climb anything that didn't move too much, and sometimes even then she would give it a try. She liked being tall, on top of the world. Cassava wondered what the top of the state's tower would be like— to have a bird's-eye view of the city bunched up around her. It would have to be fascinating. Cassava's recent climbs had been scaling the ship's rigging, but the Asylum boasted a climb wall which Cassava had the time to beat on. If climbing could kill, Cassava would have had the competition in the bag without any help from Ferran at all. Most of the time it was impractical to scale something to get to a target since Cassava liked to work close up, but she would scout from perches in the city and come to understand her target's patterns and behavior.

The wall here was tricky but not impossible. There were bits of smooth where not much stuck out from the wall—places where the bricks were placed perfectly in alignment so there was no gap. Occasionally, the bricklayers had been sloppier, and a piece stuck out with a little give and small crevices to squeeze a finger or toe into. But that would only be between window ledges—at least if Cassava plotted a route to ones that still had some ledge to speak of. Here the lower bricked off windows were superior—no doubt they had done that purposefully so that no mere passerby could pry a window open and have at the interior. But they had been cheaper higher up, so that was where Cassava had to go.

Cassava tightened the laces on her boots, readjusted her belt, and climbed on. Climbing without a rope was always more dangerous, and ideally in a situation like this she'd have both a rope and a spotter. But dragging Ferran along would have been a mistake—where would she have put him? He was liable to get into trouble, and he had not the systemic privilege that Cassava did; were she to get in trouble with the law, Veran would not leave her to the wolves. She was far too valuable an asset. Ferran, on the other hand, was disposable.

It was not the first time the difference between them had bothered Cassava; she knew she was to use the skills the demon had granted her for good, that she was a piece of the Priest's story of redemption. But why not Ferran? Why could he not use his own gifts? Why was he valueless? He could cook well, and his drawings were lifelike. And yet the Priests had deemed him too great a risk—the boy who had risked his life for a small kitten.

These thoughts troubled Cassava as she made her tricky ascent. Ferran, who had never hurt anyone, was doomed. And yet he need not be, Cassava thought. For here in this vile town, villains were held in high esteem. Your fortune seemed to be your own here, a fate Cassava was not entirely convinced of the merit of. Had the blind child done some great wrong to be punished on the street? Had the man in council chambers, Dasun—rude, and if Henequen was to be believed, malicious—done some great good to deserve his wealth and seat at the table? But, no, their society was not organized by good and evil, it seemed, but by the wealthy and the poor. It was a distinction that had always existed in the Islands, but to far lesser extent. Anyone free from the demon was granted boons if in need, and the rich were expected to give their wealth to the Priests who could redistribute it as their laws required. Cassava had never seen a starving child before coming to this writhing mass of sin. It made her sick to think about it.

Cassava took a bad step and was suddenly hanging by three fingers, rudely interrupting her thought process. Her foot searched and found a foothold, and she climbed with the concentration due the task now, attentive and highly aware that she had nearly suffered at least one broken bone.

Finally, Cassava wedged herself into a good position beside a boarded window. She took out her knife, supported by her legs, and dug into the board for a nail to pry up.

It was only after she had made several scraping noises

as she searched for a foothold in the wood that she remembered there might be someone on the other side who could hear her. Cassava stopped at once and listened closely. She couldn't detect any voices, so she assumed no one would take immediate notice of her presence. One person she could take anyway. It was just if there was a conference room that Cassava thought her skills might fail her. Henequen, she believed, could do just about anything. He was a force to be reckoned with.

Cassava returned to prying up the board. They were stuccoed to the window frame, which was also made of wood. Cassava was not in a very comfortable position and the angle was difficult, so she spent a considerable amount of time readjusting her grip and shaking her fingers out. Her toes were trembling with effort.

Below, a twosome straggled through the street. Cassava cursed to herself and took another silent break until they passed. Finally, she managed to pry one side of the board free. Wrenching it down with all the force she could muster from her strained position, Cassava managed to swing it down so it hung on its hinge to the far side. The gap was narrow, but Cassava had forced herself through smaller. It wasn't an Asylum window; it hadn't been made to keep people in. That was a new purpose.

Cassava tried to peer in, but with the only light coming from the slit it was hard to make out much. It appeared to be a small room with two beds and not much else. Cassava felt relief flood to her toes as she leaned her weight on the sill. She pulled herself in slowly, trying still to be quiet. She couldn't tell if the beds were occupied or not until in the silence she heard a low moan echo from one of the beds.

Cassava dropped down. She wasn't sure what she had expected to find, so this couldn't surprise her and yet somehow it did. Cassava moved like a shadow over to the one who had moaned, but if they were awake they did not seem to have noticed Cassava.

The individual in the bed, now that Cassava could see a little better as she was not blocking the light, appeared to be a ten-year-old Rabian boy. He did not look well. His skin was sallow in that way only Rabian skin could be, and he smelled of sick. Cassava could not believe the guards who worked in this house had left this boy on his own, without help. She glanced at the other bed to find an even younger girl sitting upright, clutching her blanket before her as though it were a shield, watching Cassava with frightened eyes.

"Who are you?" she spoke. Her voice was rough, as though she had been crying for some time and worn it out until there were no tears left.

Cassava, who for a moment on instinct had drawn her knife, quickly packaged it away. This girl was slight, and her hair appeared to be dark red, though it may have been the lighting. She appeared to be sick as well, but it was less acute.

"My name is Cassava," she said. "What is this place?"

The girl glanced toward the door, to Cassava, and then back to the window. "Why are you here?" she asked.

Cassava took a step toward the child, her hands open. "I'm looking for someone."

"Who?"

"A girl, like you. Older, though, with blonde hair and green eyes."

The girl shrugged her shoulders. "I don't know who's here. This is my room."

"Don't you ever go out?" Cassava asked.

The girl stared at her for a second, then walked to the door and twisted the knob, pulling with all the strength such a small girl possessed.

Cassava was duly reminded of the Asylum, of waking upon that place, tied to the bed, barely able to lift her head, her face on fire.

"What are they doing here?" she asked. "Why are you here?"

The girl wandered back to her bed and sat on it. "I thought maybe you were a gesu," she said, "but you don't know anything."

Cassava tried not to be frustrated by this child, but it was difficult. Nimmory could be anywhere and anything could be happening to her—looking at the evidence, likely something bad. "So, explain it to me."

"My mom wanted them to take my magic," she said. "So, they sent me here. But I don't think she knew how much it hurts."

"So there is a—" Cassava didn't want to call it a cure, Nimmory had been dead set against the notion, even if that's all Veran could think about. "—a way to get rid of magic."

The girl brought her blanket to her chest again, a protective posture that Cassava understood. She too desired at times to hide under a blanket, to curl up in a puddle, to put a wall up between her and the world through which nothing could pass. "What are you scared of?" Cassava asked gently.

She extended one arm and her finger pointed sharply. For a moment Cassava thought she was indicating herself, and wondered what wild tales these Triking people told their children of the Black Sins—it couldn't be any worse than what the Rhimeons told their children. But she realized that the girl was looking past her, to the boy laying on the bed. As she watched, he moaned weakly again, shifting slightly under his blanket.

Cassava swallowed. Nimmory had said it made people sick. This was more than some simple illness, Cassava thought. She had been in close quarters with many who were ill, but this boy was another level. She could sense his body giving up the fight.

"He's going to die," the girl said with a frightful finality to her tone.

"How do you know?" Cassava asked.

The girl twisted her hands together. "One of them is a healer. They said there was no use helping him."

"How many are like this?" Was Nimmory already one of them? Cassava couldn't waste any time.

The girl shrugged her shoulders. "Many," she said, her voice hollow.

This was more than sickness; it was outright murder. Even for all that it killed, Cassava's skills were reserved for the few—the truly dangerous, those that could not be kept safely with others. It was not murder when a soul had been so blackened by the demon there was no hope for them, no functionality, no relief. Cassava was a killer, and she killed in cold blood, but it was a defense mechanism of the Priests. It was necessary. Here they were murdering children and upright people like Nimmory. Something had to be done.

Cassava nodded tightly, her mind racing. Somewhere in this apartment complex was Nimmory. Whether she had been injected yet or not, Cassava did not know. But she was going to find out. "What's your name, little one?"

"Saraj."

"Have they gotten to you yet?"

She nodded. "They're keeping me. To see if it comes back because I'm so small."

They might not have given her a full dose. Interesting. At least they didn't seem to be totally throwing caution to the wind. Cassava tested the door herself, but she had never learned how to pick locks. Having the keys to most places made that more or less irrelevant. Besides, she had no tools to work with. Cassava paced the room for several minutes before turning back to Saraj. "When do they come?"

Saraj shrugged. "Morning. Someone brings food."

Well, there was nothing to do but wait then. Cassava didn't think she could bust through that door, and any other window she tried was liable to be the same story. Hopefully, Henequen and Veran would forgive her absence. But there were more important matters to attend to here. Cassava doubted Dasun, if he were to make a move, would make it now. He seemed like the slow, lecherous beast that no one saw coming. Which, while certainly a problem, was still a problem for another day, when Nimmory's life was not on the line.

Cassava sank down against the wall, feeling disgusting in her sopping clothes. She felt naked without her cloak, and glancing over at Saraj, she saw the girl was staring intently at her. Even when Cassava scowled, she did not look away.

"Are you evil?" the girl asked abruptly into the night.

Cassava half opened her mouth, not sure how to respond to such a question. No one ever questioned her on the Islands. They didn't need to. Their parents told them stories where Cassava was the lead villain: the monster that would destroy them if they misbehaved. Children did not react to seeing monsters well. Cassava had made children shake, cry, tug on their mother's arms to leave, anything to get away. Heck, even adults avoided her like the plague, and if it wouldn't have been a crime to deny her service, everyone would have.

Beyond a child's understanding however, the question of evil was another thing entirely. Cassava might be taken by the demon, marked by the Priests, and given over to foul forces she could not control. But that wasn't *her*. It was the demon in her. She fully believed her companions, the Black Sins and the other Sins who dwelt in the Asylum, were not evil but struck by a great affliction. Permanently sick. It had nothing to do with morals. And that was not to say they were all good people; Kazini came to mind as someone truly evil. But even that was not straightforward. Kazini was burdened with her own illness, one Cassava did not understand the extent of, and carried her own trauma that she reflected to others. Was that evil? Or was that too just an inescapable manifestation of the demon?

Saraj was still looking at her, staring at her face. Cassava felt the weight of the brand, a legacy she could never shake no matter how she might try to reinvent herself. However she clothed herself, however she talked, she would still be marked for all to see. Even here, where it did not outcast her completely, it marked her as strange, different— someone to be wary of. Cassava was so, so tired of that reaction.

"No. I am like you," Cassava said finally, searching for some way to connect to this child, to perhaps have the chance of being seen as she was by someone who was not marked the same as her. "Something was different about me, so they didn't want me mixing with other people."

Saraj put her hand to her face, mimicking feeling the marks on Cassava's face. "It's not a tattoo," she said.

"No," Cassava said. "They're scars, from people who hurt me."

"They hurt me."

"I know," she said gently. It had been some time since Cassava had spoken with one so young. It could be difficult to follow conversations, but Cassava knew Saraj was following and working hard to keep up with what she was saying. It was a lot for a little brain. It was a lot for Cassava's brain. "It doesn't seem right, does it?"

Saraj shook her head. "I just want to go home," she said with a slight whimper.

Cassava took a deep breath. She had wanted to go home too. She had wanted to go back. But that wasn't an option for her. Perhaps Saraj would get out of here. Perhaps she would survive and be brought back to her mother safe and sound. Perhaps her mother would still love her. Cassava looked away. "You should sleep."

Saraj tucked her knees up to her chest, her blue eyes wide. "What are you going to do?" Saraj asked.

"Something they won't see coming," Cassava said. She didn't have a grand plan. She rarely did. She just acted and then saw how things fell into place. Cassava didn't know what it looked like out there, how many people there were, but she knew she was going to fight to get Nimmory out. That was all that mattered—to make good on her word. There were so many things between the two of them that had yet to be said, but Cassava believed they would still have a chance to say them.

Cassava's mind flew through the night, and she found it impossible to get comfortable. If she wasn't waiting, she would have gone for a run to clear her mind. As it was, she paced the room. Saraj watched her the whole time, keeping her own counsel. Cassava did not suspect she would be any threat; she only hoped Saraj made it through too. She hoped they all did. There was a great darkness here, and this was a pit the Demon had made.

Where had the magic come from? Why had it come back? Was it truly the world's descent into darkness that had pulled free this source? Cassava couldn't believe Saraj was meaningfully communicating with the Demon. She was nothing but a child. She, like Ferran, had fallen unwittingly into a place of deep darkness that threatened her life. She was not an actor—not like Cassava—this had happened to her. It wasn't right.

None of this was right. Cassava didn't know what to do about magic, didn't know whether it was good or evil, but she did know that what the Trikingdom was doing was pure black of heart. Whoever authorized this complex, whoever worked for its upkeep, deserved to be brought low. They were demons of their own making; they were the kind of people Cassava killed. She would have no remorse over her mission here tonight. No matter what it took.

Chapter Eight

From the sun, Cassava guessed it was around seven in the morning when she finally heard noise outside the door. Cassava was on her feet in an instant, her hand going to her knife. She stalked to the side of the door, lying in wait for its opening. Her whole body thrummed with impatience as she heard the slide of a key into the lock and the subtle twisting of metal on metal, tumblers rolling.

Cassava let the attendant enter unmolested. His hands were full with a bowl laden with some sort of soup and a great glass of water. He moved to set them down on the floor by Saraj's bed, and that was when Cassava struck.

She stepped swiftly behind him, one arm curling around to keep his arms out of her way, and the other coming tight around his neck with a blade focused on it. He let out a squeak, but Cassava was quickly at his ear. "Not a sound now, if you don't want my blade through your throat."

"Who are you?"

"That is hardly your concern," Cassava replied. "What is your concern is that the slightest prick from this knife could end your life."

"You're one of the Black Sins," the man said with a sudden quake in his voice.

"So I am," she replied. "I'm sure you're well acquainted with my particular skill set."

"What is it you want?"

"A girl was brought in here yesterday. I want her back."

"Surely, we could find someone else to satisfy you. I can show you to the many brothels—"

"I want her. Now. Do you understand?"

"I'm afraid that's really impossible."

"And why would that be?" Cassava asked, her voice low.

"She hasn't been seen to yet. I reckon you wouldn't want her, dangerous like she is. Unwilling to bow—"

Cassava's hand jerked at once and she felt the blade bite gently into his skin. She had not meant to move, but it had happened all the same. Cassava regretted it for a moment; perhaps it was unwise to use poisoned blades in all circumstances. But the moment passed quickly. Nimmory was not dangerous, and the jut of her chin had come to mind at the word "bow". Cassava could not see her bowing to anyone, and it seemed so unearthly beautiful that Cassava was at once desperate to protect it. "Where is she?" Cassava asked.

"Why should I tell you that?" he asked, "I'm already doomed, aren't I?"

Cassava held in a frustrated sigh. "Yes, but I could make this much more unpleasant for you. I can make it quick and painless, if you like. As things are, it'll take a long, long time."

The man shook a little under Cassava's hand. "Not going to offer me a cure?" he said with a shaky breath.

"I've never needed one before," Cassava said with a twinge of regret. She let go of him and he stumbled down to his knees, hands wide.

"Am I supposed to be this dizzy?"

"It starts quickly but it finishes slow."

The man listed sideways. "Heartless bitch."

Cassava had heard far worse. "Tell me where she is," Cassava repeated, "and I'll put an end to this."

He shook his head. "I'm not sure. They were keeping her on the third floor last I checked. But I don't keep tabs."

"What is this place?"

"You don't know what you just broke into?"

Cassava sighed. This guy was asking for it. If he hadn't already been dying, she would have made it happen right then. "Look, I usually get a dossier about people, so this is all new to me."

"It's the Yegada headquarters. We take kids reported to be with powers and we treat them."

"You mean you kill them."

"We cure them. Sometimes, unfortunately, yes, they die. But it's a small price to pay for safety."

"What if they don't want to be 'cured'?" Cassava asked.

The man shook his head. "Well, if they're of age, of course, we won't force them. But if they don't agree to help us out, they can't be trusted."

"And then what do you do?"

"Well, we try to make them see sense, but if there's no talking to them, it's safer for everyone if we just—"

"Kill them?"

"It's not a perfect system."

"Sounds like it leaves a *lot* to be desired."

"As if you Sins are better? You kill people over nothing! Minor deviations in behavior, physical illness—"

"No! No—you don't get to do that. No. We take people and we put them somewhere safe, somewhere that protects them and looks out for them. You treat your people like garbage. You kill them, or lock them up, or leave them in the fucking streets to die! What kind of society does that to the vulnerable?" Cassava exploded in a wave of furious anxiety. What if they had already killed Nimmory? "What we have is damn respectable."

"Says the assassin."

"I kill my victims out in the open. I'm not trying to keep what's happening a secret. I have a hard time believing this girl's mother sent her off to possibly die. I'm guessing that's not something you're advertising."

"As if anyone would listen to a freak like you. Look at your face—hideous for the world."

Cassava decided she'd had enough. She slid forward in a single swift motion and swept her knife deep across the man's neck. Blood burbled up quickly, and it was only Saraj's little scream that reminded Cassava this was supposed to be a covert mission. She wasn't used to this— yes, she was an assassin, but she was a state-sanctioned one. Here, she would not be protected. "A little louder, Saraj, maybe the whole place can hear you," she said pointedly.

Saraj did not reply, but stared at the man who had collapsed with blood flowing freely from his neck.

Cassava sighed, and pointed with her blade to the bed. "They're both dying," she said, "who would you rather be?" Cassava did not wait for a response, but took a moment to reapply the poison paste to her blade. She was not looking to leave survivors. Anyone she attacked, she would mean to kill. The world was easier taken in black and white.

Saraj stared back at her. "Kill them all."

Cassava gave the girl a little captain's salute and poked her head out the door. The hallway was clear, and Cassava took advantage. They were on the fourth floor now, so she just needed to go down one level. It didn't take long to locate the staircase. Cassava wondered how many kids were behind the doors she passed. Too many. It wasn't right.

It bothered her in a way the Asylum never had. Maybe it was cultural, but Cassava felt a deep disgust that burned through her blood. She had felt angry at the Asylum before, she had raged and screamed that they had torn her away from everything she cared about. She had been desolate. But she had been desolate for other reasons. She had been desolate over Visea. Now she had another passion.

For a moment, as she hurtled down the staircase not bothering to conceal her footsteps, she felt disloyal. But Visea had never loved her—not the way Cassava had loved her. She would have never said the things she had otherwise. Nimmory was different. There was no expectation there; Cassava was aware she might be building things up in her head, but there had been no promises between them except for one—Cassava would have her back. Cassava didn't go back on her promises. She didn't.

The third floor was empty for the moment. Its layout

was identical to the fourth, which didn't tell Cassava a lot. She could only assume this used to be a hotel that had been repurposed to a murder den for children.

Cassava tried the nearest door, but it was locked. She should have thought to look for keys on the man upstairs. But Cassava didn't want to move backward. "Nim!" she shouted. "Nimmory!" She walked down the hallway, calling Nimmory's name over and over again.

Cassava heard a quiet but distinct "Barli?" followed by heavy footsteps on the stair coming up from below.

Cassava hurried away from the footstep and toward the voice. It had come from somewhere down the hall. Cassava pulled a second knife from her belt as she ran, periodically checking in the direction of the stairs. "Nim?"

"Barli!"

That was definitely Nimmory. Good. She wasn't dead or devoid of life yet. There was still time. Cassava tried to pinpoint the sound as the footsteps came louder on the stair. Fairly confident in her choice, Cassava stomped the door hard. After three kicks it caved in, just as Cassava saw a woman enter the hallway from the stairwell. Cassava stood by the door, took a moment to line up her shot, and let the dagger fly. For what felt like several seconds Cassava watched it turn over and over in the air until finally it collided with the woman at full force.

Cassava didn't wait to see more. She busted her way through the door. Inside was another set of two beds. Nimmory was standing next to another teenager, Belish and rather round. Nimmory was somewhat pale and her hair disheveled, but she otherwise looked in relatively good shape. They had not poisoned her yet. The window on this level had been blocked out with cement and it was extremely dark for this time of morning. A tiny light flickered in the Belish teen's hand, providing the sole light.

Cassava took this all in as the body outside hit the floor. "Come on," she said. "We're getting out of here."

Nimmory ran to her and signaled her companion to do the same.

"Me too?" the teen asked.

"If you want," Cassava replied. She frankly didn't care. As long as Nimmory was on the way to safety, Cassava had satisfied her word.

Cassava stepped back into the hallway. "I might need a little help," she said as three more individuals poured up from the staircase.

"Where we going?" Nimmory asked, striding forward with her hand outstretched.

"Up," Cassava said. "Then out the window."

Nimmory nodded. The next second a wave of wind swept out from their threesome towards the foe. The Yegada members, some dressed as guards, others in plainclothes, seemed to slow as they fought against the force of the wind. Cassava ran up, grabbed her dagger from the corpse of the first woman she had killed, and twirled it in her hand. No time for poison now.

Cassava soon found herself struggling with Nimmory's wind, and she didn't want to risk a throw with the winds acting as wild as they were. The dagger could have gone anywhere. "Focus down, Nim!"

A moment later, Cassava felt some of the resistance

cease and she flung herself forward with the fury of a wildcat. Cassava raked down the arm of a man not quick enough to parry her first strike—but before she could finish him he had a sword in hand and was making his own pass at her. She jumped quickly back, stumbling a little as she found herself touched just slightly by Nimmory's wind.

Cassava took a moment regaining her balance and the man pressed the advantage, plunging forward with his sword. Cassava felt at once a great rush of wind from the side, so strong it tore the blade from his hand, leaving him defenseless.

Cassava grinned in primal satisfaction as she raised her blade to him and brought it in with a quick twist between his grasping fingers to his chest.

One of the other guards was down, no doubt thanks to Nimmory, and Cassava rounded on the last one. But more footsteps were thundering. They weren't getting out of here without a real fight. Cassava was thrilled and terrified at the same time. She had never felt so alive as in this moment.

As four more guards appeared, the Belish teen called out, "Close your eyes."

Cassava obeyed without question, and not a moment too soon because from behind her Cassava felt a violent bright light build and shoot out in front of her. Even with her eyes closed, Cassava could see the light like an afterimage.

Then, as suddenly as it appeared, it was gone. Cassava opened her eyes to see the four that had come to join their comrades staggering and holding their eyes, blinded by the brilliance. Cassava could only guess this was the Belish teen's power at work.

"Come on!" Cassava said. She sliced deep into a plain-clothed human, the last of the first wave, as she charged upward.

Nimmory and the Belish followed quickly. Cassava let them pass her and took up a rearguard position. It was not something she was used to—guarding other people. It felt good. It felt like some deep desire in her was being acknowledged for the first time. Sure, she believed she was protecting people when she killed, but this was so much more immediate, so much more instantaneous, and it felt good.

Nimmory and her roommate charged up the stairs with proper vigor, and Cassava trailed their back. Before long they were racing down the fourth floor to the door Cassava had left open wide. Saraj was doing her best to keep up, but her legs were smaller and she wasn't as fit. "Out the window, and if you can't climb, I'm sure Nim's got it covered."

They tore into the room. The Belish teen kicked at the still plaqued over window in an attempt to widen the gap Cassava had wormed her way through. After several tries they had a much more reasonably sized hole to fit through. But the Yegada were coming.

Cassava stood in the doorway watching them approach. One of them threw something down the hallway and it exploded into smoke as it hit the ground several feet from Cassava. Cassava leaped back and quickly shut the door as smoke or gas of some sort began to curl its way through the space beneath the door. Cassava didn't want to stick around to find out what it did.

Behind her, the Belish teen was halfway out the window, and Nimmory was getting ready to head out after them. Cassava considered searching the body for keys to lock the door, but she doubted she could find the right one in time.

She looked instead for a something to wedge between the door, but the room was pretty barren aside from the beds and the corpse. More of the smoke was filtering into the room now and Cassava felt as though she was getting a little lightheaded.

The door burst open with surprising force. The Yegada who entered had masks pulled down over their faces, protecting them from the smoke. It was filtering in more quickly now, and Cassava struggled to push herself over toward the window without setting her back to her foes.

"What's going on?" came the shrill voice of a true child. Saraj. Cassava's heartbeat quickened.

The Belish teen was finally through, though no doubt blocking the way just below. Nimmory summoned a force of wind and propelled herself out of the window with grace and speed that seemed like far more than Cassava could manage at this point in time.

Cassava backed up to the window, her blades out. "Just a taste and you're gone," she warned threateningly as still more masked Yegada came through the door. It was five on one now, and Cassava's eyes were having trouble focusing.

One of them men started toward her and Cassava

threw. It struck true, and Cassava felt a deep though nauseated satisfaction thrumming through her body.

"No more," a tall non-binary Yegada said sternly. Cassava could tell from the earring placement, now that she was paying attention to them. She turned to look now. The Yegada had Saraj in one hand and a wicked knife in the other. They took it to Saraj's neck. "Stand down."

Cassava hesitated. It was the worst hesitation to have; time was running against her and the world was suddenly moving too slow and too fast at the same time. Cassava's knees buckled under her and she collapsed to all fours, trying not to breathe but needing to desperately.

"Drop your weapons," they commanded. Two of the other Yegada at a nod hurried forward and kicked Cassava's blade away. She had more tucked on her person, but her head was spinning so badly she could hardly think at all, beyond recognizing that if she didn't stop struggling, this little girl would die.

They bound Cassava's hands behind her back. They were not gentle, but Cassava barely noticed. They brought her stumbling to her feet and Cassava moved like a rock until the Yegada simply picked her up.

They went down stairs, more stairs, and finally threw Cassava into a dark room without any light. The lock clicked into place and Cassava was alone.

After she was sick, she slept.

Chapter Nine

Cassava awoke an indeterminate time later. There was no light beyond the slight hint coming through the crack in the door. It could have been any time of day.

Cassava was alone, which she hoped meant that Nimmory and her friend had gotten away. At least then she would have kept her word. Nimmory had gotten out the window, and with her wind powers she should have had no trouble escaping. Her wind would be able to dissipate the gas, and she could more or less fly. Nimmory would be okay. She sat in satisfaction for a moment before getting up.

The nausea seemed to have passed. Any other ill effects of the gas were impossible to be sure of—there was nothing there to focus on, Cassava could barely test whether her vision still worked. She bent down before the door and peered through the crack. It didn't help. All she knew was the hallway was dimly lit, just as it had been when she'd gone in. It could have been hours. Cassava doubted it had been days. She wasn't hungry enough.

Cassava tried the door just because it would have been stupid not to. Her hands were still tied uncomfortably behind her back, and she had to face backward to even try.

It took some time to line her hand up and grasp the nob, but they were smart enough to have locked it and she couldn't budge it. The door was different from the others too, Cassava realized. It was metal instead of wood, and Cassava, after feeling it carefully, was certain she would only hurt herself if she tried to knock it in. This was an upscale prison compared to the rooms Nim and Saraj had been in.

Cassava stood in the darkness for several minutes with a defiant expression on her face as if the non-binary leader would swing the door open at any moment and demand an accounting. Cassava practiced her answers in her head—snarky and short. But no leader appeared.

Cassava found herself getting more and more angry as she waited. What did they think? They could just coop her up in here forever? What was their goal? They hadn't killed her, so they wanted something from her. She wondered what.

Time dragged on, and still nothing. Cassava would get tired of standing and finally sit down only to hear footsteps in the hallway and spring up again. But they were never for her.

Cassava sat in the darkness a long time. She sat until she was quite hungry and nearly succumbed to banging on the door for some attention—anything that wasn't this dark prison. Cassava had been contained before, but this was different. Then she had known why, and although she hadn't been sure how long, she knew the what and the how and generally what to expect. She had known who her captors were, and more or less what they were going to do with her. Now she knew very little, and this little began to spin out in her head until grand stories of epic proportions were being told there in the black. She imagined she had stumbled upon some deep state secret, so dangerous that they couldn't let her live, and they wanted to interrogate her on who she worked for and why she was here. Cassava could almost imagine this was some grand mission—what if she had been sent here by some greater force? Surely there was someone else who opposed what was happening here? She couldn't be the only one with a friend who had found herself tucked away, locked into this murder hotel.

But whether that was true or not, it wouldn't help her now. Why were they ignoring her? Did they think she should still be asleep? Or did they want her to be in the dark, wondering and worrying? Or were they simply too busy to deal with her, and she was an afterthought they had no interest in returning to? Perhaps now that they had subdued the problem, they would leave her here until she rotted.

Cassava scowled. She had given up standing when there was movement outside the door, and her wrists were really uncomfortable now. Her fingers were stiff and compromised from being held in that position for so long. Cassava tried in vain to get comfortable. She wriggled her arm one way and then the next. Cassava eventually found herself on her stomach in an attempt to relieve some of the pain. It was not a dignified position, but it took some of the gravity pressure away and that was something.

Cassava was beginning to nod off again, despite the difficulties of position and hunger, when she recognized faintly a new noise. Shortly afterward, blinding light shone from an open doorway. Cassava started, struggling to get upright with her hands still tied behind her back. It was an impossible ask on short notice.

She arched her spine as a figure stepped into the doorway, blocking the worst of the light.

"She yours?" a voice asked. Cassava thought it might have been the non-binary individual who had captured her.

"I'm afraid so," said a much softer-spoken voice. It took Cassava a moment to place the voice out of context, but her mind finally supplied that it was Veran.

"Kitadu," Cassava muttered under her breath. In all her imaginary scenarios, this had never come to pass.

Veran stood back as two others came forward and hefted Cassava to her feet. If she'd been able, she would have shaken them off, but all Cassava could do was get her feet under her and straighten her chin.

Cassava looked at Veran, daring him to see what was behind her eyes, but he wasn't looking at her anymore.

"Cassava, with me," he said dismissively. He shook hands with the non-binary individual. "I'll be sure to punish her for this transaction. Believe me, this behavior was wholly uncalled for. There can really be only one response to a disobedient Sin. Cassava was already on her second chance," Veran said gravely.

Cassava swallowed, trying to tamp down the fear roaring up inside her. Was Veran serious? Or was he putting on a show for present company? Cassava had no idea. Either she was getting rescued or she was going to a new death sentence.

Cassava stepped into the hallway, and when Veran turned it was too easy to find her way into his shadow. One of the Yegada cut her bonds, and she felt blood return to her extremities. Her hands felt like they had been cramping for years. Cassava flexed her fingers, but they were slow and unresponsive, and she knew it would take some time before she was up to handling a knife.

Freed, she fell into step behind Veran, a silent shadow, quietly menacing, but for the moment harmless. Veran did not check to see if she followed; he knew she would. What else was she going to do?

Veran exited the hotel-turned-headquarters and stepped out onto the street. Cassava followed wordlessly. She could have broken off and run, but why would she do that? What did she have? A chance at some strange life in this horrible place? But what of her friends? What of Ferran and Henequen? And how would she ever find Nimmory again? That chance that Veran would be merciful was enough to keep Cassava in line.

She didn't speak. She knew she wasn't allowed to. She had no choice but to follow closely, look contrite, and behave like the perfect Sin.

Cassava found herself hanging her head out of instinct. She wasn't ashamed. Was she? It was a status. Even if she wasn't beautiful, at least she was dangerous. But here no one knew that. Here she was just a marred face among many.

Veran walked quickly, and Cassava didn't have much time to think as she was hustled along. When she did think, it was not about her uncertain future, but of her unfinished business. Where were Nimmory and her friend? What would happen to Saraj?

Finally, they were climbing the steps and arrived at the

room. Veran paused for a moment and looked back at her. "I hope you realize the gravity of this situation; the position you've put me in, and the risk you've done to this mission."

Cassava did not look down. In this moment she refused to be subordinate. Yes, she had gone beyond any order Veran could have given, but based on what she'd found, things were far more serious than Cassava could have imagined. Surely, Veran had a heart somewhere and could see that. "This cure isn't the answer we're looking for," Cassava said. "It'd be against everything good to support it."

Veran's face was impossible to read. He reached his hand out for a moment, and for an instant Cassava thought he was going to touch her, but instead he turned away. "We have much to discuss," he said.

Cassava couldn't tell if it was rebuke or wariness, and as he raised his hand to the door a torrent of fear overtook her. "If you're going to have Henequen kill me, at least hear what I have to say first. As a Black Sin, I recognize my like and I know when it goes too far. I have information. Information you need."

"I do not need your information," Veran replied stiffly. He pulled the door open in a swift fluid motion, and Cassava saw several people jump to their feet. Henequen, Ferran, and then to Cassava's surprise the non-binary teen from earlier. As Veran stepped into the room, she saw the not yet familiar enough form of Nimmory. Her hair was tied back in a tight braid and it was dyed a dark brown that was strange but not unbecoming. "We have multiple informants, as you can see," Veran finished dryly.

Cassava knew it was improper behavior for a Black Sin

to react as her heart desperately wanted, but she could not help the wide smile that slid onto her face, and her feet took her quickly to stand square before Nimmory.

Nimmory's familiar green eyes danced and she closed the distance between them, her arms coming in and wrapping Cassava up in a tight embrace. "I was so scared they'd killed you," she said breathlessly.

Cassava felt the strong and steady beat of Nimmory's heart beneath her hand and swallowed hard. She was soft and warm, and smelled crisp and fresh like an apple on the wind. Cassava closed her eyes for a moment and just felt.

"Cassava." Veran's stern voice brought her back to her body. "As I said, we have much to discuss. Sooner would, I think, be better than later. You can enjoy yourself when you're relieved of duty."

Cassava stepped back, her eyes shining. "I'm glad to see you're safe. I assume Veran is the reason you're here?"

"Partially," Nimmory said.

Veran swept his hand over the living room. "Please. We have much to discuss."

They all took seats. Ferran sat in a seat beside Cassava; Nimmory was across the room and it was hard for Cassava to keep her eyes off her. Henequen stood behind Veran, his eternal shadow.

"Now this is an odd collection of individuals, and normally I think we would not have a gathering like this. But this is not normal, is it?" Veran looked them over. "Cassava, I think we start with you."

Cassava rolled her neck. "I went investigating," she said. "I knew from Nim this cure wasn't a walk in the park, and I thought reconnaissance on that issue would be helpful. I figured out where the facility was and I snuck in. The first room I entered had a boy who was dying and a girl who might be soon going the same way. The conditions were miserable and they kept them locked in little rooms where people were dying."

"In all those rooms?" Veran asked.

Cassava nodded. "I think so."

Veran steepled his hands. "Children?"

"Some not but five years old," Nimmory said. "Yes, they can be unpredictable. But they don't mean harm; they can't."

"The demon means harm, the demon inside them."

"But they should get a chance, shouldn't they?" Cassava said. "To figure out what they're going to do? If they're going to hurt anyone?"

Veran looked at Nimmory and her friend. "And you? Are you dangerous?"

"Only to people who are about to destroy us," Nimmory replied.

Veran shook his head, and Nim glanced sideways at Cassava, as though trying to gauge Veran's response. But Cassava wasn't sure. She wasn't even sure she knew what the right answer was, but she knew these kids didn't deserve what was happening to them. It was unnecessary and cruel.

"Veran, if this is the demon, it's not like we were told," Henequen spoke up for the first time. Cassava had forgotten he was there. "These kids who don't know who the demon is aren't contacting him. They're like me or Cassava. They have defects caused by the demon, but three can contain it, challenge it, channel it." His eyes were bright. "I know I'm crazy, but I can see this. They aren't evil. You know I have senses about this."

Veran turned to Nimmory and her friend. "You two—how did this start for you?"

"Xiben and I were both just kids—it started a few years ago. I was scared, tried to keep it under wraps, didn't understand how it worked. Until the Yegada snatched me up. They thought I would make a good soldier someday, and my parents wanted that too, so I went along with it for a while. I learned how to control it. But as I grew up, I realized what was happening to others, and I didn't want to be a part of it. So, I ran as far as I could, to an island that hadn't heard of magic, that didn't have some tyrannical system—that didn't have me *in* the system, where no one would think to look for me. But clearly that didn't work out."

"Xiben?"

"It wasn't something I noticed as me for a long time. Bright lights would emit, I would read late into the night with no problem. Light just seemed to work for me." Xiben, the nonbinary teen, gave a little shrug. Xiben was strawberry blonde with chin length hair and crystal blue eyes. They had a crisp Adam's apple, but a round face, with a shadow of a beard. "I suppose looking back it should have been obvious. I think my family knew, but they didn't want any trouble and they tried to ignore it." Xiben sighed.

"But eventually there were just too many coincidences. I still don't fully understand how it works, and I expect I never will. Although, I have a chance now. When my parents were confronted about me, they didn't want anything done. But our neighbors called the Yegada in, and they took me here. I'm from the country. I've never been in the city before. Not that I've seen much of it. They snatched me from my home and locked me in a room and demanded I either pledge myself to the army or be given this 'cure.' I didn't understand much about it. I didn't know what to do. I just wanted to go back to my family, and I was going to do it, but then I met Nimmory, and she explained what happens if you do. I don't want to fight for a government who does this to their people, and I don't want to risk dying so they can take away some piece of me that's not hurting anybody."

Henequen started suddenly and turned to the door. "They're outside," he said quietly.

"Who?" Cassava asked.

Henequen put his finger to his lips. Veran got to his feet, and the rest of them followed suit, standing and facing the door. Henequen had his thin rope in one hand and a knife in the other. Cassava stepped in front of the two Rabians. "Get down," she said. She didn't want them getting caught by the Yegada again.

Veran nodded to Henequen, and the Black Sin pulled the door open in a quick motion. A very caught-off-guard Faita stepped back from the door, looking at Henequen and Cassava, with their weapons readied.

"I-I was just coming to ask if any of you wanted to hang out tonight," Faita said.

Henequen did not lower his weapon. "We don't," Cassava said.

Faita brought his hands up in a gesture of surrender, but his tone did not seem particularly contrite. "Just trying to be nice," Faita said. "I'm a lovely host, I promise."

"We keep our own counsel," Veran said. His hands were folded before him like a serene prayer. "I know this might not be your custom, but please respect ours."

Faita nodded his head slowly. "Sure. Sorry to disturb. Just wanted to be polite." He stepped back from the door then walked quickly down the hallway.

Henequen stared after him until he was well gone, then shut the door again. "Snake," he said.

Veran looked uneasy. "Maybe, Henequen, but keep your line to yourself for now. We don't need to get in any more trouble in this country than we already have," he said with a pointed glance at Cassava.

"How did you get me out of there anyway?"

"Well, Henequen knew something was wrong when you didn't come back. He didn't know where you'd gone, of course, but he knew something was amiss. We couldn't do anything about it. The next day, though, Nimmory showed up with Xiben, saying how you'd been locked up. They wanted to try to bust you out, but were afraid reinforcements had been called in—which, given what I saw when I was there, was an accurate statement," Veran said. "I worked my contacts here, and was informed someone matching your description had been caught breaking into a secret facility."

Cassava grimaced. She still wasn't sure how Veran would deal with her, though it seemed she had escaped immediate execution. There was a lot in between that and a slap on the wrist, however. "Sorry."

"You should be," Veran said stiffly. "It was completely unprofessional and unacceptable. Do you know what strings I had to pull to get you back? Of course, they didn't want to *kill* a dignitary's bodyguard, but understandably they couldn't free you with no guarantee you'd keep your mouth shut."

"I won't."

"You *will*," Veran replied, "if you want to ensure your friend's safety." Veran gestured for Cassava to sit back down. "We have to move carefully now."

"People are dying *right now*. Kids, Veran."

"Cassava," he said sharply, "remember your place."

"You're only a few years older than me," Cassava said sourly.

"And I'm in the position of power," Veran said. His voice was cold. "Cassava, do you need to be reminded of your position? I think your time here has been very unsettling for you."

"Because people actually look me in the eye? Talk to me? The horror."

"Because you are coming to believe you are something you are not. You, Cassava, are a tool. You are full of evil—brimming with it. Remember how broken you were when you came to us? That is what your life is—where you will return. You are nothing without us. You would be dead. So don't for a second think you don't need me. I saved you today. I could have had them kill you. I could have had Henequen kill you, which he would have done without question. But I believe there is something more to you, Cassava, some piece of the darkness in your heart that we can use for good. So be patient. Be obedient. And you might see something good happen from your dark and twisted body."

Nimmory had popped up from behind the couch now, and was staring between Cassava and Veran with wide eyes. "Cassava, what's he talking about?"

Cassava looked at Veran and saw it in his face. He had no problem with informing Nimmory exactly who she had been. But Cassava couldn't have that—she couldn't have the reputation that she'd built for herself destroyed, she couldn't bear for Nimmory to know the truth. So, she swallowed and sat down and did not meet Veran and Nimmory's eyes. "Let's hear your plan," she said contritely.

Chapter Ten

The next few days were like nothing had ever happened. Cassava and Henequen stood behind Veran in his meetings, and Veran treated them with his normal reticence. Cassava was impatient, but she could feel the dark at the edges of her mind, and she struggled to stay afloat. She found herself thinking of Nimmory more and more frequently in her meetings. She knew Nimmory was potentially in trouble every time she moved between the safety of their chambers and the outside world, but Veran had requested her assistance and Cassava was not allowed to go out on her own.

The suite was not designed to sleep their full number, but Nimmory and Xiben had bunked up together in the spare bedroom. Cassava might have privately preferred different arrangements, but Veran hadn't exactly been open to debate. His whole plan was scaffolded by various details, and he had not left much to chance.

It was in some ways a relief to have no secrets from Veran—although Ferran's identity had never been explicitly discussed, Cassava did not see how his branding would have escaped Veran's notice. Still, out of habit or an abundance of caution, Ferran did not speak when Veran was around. Cassava wasn't sure what Ferran did all day, but he would leave the rooms and sometimes not be back until late in the evening. Cassava wondered if he was playing cards or finding new inspiration for him to draw. She had seen his room in the suite, and there was a growing collection of detailed pictures—pictures of the market, the docks, a busy bar, all the places Ferran had visited. It was like a visual record of their stay in the Trikingdom. Cassava thought he could really be something with a bit of training.

Cassava tried to follow the political talks, but Dasun made it relatively impossible to follow. Everything was so technical, and the numbers were everywhere. Cassava found she had no head for such things, and they were discussing quantities of things she that she couldn't identify. Cassava often tried to catch Henequen's eye during these long meetings, but he was stoic and focused in a way Cassava found unnerving.

Cassava usually gave up listening after the first hour and turned her mind to other matters. When she wasn't thinking about Nimmory, she was thinking about Saraj. Cassava didn't particularly like children, but she didn't dislike them either, and she had become somewhat fond of Saraj and her story even in that short amount of time they had spent together. Maybe it was because Saraj was her key to Nimmory—or had been for that short period of time— or perhaps it was because Cassava saw some piece of herself in Saraj's story. She hoped if there was the chance to fix her, her parents would want her back. But she wasn't sure. Once damaged…always broken. Cassava's hand moved to the faded scar on her wrists where once she had tried to let her life seep out. It had healed, yes, but some part of her had changed that day, and she wasn't even sure she could have gone back to her parents.

When Cassava had thoughts like this, she pushed them away and refocused on Saraj. That was when a heavy sense of purpose settled over her. She was here to rescue Saraj. She was going to rescue all of them. That was her reason for being. That was the reason she had survived this long. It had never been to be a Black Sin. It had never been for Visea. Those were red herrings—purposes that came before this one, the one that would matter. Cassava knew it was Veran's plan, but it was all because of her. She had given root to the idea. Her breach into the Yegada headquarters had kicked off this whole adventure. Her falling into Nimmory's arms, making that deal, being the one to find her, it was all connected. It was all part of the plan dragging her here.

Cassava was the lynchpin of it all. And these magical kids—they were hers. They were her responsibility now. Cassava was their savior. She was just biding her time now, waiting for her moment to shine, to fix all the problems, to rescue these foreign kids and take them somewhere safe. They didn't need to be fixed.

And Cassava didn't need to be fixed either; she was a hero, wasn't she? Or she would be. She was. She'd rescued Nimmory and Xiben, and that was only the beginning.

A startled response brought Cassava's attention back to the meeting.

"I'm sorry, you—you want our kids?"

"Yes," Veran replied. "In simple terms. We've examined this 'cure' and frankly we don't trust it. It might not stick. We need to contain this aspect of the demon. It's coming to our borders, and who knows who they could be? Obviously once identified we need them to be quarantined from the rest of society. We're set up for this. It's a different form of the demon, but it should be simple enough to add them to our existing infrastructure. How many would you say there are?"

"There are maybe thirty in the facility right now, but it changes. We let them go when they aren't exhibiting symptoms, but it can be hard to tell if they're cured for sure. So, we hang onto them for a long time. We don't want to go releasing anyone who might be hiding the fact that they still have powers."

"That seems like a high rate of error—and a drain on your resources."

"It is," the King agreed. His fingers steepled together. "Still, I'm not sure you realize what you're requesting."

"I know our normal policy is no interference, but this is frankly a problem that transcends borders."

"And do you endeavor to go into Meinweit and do the same?" Dasun asked sharply.

Veran shifted. "I don't know what Meinweit's policy on this matter is, but I would not presume to take what was not offered. I'm merely suggesting an alternative to current operations. We are accustomed to dangerous individuals, we treat them with respect, keep them safe, allow them to live lives with communities of their own. We find this keeps them settled better."

"They do become troublesome, especially the older ones," the King allowed. "What of our possession of those who do wish to serve? They are a valuable asset to our country and we would be loath to rid ourselves of them. We would find that an imposition beyond politeness."

"By all means, save those who wish for yourself. I will be content with knowing they are settled into their life in service. After all, we too put our Sins to work, and we recognize that labor force should not be denied."

Cassava flushed at his words. A labor force? Yes, the Sins did labor, those who could, anyway, but it was hardly the same. Being a Black Sin was a position of merit, it had to be earned. And not everyone was cut out for it. Cassava almost hadn't had the stomach for it, but Henequen had made her see the light. She wondered if he had ever struggled with killing people, or he had just been born ready to lay waste.

"I'm glad you understand. But still—taking our citizens is quite the notion. I would hate to think what would happen if our citizens were to find out we were giving them to Filoli."

Veran inclined his head. "You're not giving them away. Think of it as an additional choice—if they don't want the risks of the cure, and they don't want to serve you, you can send them to us. You know our policy. We don't want any of that in the wild. We're not movers and shakers. We don't get involved with politics. You don't have to worry about us using your resources against you."

"True."

"Please, you can't seriously be considering this?" Dasun

asked. "Just think about it—sending your citizens to languish in some Filoli prison?"

"They're not prisons," Veran protested. "They are secure facilities for the safety of our citizens—and yours."

Dasun waved his hand. "A matter of semantics. Besides, who knows when Filoli will change its mind?"

"And become, what, world domineering? A small nation like ours? We have no armies, no navy...no infrastructure at all. We would be helpless to any nation who decided we were worth invading."

Cassava had never considered Filoli's position before. She had never experienced the wider world, and she didn't even know what these words they were using meant—armies? Navies? All Cassava knew was if another country did want something from Filoli, they were pretty much screwed. Filoli had only stayed independent because no one really cared what they did. They were not particularly wealthy, they bespoke no great arts, no rare natural resources, they simply existed as hard-working individuals who scraped by their livings and gave what excess they had to the Priests.

"Perhaps—"

"No, your Highness, this is madness," Dasun said.

"You are not my advisor, Dasun," the King cautioned sternly. "You are allowed in these meetings as a matter of courtesy and convenience, but I am the King here. We are not in your jurisdiction." He glanced at Novenza. "All the same, I'd be curious to hear what our delegate from Belin thinks."

Novenza glanced between Veran and the two Sins.

Novenza regularly regarded the Sins in a way that made Cassava uncomfortable. She did not write them off as bodyguards, Cassava was sure. Whether this would cause them trouble or not, Cassava was not sure. "I can't say what you're doing now doesn't trouble me, but I understand the reasoning behind it. But perhaps this would be a better alternative. The Queen believes we shouldn't interfere with these things, beyond respecting the parent's wishes, but to keep working on refining the process so the cure is more predictable and helpful."

Cassava wasn't sure what to think of the Belish representative. Something about her seemed off, but she seemed genuine in a way Dasun was not. She was also never aggressive, speaking clearly and persuasively, but without incitement.

The King nodded slowly. "I will think on this proposition, Priest Veran. It is of course a generous offer, to take on that burden and danger."

"Such is always our position," Veran said with a nod. Then the topic of conversation changed, and Cassava was no longer interested.

Later, they gathered back in Veran's chambers. "It is as much as I could expect," Veran said. "To make such a decision without time to consult and think and consider my motives is only natural."

"You say this as if you've negotiated for people's lives countless times," Nimmory said with a little laugh.

"I have," Veran replied seriously. "That is the duty of a Priest. At least, one of many."

Nimmory sobered quickly. "Do you really think this will work?"

Veran sighed. "I don't know. Dasun was quite the opponent. I wonder at his anxiety. Perhaps he had other plans we are getting in the way of."

Henequen snorted. "He is an evil person," Henequen said, "any plans he has should not be seen through."

"You don't know the man," Xiben objected.

"Yes, I do," Henequen replied stiffly. He folded his arms, glancing around the room as though he expected someone to come leaping out from behind the curtains.

"What do we do if he says no?" Cassava asked.

"Then that is the answer," Veran said, "we can't take further action."

"Why not?" Cassava demanded. "They're doing wrong, and they're putting people in danger. How can we let that go by?"

"We let many travesties go by. Surely you have seen the suffering in this city. It is simply beyond our reach. We must trust that those who cannot stand to live in such sin find their way to us."

"They can't find their way if they're locked up," Cassava replied hotly. "What are they supposed to do?"

"And what would you suggest, Cassava?"

Cassava's frustration was building. "We go in there and we free them."

"Think, Cassava. That might work—if we were able to do so, which is questionable as they've no doubt upped their security. But what would happen next? They would know it was us who came, and they would not let us leave until they found and punished us and any who had helped. And even if by some miracle we managed to escape, we would only get away with the people who are being held now. This is an ongoing issue, and after one escape attempt, do you really think they'd leave themselves open in the same way? It would be highly dangerous, and we can't afford to sacrifice two Black Sins to this pursuit. Your skills are invaluable."

Cassava knew he mostly meant Henequen, but she found herself at least somewhat satisfied by Veran's explanation. Of course, if things didn't go according to Veran's plan, Cassava might need to step in. But hopefully that wouldn't be necessary.

Veran said he was feeling poorly and went to bed early that evening. Henequen disappeared into his own room for a nap; he told Cassava to wake him when she went to bed. Henequen was taking his duties very seriously, as per usual.

Xiben stretched their arms out. "How long do you think we'll have to keep sneaking around like this? I don't like being cooped up."

Ferran snorted. "This isn't cooped up."

"You talk?" Xiben said, falling sideways in surprise. "I thought you were mute."

"So does Veran," Ferran said. "And I hope it'll stay that way."

Xiben nodded. "I know about secrets. It must be hard pretending to be mute."

Ferran shrugged. "I am used to not being listened to, so not being able to speak does not impact me as much as you would think."

"Sounds terrible," Xiben said. "I talk nonstop."

"Yes, we all know," Nimmory said with a roll of her eyes. "Chatty Xi."

Xiben stuck their tongue out. "What do they say about you, Cassava?"

Cassava thought about what Visea had said, what the Priests said, what her mentor had said. None of it was something she wanted to repeat. Cassava's flaws were a mile long, and none of it did she want aired in front of Nimmory. "People don't say a lot about Black Sins. They're too afraid."

Nimmory waved her hands over Cassava. "Oooh yes, you're so scarrry," she said. "They don't know you at all. What about you, Ferran?"

"Cassava is very loyal," Ferran said. He met Cassava's eyes and smiled slightly. "Xiben, do you like playing cards?"

"Who doesn't?" Xiben said. "I play wicked Cloudfire."

"Come on," Ferran said, "let's go to my room."

Cassava watched the two of them leave and the door shut behind them. All the sudden she was alone with Nimmory, for the first time since their journey on the seas. Cassava found all her butterflies back.

"Nim…"

Nimmory smiled sweetly at her. "You want to know what they say about me?" she asked, leaning forward on the couch.

Cassava swallowed. "Tell me," she said, her mouth dry.

"They say I'm like wildfire," Nimmory said. "Always ready to go."

"Go do what?" Cassava asked.

Nimmory laughed. "Oh, you're so innocent, Cassava. Have you even had sex?"

Cassava blanched. "Well, I—" she had never felt accosted by it before. It wasn't...she wasn't *supposed* to have...Cassava felt any of her confidence abruptly evaporate. "So, what if I haven't? How many people have you killed?"

Nimmory laughed again. "I'm sorry, Cassava. I just forgot...which honestly I don't know how I could have. You're not like any girl I've...you're not like anyone."

"Is that...a bad thing?"

"No! No, it just means I don't know what to do exactly. I...falls, you get I'm flirting with you, don't you?"

Cassava blushed. "You are?"

"Of course! You're gorgeous and strong and brave and mysterious...seriously sexy."

Cassava was not in control of her face. It was making all sorts of expressions she wasn't accustomed to. "Me? I mean…beautiful?"

Nimmory reached her hand out slowly and touched Cassava's face. "I know you probably think this makes it difficult, and, honestly, I was a bit put off at first. But now it's just a part of your face—a face I...really like. I mean, I've been with a lot of people but none of them have done anything like what you did, over a lot less." Nimmory looked away. "You saved my life, you know?"

"You don't know that."

"Every chance you could have, and even if not, you kept something I hold dear from being taken away from me. And it wasn't for some reason thinking I'd do something for you. You never talk about money, you never have demanded anything from me beyond our deal, and that-that's rare in a person." Nimmory bit her lip. "I've been trying to find a moment with us since it happened. I was so scared, like I've never been, when we waited for you to come out of that window and you didn't. If they'd done something to you...and I'd never even gotten the chance to..."

"To what?" Cassava asked breathlessly, her face flush. These were things she had dreamed Visea would say to her, but it was so much more magical now, as they sat on the couch together, legs nearly touching.

"To kiss you," she said. And she did.

Cassava had never been kissed by a girl before, and now she felt the soft gentle touch of Nimmory's lips on hers. They were a little chapped, dried from the sun, but soon Nimmory was pushing into her mouth, her tongue wet and slick as it slid between Cassava's teeth and licked at the inside of her mouth. Cassava felt as though her whole body was flushed, right down to the curve of her toes.

It was so different from a boy. That had felt awkward and difficult, and a little like kissing sandpaper, with the juvenile boy's face stubble not quite sure what it was doing. Cassava let her own tongue free from its cage, exploring gently. She could smell Nimmory—the sharp tang of a sheer wind that never really seemed to leave her, the fresh burst of air one got opening a door to a cooler atrium. It was like entering into a beautiful building, a palace even the Trikings could not construct.

Cassava had wished to be kissed like this, but this, it actually being there waiting for her, not waiting anymore but coming on, made her impossibly heady. She broke away for a breath of air and to lay her eyes upon Nimmory.

"I don't know how to have sex," she said in a rush.

Nimmory laughed. "Slow down, *yesha*, we're just kissing. I don't think I'd feel comfortable deflowering you so publicly either," Nimmory said.

"Oh," Cassava said, at once alarms racing through her head. Had she done a bad job? Did Nimmory not want her? Had this all been some dreamed up mistake?

"Cassava," Nimmory said, and her voice sounded sweet, it sounded tender, and yet…

"Sorry to disappoint," Cassava said flatly. "I'm getting tired, perhaps I should wake Hen—"

"Barli, please. You're not a disappointment, not at all. But I am a loud partner, and we've got a lot of neighbors. So maybe we kiss, and we talk, and we get to know each other, okay?"

Cassava's hands twisted. She was hung on this girl, she knew it now. There was no denying that when Cassava fell, she fell with her whole being. So here was Cassava, falling. And you know what? Falling felt a lot like flying. "Kiss me again?" she asked hopefully.

Nimmory grinned. "Of course, my lovely assassin."

Chapter Eleven

Cassava spent the next few days floating on a cloud of bliss. She and Nimmory stayed up nights, talking, kissing, and just being together. Cassava had welcomed the Rabian girl into her bed—that was the literal bed. It had been strange the first night, but before long Cassava found it only natural to reach out and find Nimmory there. Nimmory was a wildcat.

When they weren't on guard duty, she and Cassava went out with Ferran or Xiben. Those nights were some of Cassava's favorites. There was drinking—more than Cassava had ever done—and dancing! Cassava missed her homeland's music and the familiar tunes it brought with it. Here everything was loud and clashing, but Cassava still found a way to groove. Dancing with Nimmory was fun. Nimmory danced the same way she did everything else— with reckless abandon. It was sultry too, this style they had of dancing here. It was up close and personal, with so much touching. Cassava liked touching Nimmory.

During the days, Cassava stood behind Veran and didn't say a word. She was the model Sin. Of course, if that was because she was nursing a hangover, what did it matter? She was on two feet. Still standing.

And while she stood, her mind had only two tracks: Nimmory and Saraj. Cassava could not forget Saraj, and for all the bliss that she felt from her fledgling relationship with Nimmory, Cassava knew it was another day Saraj might be dying. Sometimes that was what Cassava thought about when she knocked back another shot. She had to remind herself of Veran's words, his sensible details. But with Saraj on the line, Cassava had trouble thinking about the future generations. Every day felt like another agony, because it could have been a day Saraj lost her fight with the cure.

"Barli?"

They were eating dinner, Veran having retired early with Henequen to keep him company as per usual. The magical twosome was upstairs keeping out of public sight, and this was the first time Cassava had been alone with Ferran in some time. "What's going on?"

"You've been different lately."

Cassava blinked. "Have I been ignoring you? I'm sorry. I get so obsessive sometimes, it's hard for me to think about anything else."

Ferran put his hand out, and Cassava touched it gingerly. It felt good to connect with someone solid and steady like Ferran. She knew he wasn't going to move, he wasn't going to pull away. Ferran would always be here, and that was comforting. She grasped it more firmly. "I do miss some things, but that's not what I'm concerned about," Ferran said.

"What are you concerned about?" Cassava asked. "We're having a good time."

"I don't know a lot about relationships, but I do know you haven't known her that long. Do you even know what she wants to do once she gets out of here?"

"Well, she'd come back to the Islands, of course, that's where we're taking everyone." Cassava said. "It'll be like any other Sin-Black Sin pairing. They make it work."

"Barli, do you really think Nimmory would ever be happy in captivity? She's like you. She doesn't handle it well."

Cassava frowned. She hadn't thought about that. "Maybe she can be a Black Sin too—I mean why not? She'd be great at it."

Ferran lifted an eyebrow. "Maybe. Look, Cassava, just be careful. I don't want you to end up hurt."

"She's nothing like Visea. Visea was so timid and uncertain...Nimmory isn't like that at all. It's completely different. She won't deny me."

"There's more than one way to get hurt, Cassava."

Cassava lifted her chin. "Maybe," she said. "What about you and Henequen?"

Ferran shifted. "That's not important."

"Henequen's been obsessive lately, hasn't he?"

"He can hardly focus on anything but Veran. I think this place has really been messing with him. His mind is coming apart. He needs a break. A real break—not just a few hours of sleep."

Cassava thought about it. Henequen had been terse and uncommunicative lately, his general energy had been dour, and he was spending half the night up watching Veran, and pretty much every other waking hour. Cassava really had been taking advantage of him. "You're right. You should take him out tonight; I'll stay in and keep watch. Get him out of the city, I think that might help. Far enough away that he's not worrying about all the people that might do something next."

Ferran's face went a little red. "Me and Tane?" That was the name Ferran had known Henneqiun by—before he'd become a Black Sin.

"You've been alone with Henequen before."

"Yes, but...but it was different, he was always there to do something. Not just...I don't keep company with people, Cassava, I don't know how to do that. You're the only one I talk to like this."

"What are you talking about? You make conversation with all those people you're playing cards with."

"No, I don't," Ferran said. "I'm used to the mute role, and it's kind of my calling card. It's just easier that way."

"Easier not to talk? Ferran, talking is how we relate to people, how we share experiences...how we fall in love and deepen friendships."

Ferran shrugged. "So, you think people who actually are mute can't make friendships?"

"No, that's not what I'm saying, but you'd better believe that those people are *communicating* however they can. They're not just sitting back and letting life happen around them. That's a sure way to not feel connected."

"I don't know how to do this," Ferran protested.

"You just need some practice. And this is perfect. Look,

Henequen's crazy. He won't mind if you don't have much to say or there are long pauses in conversation—he's got enough going on in his head. You know he needs someone...stable."

Ferran bit his lip. "But I don't feel...stable around him. My insides get all tied up."

"I believe in you, Ferran." She squeezed his hand. "And I want you to succeed and be happy. You've been getting along with Xiben, haven't you?"

"We play cards. They've taught me some new games. It's...nice." Ferran shrugged. "It's nice hanging out with another outcast."

"What am I?"

"You're...a Black Sin. You're the pinnacle of what we can be. You'll have freedom when we leave here and go back home. Me? I'll go back to living out a private existence with only you and Henequen to visit me. What do I have to look forward to, leaving here? I won't even be able to play cards with Xiben, because they'll be locked up in another facility. I don't even have that community."

"Maybe..." Cassava cast around for straws. "Maybe we can talk to Veran, tell him who you really are, and then he'll know you're safe and you don't need to be locked up. Veran seems reasonable."

"No. Not only does that screw me if it goes wrong, but it's the end of the line for both you and Henequen. I can't risk that for you, and I'd rather be alive and shut up in a house in the middle of nowhere than dead."

They sat quietly for a little while, Cassava feeling guilty about forgetting about Ferran's delicate situation in light of everything else. Why could nothing go smoothly? She was Ferran's only chance, and Ferran was her first rescue, her best friend, and she owed it to him to take care of him as best she could.

"But that's not the only thing I'm concerned about, Barli."

"What? What else did I do?" Cassava asked. She'd been prepared for the other topics, but now she felt floored.

Ferran frowned. "It's not something that you did," he said. "It's just something about you that seems...off."

"Something about me? You mean that I'm happy?"

"No. You weren't happy. I mean, you are, sometimes. But sometimes...sometimes it's like there's something else in your head."

Cassava scoffed. "I'm fine, Ferran. I'm just stressed about this Yegada thing. I mean, my girlfriend's future is kind of tied up with it. Girlfriend." Cassava smiled. "It's fun to say that. I've never gotten to say that before."

"Are you sure? It feels like something's wrong. It reminds me of how you were when you were training to become a Black Sin."

"And I was fine then, I'm fine now." Cassava shook her head. "I appreciate the concern, Ferran. I just get a little obsessed sometimes. It's not the end of the world. It's not anything bad at all. In fact, I need it. It makes me tick."

"I suppose it's fine. It just worries me a little."

"Ferran, I've got it all under wraps. I know you don't know people that well, but people like me are just...like this. I'm happy, I'm stressed, and those things can be true at the same time."

"Life on the outside is complicated," Ferran said.

"Yes," Cassava agreed, "it definitely is." Cassava glanced around the dining hall, spotting Dasun and his family at another table. Dasun was speaking quietly with his son, looking around every so often at the other tables. He scowled when he saw Cassava looking and stood up. Cassava wasn't sure about him. Yes, he was a despicable person, and every encounter she had with him made Cassava dislike him more. But he seemed straightforward enough. He always said what he meant. Henequen was just overreacting. He did that a lot. Everything was a threat when Henequen was around...though Cassava had never known him to be wrong. He had a special sense about people she probably shouldn't ignore.

"Come on, Ferran, let's go," she said. They got up together, Cassava glancing back over her shoulder as she left. The Dasun family was coming along behind them. They were talking, but stopped when they realized Cassava was so close. Cassava stopped outside their door and lingered for a moment. "Faita, not interested in hanging out tonight?"

"No," he said quickly. "I'm going out tonight."

"Me too," Cassava lied, driven by a sudden impulse to play with the boy. "Maybe we should go out together?"

"Ah, no, no need for that." He stammered for a moment, and then seemed to find himself. "I wouldn't be caught dead in the same scene as you."

"Actually, I think you would," Cassava replied with a brittle smile. She put her hand to her belt, touching the hilt of one of the many knives she kept on her person. "Have a good evening," she said sweetly as she entered the suite and locked the door sharply behind her.

Veran was buried in paperwork in his room, a job Cassava wasn't sure whether he had given himself to stay busy, or it was actually important. He always seemed to have something to do. Henequen, face drawn and with bags under his eyes, nodded to Cassava. He really was worse for wear. While Cassava went out and partied, he was here wasting away. Thoughtless of her to forget how this place might be affecting him—he who had never done well with crowds.

"Hey, Quen," she said softly as she approached him. He seemed to start a little, and blinked blearily back at her, then almost through her. "Quen?"

"Something's happening."

"Nothing's happening," Cassava said gently. "We just got back from dinner, and me and Ferran think it would be best if you took a night off."

"A night off?" Henequen responded slowly, as if he was processing her words on a delay. "The night doesn't go off."

"But you can. Henequen, you need a break. I'm a Black Sin too, you know, I can take care of Veran. Relax. Sleep. Go somewhere quiet. Run." Cassava spread her hands. "Do whatever you want, but I don't want to see you for at least twelve hours."

Henequen looked like a lost boy in a busy market for a moment. "Be careful, Cassava."

"I will, Quen."

After a bit more convincing and placating, Henequen and Ferran finally left. Xiben looked at Cassava and

Nimmory and rolled their eyes. "Great. So, I get to third wheel," they said.

"We can do something for all of us," Nimmory protested.

Xiben made a rude gesture. "Don't bother. The stench of lovebirds is already soaking the room. I swear I can taste it." And with that declaration, Xiben shut the door to their room, leaving Cassava and Nimmory to their own devices.

"We're alone," Cassava breathed.

Nimmory wrinkled her nose. "Kind of. I mean Veran could hear anything and I don't think you want that. Plus, he *could* come out."

"But he's not going to," Cassava replied. "He never does—whatever we're doing."

Nimmory kissed her. "I suppose that's true," she said, a soft purr in her voice. Cassava's spine shivered. "You're a little minx, aren't you?"

"I don't know what that is," Cassava said, gasping slightly as Nimmory nibbled on her ear.

Cassava could feel Nimmory's smile in the curve of her neck, the soft part of her lips, a little flash of teeth. "It means," Nimmory said quietly, "that you'd flirt your way to anything."

"If anything means *something* in particular, then yes."

"My beautiful little assassin." Nimmory's hand crept up Cassava's thigh, slowly edging higher and higher.

Cassava moaned. "I'd kill for you, Nimmory."

"You already have. You're such a good assassin, and no bells and whistles just...straight blood. You're used to getting what you want."

"Not really," Cassava replied with a laugh.

Nimmory put a finger to her lips. "Shut up, you're ruining the mood." She tucked her hand around Cassava's waist and pulled her closer. "Do you want me?" she asked.

Cassava's mouth was dry. "Yes."

Nimmory kissed her deeply, and Cassava felt as though a little piece of her soul was being drawn out. "Are you sure you want this?" Nimmory asked. "We don't have to. I know it's a big step for someone like you."

Cassava stayed her hand. "What do you mean someone like me?"

"You know," Nimmory said awkwardly, "I just mean...I don't expect you've done this before. I know in some cultures it's a big deal."

Cassava brought her hand defiantly to Nimmory's breast and stroked her softly. "In another world maybe. But I'm a Black Sin, the rules don't really apply. Besides, you're not going to get me pregnant."

"Okay," Nimmory said, "as long as you're sure."

"I'm sure." Cassava took her hand and moved it down Nimmory's body, further than she had ever gone before. She reached the waist of Nimmory's pants and fumbled with the button. "Why do they put buttons here?"

Nimmory found Cassava's waist and the tie that held Cassava's pants up. "And a knot is better?" she replied. They both struggled for a moment before freeing the respective attachments.

"I'll admit I don't know quite what to do," Cassava said. She refused to feel embarrassed by her inexperience. It was not scruples that had kept her from taking the plunge, but lack of availability. Cassava simply didn't know that many queer people, and certainly not any that had taken an interest in Cassava.

Cassava felt somehow that this experience with Nimmory was fleeting. Some part of her believed she would only have so many chances. Life was not certain, and Nimmory seemed too good to be forever. So, Cassava knew she had to take this moment and live it to all it was worth. She felt good, and that wasn't always the case. She wanted to be up, up higher than she'd ever been before. This was the moment to fly.

Nimmory kissed her again and pushed her back onto the couch. "It's not that complicated, I'm sure with an example you'll be able to figure it out." She proceeded to divest Cassava of her undergarments. She touched Cassava's breast with just chilled fingers that made Cassava's whole body shudder. She took her other hand and moved it lower, lower, and then she was brushing along Cassava, and Cassava moaned. Just the barest tingle of her fingers over a particular spot made Cassava see stars.

"Quiet now," Nimmory warned, kissing and sucking on Cassava's neck. "We don't want Veran to hear. He mustn't think anything is wrong."

Cassava swallowed her sound, and it seemed to fill her body instead. Cassava's body trembled with each stroke of Nimmory's fingers. So small, so powerful. It was like a knife, but instead of giving pain it brought pleasure, slipping into just the right place and the result was incredible.

Cassava was biting her lip when something shifted; the wind or something else gave her pause. She struggled to sit up, but Nimmory held her down. "Not yet, my assassin," she said lowly, "just wait."

There was another creak and now Cassava couldn't ignore it. She pushed Nimmory off her and sat up. Xiben? The door remained closed. Veran?

That was when Cassava saw the slightest movement of a door clicking closed. Closed? Had Veran seen? But then Cassava looked to the hallway and saw the door agape.

"Come back—"

"Nim!" Cassava hissed. "Stay here." She got quickly to her feet and padded to the door. "Moan," she whispered.

"What?"

"Just do it," Cassava replied. She put her hand to her hip, but there was nothing there. She wasn't wearing anything but a loose shift.

It took Nimmory a moment to recognize there was a danger, but she obeyed. Cassava twisted the door open.

Inside, Veran was asleep—at least Cassava hoped he was asleep—at his desk. A figure stood poised with a crossbow behind him, readying the shot.

Cassava wasn't used to being weaponless. She didn't even sleep naked. She always had at least one knife on her. You never knew what to expect as a Black Sin. Now, she was standing in a state of undress behind an armed assailant.

There was nothing else for it. She rushed forward and swept out with her leg at the figure's back leg.

Closer now, she could see that this was Faita. Cassava wished she could sink her blade into his ample stomach, but instead she was left grabbing for the crossbow. The bolt displaced as he staggered back, falling to one knee.

"I thought you were out," Faita snarled. He dropped the crossbow and swung a fist at Cassava that collided with the side of her head.

Cassava reared back, her vision going black momentarily. But she couldn't waste a second. She lifted her knee up into Faita's crotch, to which he gave a wild shriek.

Faita cursed loudly in Meinish. "You weren't supposed to be here," he said. "You were going out."

"Plans changed," Cassava said, panting a little. He wasn't attacking her and she didn't quite know what to do with it. Normally she would have knifed him, but she didn't have a weapon on her.

"It doesn't matter," Faita said, "you'll be asleep soon enough."

"I don't—" Cassava began, but Faita stretched his hand out and suddenly Cassava's eyes were incredibly heavy. "What…" she tried to stay upright, but staggered slightly, using the wall to support herself. "You have magic?" she managed.

Faita grinned. "Don't you feel foolish now? How could you hope to protect your precious Priest when you're dead on your feet?"

At this point, Cassava heard steps behind her. "You're not the only one with magic," Nimmory said. A sudden wind bellowed through the suite and slammed Faita against the wall. Faita groaned, but held out his shaking arm again. "Sorry, bitch, but I beat you."

Cassava was desperately trying to take a step forward as she saw Nimmory keel over beside her. Cassava hoped it was just sleep and not something more sinister.

She tried to form words, but it was so, so difficult. As her eyes began to close, she saw something rise behind Faita and then a resounding smack echoed through the suite. Cassava saw Faita crumple. Behind him stood a surprised-looking Veran holding up one of the heavy books of obscure lore he favored. His eyes blinked sleepily with the effort to keep them open, still recovering from his time under Faita's spell. Cassava didn't know much about magic, but she guessed it took more than a few minutes to shake off entirely.

It took far longer than it should have, but Cassava slowly made her way over to Veran, trying to shake off the effect of Faita's magic. "Sorry, Veran," she said, her words slurring a little.

Veran yawned. "Let's tie him up and then...think about this in the morning."

Cassava and Veran took an extraordinarily long time canvassing for Henequen's rope and tying Faita to their satisfaction. Nimmory had not stirred from her spot on the floor, but Cassava had checked on her and she appeared to still be breathing.

They relocked the door and sat in the sitting room, blinking tiredly at each other. Cassava at some point realized she was still mostly undressed, but it seemed too late to do anything about it.

"Good hit," Cassava said.

"I didn't think it would be enough," Veran said frankly, "but I had to try something. Who knew books were so dangerous."

"I like you," Cassava said, not entirely sure why she was

talking but feeling like she had to. "Most of the Priests are stuffy and rude. But you treat us like actual people."

"My father was a Sin," Veran said quietly.

"Wait—I thought offspring of Sins were always Sins."

"It happened when I was a kid," Veran said. "My mother argued for us, and she won. And I became a Priest. It was the only way to see him again," Veran said. "I don't think most Priests realize how close they are to becoming a Sin."

Cassava was bleary-eyed enough that she put her hand out to pat Veran's leg before she remembered she was a Sin and hardly allowed to speak to a Priest let alone touch one. "I didn't see it coming," Cassava said. "I mean, I knew I was different, but it still took me by surprise. And then I wanted it to be wrong. But...I am sick. So...so, maybe I should be kept away from people who aren't."

Veran studied her with half-glazed eyes, though she had a feeling he was more awake than her. "I admire you, Cassava. You've wrestled with the darkness and you're doing so much better now. I wonder if it hasn't left you."

"I didn't think such a thing was possible."

"If people can become demon-touched I think it stands to reason they can free themselves of the touch. It's a minority school of thought—most Priests would disagree, saying the taint is intractable. That's why I haven't said anything about Ferran—yes I know his name and that he is not mute—I disagreed with the decision to terminate him, and now I do all the more. Did you really think you could hide that face from me?"

Cassava blushed. "You pay more attention than most

Priests. And I had thought, if things went south, he could just escape and live out his life here, in the Trikingdom. There are more helpless creatures that eke out a living here. Will you tell on him?"

"No," Veran said. "I think that boy has served a harsher sentence than any deserve, for no crime at all."

"You are a strange Priest."

"I am and I am not. There are others among my brethren that desire change, change I believe could well come on the backs of this newest venture. We are smaller in number, and not given teaching roles, which is why you won't have heard our particular philosophies. Some Priests come for the power, some from a strong desire to be good or even the best, and some of us come because we care about the broken pieces of our society. I believe change is coming, Cassava. How long it will take, I do not know."

"What kind of change?"

"Changes to the way we deal with the demon, the way we regiment people. I believe the Priests, with the magic spelled out before them, will find something there worth harvesting in a way they have not seen fit to utilize people before. How this will play out, I do not know. All I know is I am bringing back a storm of trouble to our tranquil waters, and whether I will be crucified or praised I cannot say."

Cassava had frankly never thought about Veran's position in this mess. She had only ever seen him as an obstacle, as a faceless mass getting in the way of everything she wanted. But Veran was different than she had built him in her head to be. He demanded obedience, yes, but he listened to her and Henequen. He asked after them, and though they were by no means friends he was arguably friendly. Now, sitting side by side, Cassava thought about all he had done for her, things he had no obligation to do. Perhaps they could be...Cassava shook that thought away. It was too strange. Clearly this spell Faita had them under was messing with her.

Cassava opened her mouth to say something, perhaps apologize for the way she had portrayed him, but when she looked over at Veran again he was asleep. Cassava gave a large yawn. But she couldn't afford to fall asleep. She had already failed her duties once today.

It took substantial effort, but Cassava managed to stay awake until the door slipped open again. Cassava started a bit all the same and took her knife in hand, relaxing only when she saw it was a sated Henequen and a confused-looking Ferran.

It took Henequen several seconds to register that something was off, but then he straightened up. "What happened?"

"Faita. He has sleeping magic...he got to most of us. He might wake up soon and I don't know if it'll work with his hands tied or not but I *really* have to sleep, so, you got this, right? We can figure out what to do later. I'm just afraid of a second wave."

Henequen took out his string and a boning knife. He kicked a chair under the door to brace it and nodded to Ferran. "Keep an eye on the prisoner. Shout if he starts rousing." He took up a position in front of the door, readied.

"Thanks, Quen."

A few moments later, Cassava was out cold.

Chapter Twelve

Cassava awoke the next morning to the smells of sweet rolls and bacon. Breakfast was normally a downstairs affair, but this morning—late morning—someone had ordered in and it had been delivered. Henequen was standing by the door with a chair in front of him. In the chair was Faita, with a rope around his neck. Henequen held it with the barest tension, ready to tighten at a moment's notice.

Veran was eating along with Xiben, Nimmory, and Ferran. It was surprising to hear Ferran's voice mixed in among Xiben and Nimmory, but it seemed that Veran had told them he knew about Ferran's situation. Cassava was happy she had the chance to see Ferran wreathed in society and friends again. Maybe it would last. Cassava joined them at the table. They were talking about food, which Cassava thought was a nice safe topic, and one Ferran could actually contribute to.

"Bacon is hands down the best part about the Trikingdom," Ferran announced. "We need pigs in the Islands."

Xiben groaned. "You're telling me there's no pork in Filoli? Great."

"Why don't we have pigs? We trade."

"Meinweit believes pigs are dangerous and spread disease, and Filoli descends from those traditions, even though our religious conception is now very different." Veran said. "It's truly fascinating that it has lingered as a superstition when pigs would thrive on the Islands."

"Do they spread disease?"

"They've been linked to diseases before, but if you keep them in clean areas they usually present no problems."

"Falls, Veran, is there anything you don't know?"

"Plenty. But there aren't a lot of historians in Filoli. We don't spend a lot of time on it, and the Priests are some of the only people who care. I got relegated to copying old manuscripts for a year, and some of it stuck. There's plenty I don't remember." Veran took a sip of paiga juice. "Well. We're all awake again, shall we get down to business?" He pulled his chair away from the buffet and sat down in front of Faita.

"Now, Faita, I think you understand how this works. If Henequen starts to feel tired, it's the end. If you put any of the rest of us to sleep, also the end. And if you put Henequen out before he can kill you, Cassava still throws knives, and she's got them today. Got it?"

"Yes," Faita said, surly.

"Good. Let's start with who you work for. Your father, I assume?"

"Yes."

"I know your father doesn't like me, but what exactly is he hoping to accomplish?" Veran asked.

"I don't know exactly. He doesn't share everything with

me. He thinks you're dangerous, and this ploy by you to steal kids away from the Trikingdom is part of some greater plot."

"And what exactly does he think I'm going to do with these children?"

"Attack our interests."

Veran nodded. "I see. Why does he think that?"

"I don't know. He just said you were shady and this deal needed to die. He tried to work on the King, but it wasn't working."

"The King came to a decision?"

"Yes. We aren't supposed to know yet, but my father has ways."

Cassava bounced in her chair. "He's going to do it?"

Veran glanced back at her with a glare before turning back to Faita.

"Yes, that's right. He decided yesterday afternoon."

Xiben, Nim, and Cassava let out little whoops that Veran squashed with a crisp hush. "And, so, you decided you had to move now, before it was too late."

"Cassava is always out with most of you, and we knew Henequen uses a rope. I figured I could get to him before we were in close quarters. But it wasn't Henequen, and nothing went to plan."

It was all true, and well thought out. Cassava thought if it had been any other night, Veran would be under. And then where would she and Nimmory be? Ferran? Any of them? Cassava let out a breath. They would both have to guard Veran very closely until they were out of here. If Veran died now, the whole scheme would implode, and

Cassava, Henequen, and Ferran would be trapped in the Trikingdom. Well...maybe *that* wouldn't be so terrible. But for Nimmory and Xiben? Not to mention the rest of the occupants of the old hotel? It would be a disaster.

"I assume your father has other agents," Veran said.

"Several," Faita agreed.

"Then I think we'll have to hang on to you until everything's settled."

"What?" Faita said, struggling in the chair for a moment before he remembered the rope taut around his neck. "No—listen—I don't care what my father wants, I don't want to die. I promise if you let me go, I'll be good."

"You might be good," Veran said, "but I have no illusions about your father. And you have a sister, I believe, who may well be practiced in magical arts herself."

"No. Beiru has nothing to do with all this, I promise."

"Be that as it may, I'd prefer insurance. Of course, there's always the chance your father doesn't favor you, but I'll take that risk."

Faita looked pale, as if it was not a risk he wanted to take. Cassava didn't have to wonder what her parents would have done. They would have never asked her to kill someone, so they wouldn't have been in this position. But if for some reason she had been kidnapped, they would have done anything to get her back. Except, Cassava reflected, if that kidnapping was because she was a Sin, and the kidnappers were Priests. Then her family would abandon her, leave her to the wolves, and never try to contact her again. Cassava knew some Sins got letters. She never had.

They couldn't even stomach to have that level of contact with her.

Veran interrogated Faita a little longer, but it was clear to Cassava he was being honest and had told them all he knew. He just was a pawn of his father's, and his father wasn't there. Faita was not particularly brave or abrasive; in fact, he seemed just about on the verge of tears a few times, and made at least one more plea for Veran to let him go. But Veran held firm.

It was nearing noon when Veran had finished, and there was a knock on the door. Veran had Henequen scoot Faita to the side before gesturing for Cassava to open the door. Cassava walked up with her knife ready.

"Yes?" she called through the door.

"It's Zoal. The King was wondering where Veran was this morning."

Cassava opened the door just slightly. "Veran was feeling under the weather, but he's recovered now and will be in afternoon sessions."

"Very well. I'm glad he's feeling better." They gave Cassava a stiff nod and walked away.

Cassava shut the door with a snap. "Do you have other business here, Veran? I think it would be best to leave while we have the advantage. For all we know, Dasun thinks your absence is his success."

"I think you are right, Cassava. Although I could stay longer, given the current risk to my health—and all of yours by association—I believe we should leave as soon as arrangements can be made. I will attend meetings this afternoon and see how quickly the children can be moved."

They made arrangements for the afternoon; Xiben and Nimmory were given the task of guarding the prisoner and the apartment from anyone who might come to rescue him. Henequen and Cassava would attend Veran as normal, pretending as though there had been no attempt on his life. It would leave Dasun uncertain whether his son had chickened out, or something fouler had occurred. Cassava liked the idea of plaguing Dasun with doubts. He deserved it after what he had said and done.

When they arrived in the meeting room, Cassava saw Dasun's eyes widen with uncertainty and fear like the eyes of those who saw her just before she killed them, but it was quickly gone. He was a master of his emotions, in a way Cassava had never been, and she found herself vaguely envious of him.

"Veran, so good of you to join us. I'm sorry you've been feeling under the weather," the King said graciously.

"Yes, temporary, luckily. I think my stomach does not wholly agree with all the rich foods here; the cheeses can do something nasty to my constitution."

"I learned that one the hard way," Novenza agreed. She smiled politely at the Black Sins, the way she always did, and Cassava wondered if she was in on it too. "Some of us don't digest milk very well, and it's in nearly everything here it seems!"

"Now, now, Novenza, don't criticize us for taking advantage of the bounties of the world. What fun would there be without some indulgence?"

"What world would there be without some circumspection?" Novenza replied.

The King laughed, though Cassava did not think Novenza intended to be humorous. "We will always have disagreements," he said, "but that is what makes the world interesting, no? What stories would we have to tell if all were free from conflict?" He folded his hands and sat them firmly on the table. "So, now we come to a matter that was put before me some days ago, on which I have heard counsel of many types, but it is the counsel of my other King that I heed most strongly. I have determined that it makes the most financial and political sense to accept Filoli's fine offer of guardianship of our troubled youths. I know they will make every effort to take care of those who refuse treatment, as they have done with their many other citizens."

Dasun was shaking his head, but he did not speak.

"Thank you, Your Highness," Veran said, bowing to him shortly, a proper show of respect, but not of sovereignty. "I assure you, should they ever change their mind, we will transport your citizens back to their home."

The King nodded gravely. "I know some have expressed their doubts, but I fail to see how the current situation is helpful to anyone, and is simply untenable. You will speak with Dillion on the details, Veran. She knows the numbers and the other finer points that frankly I don't have time for."

"Be warned, my friend, this will one day haunt you," Dasun said darkly.

The King waved his hand. "I am not haunted by my decisions; to do so over every wrong call I have made would simply be paralyzing. I simply learn from it and move forward so the future is brighter. That is all I think any of us can do, Dasun."

"I hope we can make better choices than this."

"I will ask you to leave if you can't sit quietly, Dasun. Like Veran, you are here at my invitation."

Dasun glowered darkly.

"On to other topics then. Novenza, you had a note—"

They continued on to something Cassava cared little about, and instead she found herself thinking about Saraj, hoping she was still alive and well. She also couldn't help but feel herself remembering the night before, the part before Faita had entered.

Cassava wasn't sure what to think. It had been incredible, and yet Cassava felt as though something had been missing. The idea made her uncomfortable. Perhaps it was because it had been interrupted. Somehow, they would have to try again. Cassava was sure it would work under different circumstances.

After the meetings for the day, Veran went to Dillion. She was expecting him, at least, and managed to fit him into the schedule quick enough. She was an efficient taskmaster, and they worked together to find the appropriate ship and arrange goods for so many passengers.

Cassava didn't pay attention to the details. She was alert to every movement in the hallway, and she was jumpier than normal. The night's attack had left a mark.

Returning to the room hardly set Cassava at ease, and when Nimmory suggested going out for a last night of freedom, Cassava snapped.

"No, we are not going out. Do you know what is

outside those walls? A city without fear. This place…seems wonderful, doesn't it? You can do whatever you want and who would care? But look at what it's done—look at the cost! Children dying in the streets, children dying in locked rooms with not a friendly face around, crime beyond belief, and a State King who can't even keep his honored guests safe!

"Every time we leave here, we're at risk. Someone could see you, recognize you, and maybe they'd decide you're too dangerous to live. And me? I have a job to do, a job I should have been doing last night instead of spending time with you! Now we are on the cusp of everything we could want, something to protect us both, protect *us*—and you want to put that all in jeopardy for a night out? Are you insane? No," Cassava said, shaking her head. "We are not going out. We are not going anywhere. I am staying with Veran, and you are staying with me so I can keep an eye on both of you. We're so close now. We can't risk it now."

Nimmory put her hands on her hips. "Veran's life isn't the only one that matters. I know we're going back to your home, but for me this is a big shift. I'm going to be locked up! You think I'm happy about this? Yes, I'm so so grateful I'm not going to die—but why in the frozen plains should I have to be locked up for it? I'm not dangerous. I'm just born different. And I'm about to head on a ship to a nightmare. I'm not made to be caged up."

"I'm not either," Cassava said, "but that doesn't change things. Sometimes you just have to do the hard thing, Nim."

Nimmory shook her head. "You don't understand. Of course, you don't. You've been entrenched in this language and culture of oppression. Well, I'm not like that. I know what it's like to be free, and I appreciate it. So, I'm going out. You can come if you want. I've got to have a night of freedom."

"It's dangerous. If you just wait, Veran thinks things will change."

"When, Cassava? How? It sounded like things could go very badly for me. It sounded like it might result in an even worse crackdown than there already is, and let me tell you, all the stories you've told me about the Asylum make me crazy. I'd go mad in a place like that."

"And you think I don't? You think I wanted to become an assassin? I did it because it was my only option. You have to understand, I lived free once too. And, yes, it's terrible, but it becomes easier, I promise it does. People don't kill themselves because they end up in the Asylum, Nim, they learn how to live. It's hard and it sucks, but you're alive and safe and have an opportunity for more. You could be a Black Sin, Nimmory, you could be like me. You'd be free of the walls."

"I'd have a brand on my face. A mark. Forever."

Cassava's stomach was cold. "But you don't mind it, you said…"

"For *you*. It's not something I want for myself. It's just not. And I don't want to be a hired killer. I want to be my own person, not accountable to anyone. I want freedom."

"You can't have everything you want," Cassava said, "you're acting like a child."

Nimmory reached out at once and slapped Cassava across the face. "How dare you. If I'm acting childish, it's because I *am* a child, but I grew up a long time ago. I just have different priorities than you."

"Fine. Go out. Get caught. Wind up with the Yegada again. You'll be back here, with us, because we're the only ones you have a chance with."

"I won't. I'm smarter now."

Cassava couldn't think; she only knew that Nimmory was trying to leave her. After all they'd been through, one moment more and suddenly everything was spinning out of control.

"Don't go," Cassava said, "I'm sorry, just don't go."

Nimmory shook her head. "I can't stay." And she left.

Chapter Thirteen

Time moved slowly after that. Veran was a whirlwind around her, and he took several trips up and down the stairs, back to Dillion, and even out to the harbor. Cassava watched his back, but she knew she could rely on Henequen for most of the work, and she did. She moved as though through a haze, and had anyone tried to engage her, they would have found her lacking. But no one did. She was simply ordered here, ordered there, and she moved as if by rote. A great pit of emptiness was opening up inside her, but she could not fall off the cliff yet. There were matters to attend.

Walking through the bazaar, Cassava reflected that this was likely the last time she would see this place—vibrant and full of color, with animals constantly underfoot— Cassava had learned the not-cats were called dogs and were considerably more biddable. But this did not interest her now; none of it did.

Cassava felt as though the only thing keeping her head above water was the thought of Saraj and the chance that perhaps Nimmory would show up tomorrow, her mind changed, having realized that freedom was only so good when you were on your own. Cassava had learned that lesson; it was her friends that had made captivity palatable. Ferran and Henequen made it possible to languish in captivity, they filled her life with some small amount of meaning—though she was having difficulty remembering that now, in this quiet stoicness that filled her.

The plans were laid, and Veran was still alive that evening when they went to bed. Cassava wordlessly volunteered to stand guard that night. She hadn't been able to bring herself to speak since the incident, and she didn't think she would sleep anyway. She might as well give Henequen a break.

The night was long and bleak. Cassava stood outside Veran's door, staring at the place where she had lain the night before with Nimmory. It seemed as if there would be no second chances. Cassava would forever have to wonder about what it might have been like. What all of it could have been like.

Cassava swallowed down her despair. That piece of her that was still beating was waiting for tomorrow, for a ship to carry them away to safety. Then, she could be done. Then, she could rest.

For now, she felt a fire licking at her tired bones. It was a journey she had been on for a long time, but perhaps she would have a moment of peace. Perhaps once they were on their way, she would be allowed to fizzle out.

Cassava was alert to every motion, every shift of the breeze, thinking it might be Nimmory coming back. Or another assassin. Dasun had not come to collect his son, had not mentioned Faita, and Veran had decided they would let him go the next morning, once they were all ready to board the ship east.

There were few footsteps in the hall, but every time she heard it or felt the beginning of movement in the ball of her foot, she stood fully upright, with her knife in hand. Once they passed, Cassava found herself examining her knife. It was a sturdy one, Xinpaku had given it to her as a parting gift before her test. She wondered what Xinpaku would think of what she had done now. He probably would have been more intrigued by magic than Cassava. For the first time, it crossed Cassava's mind that perhaps some sort of healing magic existed. Perhaps there was some way to make some of the Sins who were broken to become...unbroken. What would happen then?

But that was an issue for another day, far down the road. There were many questions that would have to be answered by the Priests once things were settled, but Cassava didn't care much about that. Cassava didn't care about much of anything beyond survival.

It was strange how everything had gone dim and dark. The grayscale of the night felt appropriate, much more appropriate than the bazaar had felt earlier that day. Now it was quiet and dark and sorrowful, and Cassava felt as though she could dissolve into the moonlight.

Eventually, a pale dawn streak began to make its way through the window. Cassava felt the breeze pick up, and for a moment it was like she could smell Nimmory—that crisp bit of wind reminded her of the Rabian. But no Nimmory was forthcoming, and when Cassava looked out over the city, there was no young girl flying through the sky toward her. For a moment, Cassava allowed herself to imagine it, and it was truly incredible, a wondrous sight that filled her with longing and determination. But when she blinked it was gone.

Color came back, but it felt wrong, and when Cassava took in the morning she imagined it was rather a violent blot of scorching fire that had risen; a new tribulation.

Ferran was the first morning riser, and he came out with a wandering yawn and a contemplative look. "Where's Nimmory?" he asked. "Sleeping?"

Cassava shook her head.

"Still out? Cutting it a bit tight, isn't she?"

Cassava swallowed. She could hear it inside her head, the sound of a sudden moisture pushed down.

"Oh. She's gone, hasn't she?" Ferran said softly.

Cassava crumpled into him. His shoulder was solid and firm, and Cassava felt that steady presence keenly. Cassava felt the darkness of the night that had welled up throughout the night come crashing down on her now, and she began to cry with giant aching sobs that wracked her body. She had not cried in some time, and it had been a long time since someone had held her in response. She had been private in her tears with Ferran before, seeking him out after she had contained herself. Today, in the early dawn, she listened to the beat of his heart and wished beyond measure he could do the impossible for her.

"Oh, Barli. It'll be alright."

"No. No, it won't."

"There's no fear anymore; what's happened won't

change. She'll find her way somewhere, or she'll end up back with us."

Cassava dabbed her eyes, and then her nose, which was running profusely. "If she doesn't do something more damaging."

Ferran touched her face gently. "Nimmory will make her own choices, as we all do."

"No, we don't," Cassava said humorlessly. "The Priests decide everything for us. I think it's really preferable that way, now isn't it?" she said. "After all, if I was on my own still, I'd be lost."

"Cassava, listen to me. You are going to be fine. This isn't like Visea. You have me, and Quen, though I know he can be hit or miss. But you survived before, Cassava. You can survive this time too."

"Why does this happen to me?" she asked.

Ferran shook his head. "Perhaps because some other luckier soul is having an easier go. Your sin marks you, makes you a target. But I believe in you. You can fight through this. You're stronger than those other people."

"No, I'm not. I'm not strong at all."

Ferran tutted, a noise Cassava did not think she had heard from him before. "Cassava, you broke the rules. You outplayed everyone in your Sin competition and you rescued me at the same time! You rescued Nimmory and Xiben, and because of you, so many other people are going to live. They're going to have a choice. You make decisions, Cassava, big ones, and the world owes you. Someday, you'll get it back."

"Do you really think so?"

Ferran swallowed. "Cassava, you changed my life. You didn't just save it; you expanded it, made it worth living. You gave me friends, a family, trust, safety, security, and now maybe even love. And I didn't know how to experience any of those things before you. You taught me."

"I feel like I've failed, at so much."

"You've succeeded so much more," Ferran pressed. "I know it doesn't feel like it right now, but you'll see it someday, the impact you've had."

Cassava wiped her eyes. "I fail at love," Cassava said.

Ferran sighed. "Well, there's good news on that front," he said.

"What is that?" she asked sourly.

"We're going to have a constant stream of girls coming in from the Trikingdom, the perfect source for someone like you. Surely, you can find another."

Cassava didn't want to think about that. She shook her head. "I don't think so," she said. "I just want Nimmory back."

"There's time for her to change her mind, or get caught, or both," Ferran attempted to console her.

"For her to be trapped and miserable with me?" Cassava asked. "She sounded almost as if she'd rather die." Cassava hugged Ferran close before drawing away. "I was like her at the beginning. Perhaps she would adjust, perhaps she wouldn't, but I can't blame her for running. I would have, if given the option. I wanted an escape. I wanted something far more permanent." Cassava hugged him again. "I can't blame her. I just...wish things were different."

"So do I," Ferran replied.

They sat in quiet companionship until Henequen roused from his room. Ferran did not move away from Cassava, and they stayed wound together as Henequen entered and sat across from them, followed shortly by Xiben.

"She was conflicted," Henequen said.

Cassava glanced at him, confused and then even more uncertain. "Nimmory?"

Henequen nodded.

"How do you know these things, Quen?"

Henequen rapped at his head. "It's all inside here, all the time so much, and sometimes I can make sense of it."

"You have a very strange madness." Cassava said, "mine is never useful."

Henequen gave a wane smile. "It's an overwhelming onslaught. I don't think you'd fancy a trade, would you?"

"No, I suppose not."

"Do you really know things no one else does?" Xiben asked.

Henequen shrugged. "I don't see that I do, but I know people think I have some sixth sense—when it's not confused. I'm wrong as often as I'm right."

"But he is right, sometimes. He knows things no one says," Ferran said.

"Are you sure it's madness?" Xiben asked.

"What else would it be?"

"Magic," Xiben said simply.

They were all quiet for a moment. "I'm sorry—are you saying there is mental magic?" Ferran asked.

Xiben nodded. "There's all kinds," she replied. "Perhaps Henequen can, in crude terms, read minds."

At that moment Veran's door opened and the conversation was temporarily abandoned. He looked about at them, took in Cassava's disheveled state, and promptly turned away from her. "I believe we should be off shortly. Breakfast, and then we leave."

They packed quickly, which gave Cassava little time to make herself a presentable appropriately-foreboding Sin. She thought it was useful that she wore no makeup—the eye goop the Trikingdom was obsessed with would have run something terrible. Her hair was quickly knotted back in a stiff braid, and she had her customary black tunic and trouser. Black, she thought, was appropriate for her mood. Cassava would not have wished to wear color today even had it been an option.

Breakfast was a quiet affair, Xiben had stayed back with Ferran and Faita, so it was just Veran and the two Black Sins. Cassava did not take the opportunity to take any bacon for herself, but she did think to save a few slices put away for Xiben, who would no doubt be grateful. They did not see Dasun and his family at the tables, but Novenza came over just as they were finishing up.

"I hear you leave today."

"That's correct," Veran said.

"I hope you'll consider coming to Belin in the future."

"Perhaps."

"We are making efforts with this cure, to make it accessible and safe. Athelstan needs data. We've been trying to get the Trikingdom to share it with us, but they've refused. I wanted to catch you to ask—"

"What kind of data do you want?"

"Demographic information on the patients—their age, power, when and how they acquired it, dosage of the medication and how they responded. The Trikingdom has been focused on eradicating the magic in anyone who doesn't join their army, but there's a therapeutic dose that has far less drastic effects. It's just not guaranteed to get rid of the magic completely."

"What is its purpose then?" Veran asked, leaning intently forward.

"It lessens the effects. Some people are fine with their magic, but others it seems to be too much for them. Giving a therapeutic dose can help with some of the worst parts of their magical symptoms."

"I'm afraid I don't understand."

"Do you know how the cure was created?"

"No."

Novenza sighed. "Well, it's a long story, but in short the reason for its initial creation was to assist a patient who saw the future. These visions gave him seizures and made him extremely sick. The therapeutic dose has made his life livable again."

"Interesting."

"Here—this is an example of what data would be useful to us." Novenza pulled a piece of paper off the stack she was carrying. "And here's the information on dosages for the cure. It might be helpful. There's my contact information, if you ever want to set something up, and here is where you can send the data."

"Thank you, Novenza. It's been a pleasure working with you."

"You as well. I hope we can continue a beneficial relationship in the future. Filoli is part of this world too, even if you and everyone else tries to deny it. We are a global world. We trade, we cross paths...and communication will only get faster. I shouldn't say anything but the Queen is something of an inventor and has been playing around with steam...there are interesting things on the horizon, and you might want in on them. You should at least have the option."

Veran took the papers and folded them carefully. "It is my desire to venture forth again. You can of course travel to our little nation as well, though I cannot guarantee your reception will be as polite, and we are a rather disorganized hierarchy to meet with, all things considered."

Novenza smiled. "I've been in some rough situations before. I think I'd be alright."

"It was good meeting you, Novenza, but we do have a ship to catch."

"Of course. I'll let you be on your way."

They took food for Xiben and Ferran back up to the room, which they ate quickly. Meanwhile, Ferran released the ties that had been keeping Faita in place for over a day. He groaned and massaged his wrists. "I swear, I wasn't going to do anything," he grumbled.

"Perhaps one day you will prove that to us, but it will not be today," Veran replied. "Now, tell your father he is not to trifle in Filoli's affairs unless he is prepared to bring the doom of the demon onto his and his family's head. Remind him that I employ trained assassins who would have been well within their rights to kill you for your intrusion. He's lucky he has a son still. If he tries again, that may change. Do you understand?"

Faita swallowed nervously and nodded. "I understand."

"Good," Veran said, "then I see no reason for you to linger here. I'm sure you'd appreciate getting out of here."

"Yes, sir." He raced off down the hall so fast Cassava felt as though he was aided by one of Nimmory's winds.

The five of them, business concluded in the tower, made their way out onto the busy city streets. Cassava still felt quite numb and was grateful for her group of people creating a layer between her and the bustling life of Triking City. It was unnaturally loud, Cassava thought, and beneath the shouts and jeers there was a common cry of desperation that clung to the sides of buildings, slipped between the shadow of a cart, and cloistered itself in little awnings. Cassava saw children everywhere, hungry and worn down and beaten, sick and disabled, healthy and unscrupulous. There were many here who would not be saved today, who might never be saved.

The sun was beginning to become a roast as they reached the docks, and Cassava pulled up her hood to protect her face from sunburn. Her scars could be particularly irritated by the rays.

The ship they had chartered for this voyage was not Rhimeon in make, but had the bold colors and design of a Triking vessel, with occasional fine detailing around points of interest. It was larger than the ship they had come on and seemed to be crewed by several men, women, and non-binary individuals who called out in Belish to each other; apparently there was no longer the need for secrecy.

"Priest Veran," a non-binary individual with dark brown hair shaved very short on one side and kept very long on the other greeted their party. "I am Captain Vanqui. I hope I and my crew will prove adequate."

"I'm sure you will," Veran replied politely. "Has my cargo arrived?"

"Yes, sir. It's all below decks and ready."

"Good."

They boarded the ship with no further discussion, and the captain bellowed out orders Cassava assumed were to make ready to leave port.

Veran immediately headed below decks, and Cassava followed. She was curious as to what they would see. Henequen took his leave of them, saying something about inspecting the ship, but Xiben and Ferran stayed, dragging their meager belongings with them.

The below decks was roughly divided and the first floor they passed appeared to be sleeping rooms for the crew, the kitchens, and some food storage. Cassava could hear the sailors faintly from above, singing some shanty. She could also hear something else—moaning, crying, and the clank of moving metal on metal. The noise grew louder as they approached the lower decks.

Beneath the sailor's quarters opened a large deck, filled with cargo to the left and then, on the other side, were sitting in shackles about twenty children of varying ages.

Cassava gasped. Some of the children were sitting up, but others were flat on their backs, staring up at the ceiling, or listlessly swaying with the ship's motion. Still others were dissolved in little pools, tears streaming down their cheeks. A few of the older ones were arranged to try to comfort the smaller ones, but they were limited by the chains that bound them hand and foot.

"Veran! Did you tell them to do this?" Cassava demanded.

"No," he replied darkly. "I'll see the captain about a key immediately."

Cassava approached the group, feeling a swelling in her heart when she saw Saraj among their number, coupled with a twinge of some deep sorrow that Nimmory was not there. "Hello," she called out.

"Who are you?" a teen boy immediately demanded. "What's going on? Where are you taking us?" He stood up, taller than Cassava. He had curly brown hair and a wiry frame. He looked as though he had been starved.

"My name is Cassava. You are being taken to Filoli."

"Filoli?"

"The islands?"

"Why?"

Cassava took the flurry of questions in stride. "You will be given the opportunity to live out your lives with your powers, somewhere safe and contained."

"So, another prison?"

Cassava sighed. She was not the person to explain this, but here she was. "Of a sort. A better one, I hope."

"This is *skado*," the boy said, "why can't we just live our lives?"

Cassava spread her hands. "I don't know. Because... because it's dangerous. And someone has to keep an eye on people like you."

"I don't see why. I can take care of myself just fine."

"Think about it," Cassava said, casting around for some justification that wouldn't sound hollow to their ears. They weren't versed in Sin; they wouldn't understand that approach. "Your powers make you different from normal people. Justifiably or not, it makes people scared. They're scared of what might happen if you got angry with them, or wanted something. And society is going to protect those people because, well, some of you can do some really scary things, and you're young and we don't know if you can be trusted. Just yesterday someone with magic powers tried to kill me, and I'm lucky I had someone with powers to back me up, otherwise I would be dead. Now imagine that happening unchecked."

The boy still looked furious, but he didn't immediately fire back at her. He just shook his head. "I'm not going to hurt anyone," he said.

"So, you don't hurt someone. Do you know how hard it is to live in a society with people who can't accept who you are? I bet you don't. You grew up in the Trikingdom, where everything goes. But even that has limits. You're different. That means people are going to look at you, judge you, without ever knowing you. They're going to assume you're dangerous or privileged, they're going to be rude to you and refuse to serve you, and do all kinds of horrible things, say all kinds of horrible things, because you're different. It's like this mark on my face. But it's more than that," Cassava said. "We're taking you away, yes, but we're also giving you something."

"What could you possibly give us?"

"A home. A community. A place where people will accept you for who you are, no questions asked. You're going to build that community with each other. A huge number of people with the same thing happening to them coming together. It might not look like your old lives, but that doesn't have to be a bad thing."

"You'll be safe, and warm, and have a place to live that's dry and consistent," Xiben said, breaking in suddenly. "I know you, Chail, you were on the streets before they caught you. Sure, you could bed anywhere—as long as anywhere wasn't someone else's property and no dogs or thieves or soldiers or thugs came along to rough you up. This place, the Asylum, it's got four walls, individual rooms, courtyards, a kitchen...it's a home."

The boy, Chail, bit his lip. "You're in this, Xi?"

Xiben nodded. "These are good people. They don't understand everything, but they help. They mean well. And," Xiben added, "it's not really like we have a choice."

"Well, if you're really kind, are you going to do something about Damon? He's really sick."

"We'll do what we can," Cassava said, "and no more cure, not if you don't want it."

Cassava didn't know much about caring for sick people, but she at least knew more than Ferran, so she approached the boy Chail had indicated. He was lying fairly still and crying, but not from fear or confusion but from what seemed to be pain. Cassava brushed his forehead and found him fairly warm. "Go get some cool water," she told Xiben. Ferran was rifling through his pack. "What are you looking for?"

"Petty Oka," Ferran said, "it helps with pain."

Cassava shook her head. "An herb?"

"What else?" Ferran said, "it's not like I was always healthy. I had to grow things for myself."

"You are full of constant surprises, Ferran."

"Thank you?"

Chail knelt down beside Damon. "He was at least walking when they brought him here," he said, "but it's been getting worse. They dosed him right before we came. I think they were afraid he'd set the boat on fire."

Well, that would put a damper on their plans, but this seemed extreme. Xiben returned with a bucket. "I hope sea water is fine," they said, "we've cast off."

Cassava tended as she could for Damon and the others who seemed in poor condition. Veran returned with keys some time later. By that time things had quieted below decks and there were no more tears as Veran explained what would happen next. His tone was gentle but firm, and Cassava wondered if Chail would have pressed him as hard or if Veran simply had a way about him that inspired priestly confidence.

Once everyone was unchained, they set about setting up cots for everyone. They were working with limited supplies, and ultimately there were not enough beds for everyone and they decided to sleep in shifts, which took some more ministerial finagling. After that, Veran took interviews with each of the children, and Cassava had a moment to herself.

She took to the fresh air of the upper decks, but it felt wrong to be besieged by the wind and she found herself making her way to the quarters she and Henequen would share with Veran. Cassava climbed into bed, the dark thoughts that had crowded her early that morning came flooding back, and she sank into the bed with an air of finality.

Chapter Fourteen

Once Cassava enmeshed herself in the comforting pull of the covers, she found she had no reason to revive. They were off now, and Veran had nothing to fear. There would be no Nimmory coming by. And Ferran was safe. Really, what more did she have to care about? What reason did she have to get out of bed? And, so, she stayed.

Henequen did not attempt to make conversation with her after a few times when she snubbed him, and when Ferran had come to see her, she had simply closed her eyes and pretended to be asleep. She had no interest in conversing with Ferran. She had done so before and heard what he had to say. It helped, yes, but it did not magically make everything better.

Cassava had sunken into depression before. It had led her to the Asylum. Cassava had done her best to put that past experience out of her head, refused to engage with it, pretended she was normal and had never suffered with thoughts of unspeakable things. But they didn't seem so unspeakable now. Now, Cassava thought about that time again.

It had been right after she and Visea had experienced

their break. Cassava had shared a few kisses with Visea, after years of friendship. There had been glances and second looks, and an inappropriate amount of interest in each other's bodies. Cassava had believed it was mutual. It had always seemed mutual, when they had been sitting close together watching the stars late at night, or dancing close together, their bodies touching more than once, or kissing on the pier at midnight, knowing Cassava would be off on a ship the next day.

It was painful to think about Visea, because the betrayal Cassava had felt had been so absolute. They had spent five years together, as together as anyone could be when you were living in the Islands where relationships between two women were strictly reserved for the Asylum. Cassava had shared everything with Visea. They had been each other's secret keeper, best friends, and constant companion. They had kept each other safe from predatory men, laughed together when one was asked out, loaned each other money and goods when one was lacking.

Visea had been Cassava's everything. And then something had changed. Cassava still wasn't sure why, and she didn't think she wanted to know—she didn't think anything would change her mind. Cassava had gone to her one day and Visea had been agitated. She had insisted that Cassava couldn't come by anymore. She insisted that they be done, and nothing more could happen between the two of them. They couldn't even be friends. Cassava had protested, cried, begged, but Visea had insisted. She had given Cassava back every token they had ever exchanged, and closed Cassava completely out.

Cassava had fallen apart. She hadn't had anyone else to fall back on then; her parents did not understand and could do so little for her, she had been taken into the darkness and there had been no escape. She had felt constantly like she was dying. For days and days it went on, weeks stretched out and Cassava could barely get out of bed. Her parents wrote her off as a moody teenager, but it was more than a mood. It was more than a breakup.

She hadn't been capable of getting up. She hadn't been capable of moving forward. Every day she was plagued by thoughts that grew increasingly dark. She would think about dying. There seemed to be no other solution to her problems. She couldn't continue to live in the world without Visea, not as alone and distraught as she was. Cassava had gone over every moment she had ever had with Visea, over and over, a lifetime of moments, trying to see where it had gone wrong, what she had done to result in Visea abruptly abandoning her and their long-understood relationship.

Cassava began to have thoughts about dying more frequently. She thought about getting in some accident out on the sea. She fantasized about what might happen when Visea found out—her having a sudden change of mind, a large amount of regret, and a complete destruction of her carefully constructed life as she realized she couldn't make it without Cassava, just like Cassava seemed incapable of making it without her.

It grew from accidents. At first, Cassava would be boning a fish and wonder what it would be like to miss, to slice into her arm. Weirder, stranger, more terrible things had happened to fish boners before. It wasn't out of the question. She thought about walking off a dock and forgetting how to swim, or knocking herself in the head first so her brain was too rattled to remember. Opportunities lurked everywhere, if only you had the creativity to see them.

And then that wasn't enough. She began planning. She took her boning knife home with her, worked out her parents' schedules and when she would be alone. She walked to the docks and considered who might find her body. Eventually, plan had gone to practice.

But it hadn't ended. Cassava had been found, and her wounds stitched up. She had woken up in the Asylum with no way to do anything. As terrible as it had been, it had given her the space to start again. A new life had been just the thing she needed.

But there was no restarting now, and Cassava didn't want to either. She had friends, she had a family...even if it didn't seem as if they needed her now. Nimmory was one thing. It didn't matter. And, honestly, she thought she had passed the worst of the depression. It had been difficult the first few days, the sudden absence, the coldness in her heart, the confusion, and Cassava had struggled to adjust to the knowledge that the life she had been pushing for was not going to come to pass.

She had accepted it now, however. She knew it was right. Nimmory wouldn't have been happy the way things were, and it was her choice to leave. It didn't mean she hated Cassava; it just meant Cassava wasn't her number one. And that was hard, but at the same time it had been too short a time to ask that much. It was not like Visea. They had only known each other a couple weeks, and been firmly together for a few days. Yes, they had played out life-saving schemes in that time, but they were still mostly strangers. And Cassava's number one wasn't Nimmory. It was Ferran. Everything was Ferran; Ferran was the one who had rebuilt her life, reached into that brokenness and showed her she didn't need a romantic relationship to be fulfilled. Having the chance to teach him about the world had taught her what she saw as worthwhile. That being allowed a chance outside, at a breath of fresh breeze, was worth living for. She could live for herself.

Only now it was hard to remember that. Cassava didn't want to die—she didn't. And yet she still had the thoughts. They were intrusive, filling her head without reason or context. She would imagine there was some emergency and she needed to save someone—she had one chance to rescue and that was it. She needed to get between Veran and some villain and she just happened to die in the process. But no accident happened. No villain came up on the high seas and stole anyone away. The trip was unremarkable, and so Cassava stayed in bed, trying to drown out the feelings in her head, the way it made her heart clench without reason, the way all her limbs felt unbearably heavy.

Visea was not the first time Cassava had felt this way, and it seemed it would not be the last. The oppressive nature of her thoughts were nearly paralyzing, and when she did get up to relieve herself or eat some meager amount of food, she felt sick and achy as though she was suffering from the flu.

A week later they were coming close to the end of their

journey. Ferran came into Veran's quarters and did not leave.

"Cassava. I know you're awake."

She groaned and piled a pillow over her face. "I don't want to talk, Ferran."

"Why not?"

"Because everything is terrible."

"I know you miss Nimmory, but I'm still here. There are others who care about you."

"I know," Cassava said tiredly, "I know and I try to tell myself that but it doesn't help. I'm still this broken thing. I thought I fixed myself, but apparently I can fall apart still and I wonder what is the point? What's the point if I'm just going to end up here again, Ferran? I can't just collapse every time something bad happens. I can't stop bad things from happening."

"It's not every time."

"So? It happens enough. I fall apart and I can't put myself back together. I'm trying, Ferran, this is me trying. I could have just given up, but I'm getting up, I'm moving. I just can't do anything more."

"You're sick," Ferran said. "That's okay."

Cassava lowered the pillow slightly. "I'm crazy. I'm demon touched."

"I know. But it doesn't change anything."

"Why should I be alive? My head tells me not to be. Why shouldn't I listen to it?"

"Because you don't want to. It's the demon making you think that. When you feel better, you'll be able to see that."

He was probably right. Cassava liked to forget that she

was sick, and it was easy to just not deal with it most of the time. When she was healthy, she was healthy and she forgot she was disabled. She forgot she had ever been disabled. It wasn't like a missing arm—it wasn't so blatant that you couldn't notice, it wasn't something she woke up to every day, but it was every so often. And now was the so often. She was sick.

She was sick. She repeated it to herself. This was the demon, the demon plaguing her. "I try to remember, but my head gets so muddled."

Ferran sat down on the bed next to her. "That's why I'm here," he said. "I'll help you remember."

After that, things were slightly less terrible. Ferran came and ate meals with her, and sometimes he sketched while Cassava just lay. But it was nice to have the company. Ferran did not pressure her to get up or feel better, but with his energy Cassava was able to borrow just a little and crawl her way up to the deck to feel the wind on her face. It stung a little, this little reminder of Nimmory, but Cassava still enjoyed the crispness and it took away some of the deadness from her eyes to see blue skies and sea.

She saw the children too. They had become quite a handful, but at least they were confined to a ship and had little room to go. Damon was still quite unwell, as were a few of the other children, but others ran and screamed across the decks, playing elaborate games of tag and hide and go seek. The elder children had introduced a simple hand game to the group that had taken off as well, enough so that Cassava had seen sailors take breaks from their work to play a round with the children.

Cassava kept herself distant from them, not because of any dislike, but rather a certain fear that she might be contagious. She let Ferran stay by her only because he had dealt with her before and she trusted him to be old enough to make his own judgments.

Cassava had not much experience with children and she watched them sometimes just from fascination and a means of distracting her from the torment of her mind. They were amazingly well adapted for what had happened to them, and many who had been sick had improved over the course of the journey and now played as though there was nothing wrong with them. Sometimes you could almost forget that they were magical at all, but then something truly inexplicable would happen and the illusion would be gone. Xiben had decreed magic was banned from games after too many nearly-tragic teleporting incidents.

Caring for the children had mostly fallen on Ferran and Xiben, with help from Chail and two other teens. Ferran was painstakingly patient with them, but short when he wasn't obeyed. Cassava thought he would make a good father, and then remembered that could never be, and felt inconsolable. She had cried for three hours and when Ferran had asked what was wrong she could only hug him and tell him she wished life was different.

It made Cassava think about herself too. She had grown up expecting to one day be a mother, and that was something that had been fiercely wrestled from her with the advent of her illness. She did not have great feelings of care for these scads of children, beyond believing them fully deserving of life and happiness, but when she thought of little Saraj, she thought also of her mother, and what it must be like to have your child taken from you and shipped to a small island nation not known for its progressive politics. This had set Cassava back for several days.

Finally, they reached Filoli. Veran had them land at Baroni, which was a smaller but fairly empty Asylum. Veran left early that morning with instructions to Cassava and Henequen not to let anyone else leave the ship.

Cassava was still feeling quite depressed, but had managed to dress herself today in the requisite Black Sin garb. She hoped Veran's meeting would go well, otherwise they would quickly run out of options. She wasn't sure what they'd do if the Priests refused—go back to the Trikingdom? The idea was highly unappealing, but, frankly, all Cassava wanted to do was go to bed. Traveling through the city streets seemed horribly laborious and loud and disquieting. Besides, their party was sure to attract copious amounts of attention.

She sat on the deck, feeling the spray of saltwater on her face. She licked her lips to taste it and remembered her many sea voyages with her father. She had not seen her parents since that fateful night, when she had bid them goodbye for their date. They would have returned to Cassava bleeding out on the floor. And that was the last they had seen, and as far as Cassava knew, the last they had known of the fate of their only child.

"What do you think will happen?" Ferran asked Cassava and Henequen.

Cassava shrugged, feeling almost disinterested.

Henequen shook his head. "I don't know," he said, "I don't have a sense."

"It's an awful lot to take in."

"Literally," Cassava agreed in spite of herself.

They waited until the sun had gone down and a cool wind picked up leaves from a nearby tree and brought them speckling across the surface of the deck. The children had been rambunctious all day, driven by a need to leave the confines of the ship with land being so close. Now, however, they settled into a tense but quiet puddle. Shoving and roughhousing had eased off and been replaced by a quiet tension. It did not seem to be a good sign that Veran was so long in returning. Cassava began to wonder if perhaps she and Henequen shouldn't have accompanied him just in case there was an enemy on the road. Perhaps he was lying in a pool of blood somewhere on the road. As she opened her mouth to suggest a search to Henequen, she saw several figures in the distance approaching.

Cassava heaved herself to her feet, not sure what she would do with a negative answer, unsure what would happen if the Priests refused. Kill the children anyway? Send them away? It was all possible, and none of it was good. This was Saraj's chance at a better life. Not a great one, but better.

Cassava instinctively grabbed for the child in her thoughts. Saraj had spent several days under the weather, but had seemed to bounce back by the end of the journey. Cassava wished she could say the same for herself. She felt as though only doom awaited her.

She could see now that it was Veran accompanied by

three other Priests. This would have been the brunt of the force here on Baroni. Cassava and Henequen stood like sentries; the children behind them in a loose circle, some so tired of waiting that they had passed out. It was getting late.

Veran led the three Priests onto the ship. They were all older than Veran, with white or graying hair, and lines of age. They did not speak, but came and observed the children. Chail stood defiantly, Xiben by contrast hung their head and dropped their shoulders, apparently deciding meek and unobtrusive was the best aspect to communicate.

"These are all magical children?" one of the Priests asked, sounding somewhat surprised. "They seem… normal."

"And they are, most of the time," Veran said. "As I've explained, they don't pose a threat, but brought up well they could certainly, some of them, be a boon for Filoli."

The men observed the children a little longer before talking quietly together. Finally, one of them approached Veran. "We will take them in for now. It seems the most sensible solution. A meeting must be called, however; this is not a decision that can be made without greater council." The man nodded to Henequen and Cassava. "See them to the locked ward."

"Yes, sir," Henequen said dutifully.

It took some time to manage the escort; it was quite a number of little ones, many of whom could not or would not walk under their own power. Cassava found herself with a small non-binary child asleep on her back as they took them through the quiet streets of the city. Although it was late, their strange party of parentless foreigners, this parade of blonde light-skinned children attracted a growing number of locals, who seemed at once to wish to help and keep their distance. Cassava saw at least one young mother begin to walk up before she registered Cassava's brand and quickly turned away. This was Asylum business, and no one wanted to be involved.

Getting the children settled was another matter; the locked ward was not meant to accommodate so many people, but fortunately most of the people were small and so Cassava tucked two children into a bed after they had extracted promises of play for the next day.

It was well past midnight when everything was settled, and Cassava finally had a moment to sink down on the couch and rest. She was utterly exhausted by the day's administration and fully hoped that some of the caretaking adults would take over the brunt of the care for the children now that they were in an Asylum. Soon, no doubt, Cassava would have work to contend with, something she did not even want to think about right now. It had been some time since she had killed anyone, and those she had killed had been a clear and direct threat, death done in the heat of battle. It felt different from her normal cold-blooded killing, and Cassava was not eager to return to the knife. It felt overwhelming right now. She hoped they would give her a break after this mission; it had been weeks of tedious work watching Veran's back with only short breaks, and for Henequen it had been worse. It had been some time since she had truly had a day off.

Ferran joined her on the couch a little later, having

finally freed himself of his own litter. "I'm not sure what to do now," he said.

Cassava, who had forgotten all about Ferran, sat up abruptly. "Shatung. You're back here."

"Well, here adjacent. But they're all the same. It's so small. I can't believe I lived in a space like this my whole life."

"I'll get you back out," Cassava promised, "before one of the other Priests sees you and realizes."

"I'll miss the people," Ferran said sadly. "It was nice to be in a community for once, even if it was extremely chaotic."

Cassava nodded, though right now she wasn't feeling particularly like being around a ton of people. "Was it better? In the Trikingdom?"

"In many ways, yes. I got to be myself, experience the world…go to restaurants and bars, see people dancing and playing cards. I got to be a part of the world instead of stuck on the side of it, looking down from a high tower with no way to reach in and make a connection."

"I'm sorry," Cassava said softly, "I didn't mean to give you a taste of the forbidden when I brought you along. I just wanted to keep you safe."

"I know. It's not your fault. It's just…it's just painful now, because I'll know what I'm missing."

"Maybe Veran will work his magic."

"You mean maybe I'd be allowed to be locked up and not touch anyone again? What a joy to look forward to."

"I don't know what you want from me, Ferran, I can't fix everything. In fact, most things I seem to break."

Ferran glowered at her for several seconds before turning away. "Just let me out of here. I'll find somewhere to shelter the night, and then you or Tane can take me back home tomorrow."

Cassava did so, but while Ferran was out of sight, he was not out of mind. Perhaps it would have been better for him to have stayed in the Trikingdom—but, selfishly, Cassava was glad he had returned. What would she do without her best friend?

Saving these children had not saved Ferran, and though his life was saved, the life of a hermit was not a particularly good life. Especially now that he had experienced more. Perhaps it had been a mistake to take him. But was it really better to keep her best friend ignorant?

"Cassava?" A little girl appeared in the darkness from the hallway, rubbing her eyes.

"What's the matter, Saraj?"

"This is our new home?"

Cassava hesitated for a moment and then nodded. "Hopefully a little nicer than this, but yes. This place is where you will live now."

At that, Saraj burst into tears. Cassava, who had not spent much time consoling children, put her hand out awkwardly. "It's okay," she said lamely, "there's food and shelter and nice people here. You liked everyone on the boat, right?"

"I miss my mom," Saraj said between cries. "I'm never going to see her again, am I?"

Cassava pulled the child in for a deep hug. "I don't know. Probably not," she said, not one to lie to children.

Saraj buried her head in Cassava's shoulder and cried for a long time. Ultimately exhausted, she leaned against Cassava with her eyes closed and breathing returning to relaxed. Eventually, she fell asleep. Cassava carefully shifted her to the couch and stood up, stretching out muscles that had grown weary through the process of providing comfort.

Cassava had to get out of here. The Asylum reminded her of how dark and depressing it was to be segmented off from the world, and Saraj reminded her uncomfortably of the relationships she had once held outside its walls. For all that to be torn away from so many seemed cruel.

Cassava was not sure where she was headed when she started walking, but realized halfway through where her feet had taken her—to her old home, a quaint small set-up in the middle of town, surrounded on either side by other homes set so their walls touched. Cassava's family had gotten by, but they had never been wealthy. Without her help, she imagined they were faring worse than Cassava had been accustomed to.

Cassava had not seen her parents since the morning of her attempt, and had heard not a word from them since, so it was somewhat shocking to her when she saw her mother pulling weeds from the front garden.

Valenu Soset looked more frail than Cassava had ever seen her, her hair was showing streaks of gray and her face bore new lines Cassava did not remember. Instinctively, Cassava found herself moving forward, desperate to get a better view. Her mother worked efficiently as she always had, taking each weed by the stem and digging out the root in methodical purpose. Cassava remembered fondly working in the garden—her mother had never sanctioned playing where one ate—a task her mother had slowly entrusted to her as she grew.

"Barli?"

Startled, Cassava saw her mother staring at her as if she had seen a ghost.

"Is it really you?" She brushed off her hands hastily and stood, looking Cassava over closely, her eyes lingered on Cassava's face where the brands stood out.

"Yes, mama," Cassava replied slowly. Her throat felt thick and tight and the words didn't want to escape from it; they would rather huddle inside where it was safe.

"Barli," her mother breathed. A tear slipped from her eye.

"I'm called Cassava now." Cassava wasn't sure what to do now. She had contemplated going to see her parents on many occasions, sought to demand their attention, their forgiveness, their love. But now the pain and agony of that silence seemed to jolt through her like a lightning bolt, and it made her body sharp and uncomfortable. "Why didn't you write?"

Her mother stepped up to the gate and put her hand out. It trembled slightly. "We didn't know. The Priests told us you were dead." She was crying freely now. "Oh, Barli, I've missed you so much."

Cassava knew she wasn't allowed to touch her mother, but the child in her craved it desperately. "I'm sorry, mama. I got sick."

"It's not your fault, Lili." Her hands braced on the gate. "Lili."

The childhood nickname was too much for Cassava and she turned away. She wasn't sure what to do now. She wasn't supposed to see her parents, but the Priests had lied to them! They hadn't known. The anger and the guilt was quickly evaporating, as well as any incentive to stay away from her mother. Ferran's old fear of touch came back to her, and she wondered for a moment if she wouldn't ruin her mother by touching her. But when had that ever happened? When had it been proven to be the case? Or was it just another lie of the Priesthood made to keep them neglected and abandoned, with only the Priests to rely on?

Cassava ran the last steps to her mother and fell into a tight embrace. There was no hesitation from her mother, despite the scarring, despite the fear, despite all public custom and warning, she was accepted back into her mother's arms. Cassava had held back the tears until now, until the warm press of her mother's hands on her back and the gentle hiss of her breath in Cassava's ear.

Everything for the moment felt right.

Chapter Fifteen

It was difficult to leave her mother. They had been together such a short while, but in those few hours Cassava had decided something that couldn't wait. It meant she had to go, if only to ensure she could come back later. It still broke her heart to leave. Cassava had always gotten along with her mother, and though she hadn't been able to support Cassava the way she needed in the height of her illness, Cassava still treasured her deeply and their estrangement had weighed on her more than Cassava had thought possible.

She would have liked to stick around to see her father, but he was away at sea and would be for a few days still, and Cassava didn't have that kind of time.

"Will you come?" Cassava asked.

"Of course, Lili. Whatever will help you."

"I might be busy, but I'll send someone for you. Don't be afraid. Us Sins are not as dangerous as they make us out to be."

With that, Cassava kissed her mother's cheek and departed. She found herself running, and inside her veins pumped energy from this crazy idea that had birthed itself in her mother's arms, but had truly been in the making since she had first woken up in the Asylum. She knew now that this was her true purpose; whether it brought Nimmory back to her or not was inconsequential. What mattered was the futures of her and everyone like her. Their options, their opportunities, their chances at a better life.

Ferran was right, what he was being offered wasn't a good life. And it wasn't fair for Saraj to be cut off from her family, any more than it was for any of the people Cassava had met in the Asylum. But it had always been that way; the institution was deeply ingrained. There was only one thing left to do.

Cassava got back to the Asylum about midday. The Priests were preoccupied with sending notice of the meeting, which had left minimal oversight of the current residents. Cassava had not spent much time in this Asylum, and she greeted those she saw, looking them over and trying to decide if perhaps they would be helpful in her cause.

There was chaos inside the locked ward. The cacophony was terrible as Cassava entered, and she was immediately accosted by a sobbing child that she picked up and placed elsewhere. Inside she found two older Asylum members attempting to negotiate a settlement of some disagreement between two children that had apparently also created an indoor snowstorm even in the hot weather. The madness only confirmed to Cassava that she was making the right decision. With powers like this, the Asylum would need all available assistance.

Cassava searched the chaos for Henequen, but didn't find him. "Xiben, do you know where Quen is?" Cassava asked.

"I think he went for a run," Xiben said.

"Thanks." She had a good idea where he would be. She and Henequen had similar taste in running spots, and Cassava had grown up running this island.

Xiben glanced down the hallway. "Are you leaving again?"

"I have to," Cassava said. "I promise I'll get some more help."

"Thanks. It's just been…a lot. I think the ship was just this new scary unknown thing hanging in the future and now it's here and…that's a lot of meltdowns."

"Listen, Xiben, I was wondering…I know you didn't want to fight for the Trikingdom, but are you opposed to fighting for yourself?"

They tipped their head. "What exactly did you have in mind?"

Cassava took a deep breath. "I might be crazy, but I think with your help, we might just be able to pull this off."

"Pull what off?"

"I think you'd call it a coup," Cassava said.

Xiben's eyes sparkled. "I'm surprised, Cassava. You never struck me as a revolutionary."

Cassava shrugged. "It's been staring me in the face for a long time. I couldn't count on it before. I didn't have the support. But now I think it just might be possible."

"What's the risk?"

Cassava lifted her chin. "Your life, maybe. Unless you can escape, which you might with your talents. And as a group…our chances are better. Although I have no idea where we'd flee to."

Xiben nodded. "I'll talk to some of the others and see."

"Thank you," Cassava said. "This place…what we're asking people to do…it's intolerable."

"What brought you around to that?" Xiben asked.

"Just seeing it happen, again and again, and realizing what it's done—it's not only broken the people swept up here, but everyone else too."

"It is kind of nice to have a safety net for people no one cares about," Xiben said, "that's the dark side of the Trikingdom, as you saw."

"That's not how we'll be doing things. But I really need to talk to Henequen. You can hear this spiel if you come with me."

"With you? Where?"

"Hevoni. It's where all the Priests will be meeting, and where I plan to call a different sort of meeting."

"Good luck," Xiben said.

Cassava made her way back through the locked ward and out into the Asylum proper. There, she asked after any mothers in the ward, and upon being directed to them, tasked them with oversight of the newest members.

Oli was delighted at the prospect of some new young ones, whatever their challenges might be. She smiled brightly at Cassava. "It's been a while since we've had real children here. I've raised three for the Asylum, I wanted to raise my own but sometimes you don't get what you wish for." Since she'd been relegated to the Asylum when she'd lost function from the boating incident, she had been cut off from the rearing of her womb-born children.

"How old were your children?" Cassava asked.

"Oh, well, the accident happened about twenty years ago now, I had two—a girl who was five and a boy just three. I was pregnant with another, but I lost him."

"I'm sorry. Do your children write?"

"My girl does, my boy doesn't really remember me. But my girl tells me how he's doing. He's married now, with a kid of his own. I wish I could see my grandbaby."

"Maybe you will someday," Cassava said.

Oli smiled wanly. "When the sky turns green," she said.

"I hear that actually happens up north," Cassava replied.

It didn't take Cassava long to fall into her old running pattern. Even before the Asylum, Cassava had been a runner. She ran away. She ran from her feelings, from the thoughts inside her head, and from expectations that were placed upon her. Cassava was good at running, and she did it as a matter of practice. Now, however, she wasn't running from something. She was running toward.

Cassava was well out of breath by the time she found Henequen up on Baroni's highest hill. There, in the shade of the eller tree, stood Henequen. He turned toward her as she approached, opening his eyes. Their dark brown depths seemed harder than normal.

"Why have you chased me up here?" he asked briskly. He was cross, in a manner that was most unlike Henequen, for normally it was impossible to tell whether he was mad or not.

"I need your help."

"I am done helping people."

"Just...done?" Cassava asked. "Quen, what's going on?"

He looked away from her. "My brain is erratic. It always has been. Now there's some question that I'm stealing into people's minds and taking their privacy? How would I feel if someone were to lay me bare like that?"

Cassava was confused for several seconds until she remembered the conversation back in the Trikingdom about whether or not Henequen's sixth sense was actually magic. "You don't mean to pry, and there isn't any proof of that."

"It makes sense, doesn't it? How else would someone like me get along so well? I'm so often distracted and plagued by visions of things that aren't real, it's my only sense of footing in this world. If it was me, surely it would be a lie, like everything else I see."

"Quen, now's really not the time—"

"I shouldn't be here. I shouldn't be anywhere. Cassava, everything I've done, everything I am, is built up by this little piece of knowing. I thought that was some piece of good in me, but it's actually the demon's work. Everything is the demon's. I should have been killed as a child. It would have been better."

"Henequen. You can't think like that—if anything, that's the demon, not the magic. I don't believe magic is evil, and I don't believe our diseases are deadly either. I think we only view them that way because that's how we were taught to perceive them."

"Cassava. I have the demon in my head. It shows me things that aren't real, makes me believe things are true that aren't. I feel the demon watching me, all the time. It's terrifying. And you think that's not real? Then tell me why I feel this way."

Cassava opened her mouth to argue but found she didn't know what to say. Henequen was right. There was wrong in the world, hurting people. He was a victim. So was she. "No. I just think…it's not as dangerous as people think it is. You're more of a liability to yourself than anyone else, same as me, same as most people in the Asylum. The truly irredeemable are the ones that don't get a chance to live out with society, right?"

Henequen drew his eyebrows together. "Yes, we vet people on whether they are a safety concern or not," he allowed.

"And you've been vetted, and so have I, and just because we're dangerous doesn't mean we can't live with other people. We just lived like semi-regular people for weeks in the Trikingdom, and the only bad thing that happened was someone tried to kill Veran—which was not our fault!" Cassava said. "Listen, Quen, I think treating ourselves like we're damaged goods is what's doing the most damage. Take Ferran, for example, he was a wreck when I met him, and now he's a functional human being because the people around him treat him like one. It's a mental game, Quen, one that's been stacked against us."

Henequen shook his head. "The Priests can't be wrong. They're the Priests."

"And you're a Black Sin so you've never been wrong?"

"It's different."

"Why?"

"Because they're not crazy!"

"You don't have to be crazy to make a mistake. Adults aren't infallible just because they hold more knowledge generally. The Priests don't get to be us. They don't know how it feels. And we've been doing things this way for so long that no one can remember what it's supposed to be like. No one knows what it's like when things are different. Except us, because we've seen it. We saw it in the Trikingdom. You see it in Ferran, don't you? You recognized they were wrong about him and you were right. Maybe they've made this mistake before, over and over again."

"What are you suggesting, Cassava?"

"I want you to get all the Black Sins together. I want to talk with them."

"All of them?" Henequen asked.

"Yes. You can do that, can't you?"

Henequen nodded. "The Priests are meeting in two days."

"Good. We'll meet then too, if not a little earlier."

"You're planning something. Something big. Something to shatter the world."

"Yes," Cassava said, "I am." And with that she turned away from him. If they were meeting on Hevoni in two days, she had some stops to make before then. Hopefully, it would be enough time. Hopefully, she would have people on her side, enough to turn the tide.

Chapter Sixteen

It was a two days of talking and wheeling and dealing, the likes of which Cassava had never experienced. Her time in the fish market only went so far—there the deals were small, over quantities of fish and the shape of the catch, here they were life altering decisions about the future of a nation.

Cassava spent her time shuffling between island Asylums, checking in with her duties at Beroni, to going back to her home Asylum and speaking with her mentors there. Faces she had not seen in some time crept back into placement.

She still felt a deep sorrow in her bones when she stopped to think of it, but that was at odd minutes between her travels when she had commandeered another boat to take her to her next destination. Even then, there was a stronger underlying song that beat itself deep into her bones. She knew she was not acting because of Nimmory, and yet at the same time she was, because it wasn't a fair choice for Nimmory to have to make. Whether or not Nimmory returned after the dust had settled, Cassava knew she was making the right decision.

The day of the meeting was stormy. The heaviest rains

of the season had passed, but today was looking to be dark with erratic thrills of lightning. Cassava woke up early after very little sleep; she'd hardly been sleeping at all lately. There was just too much to do and think about, too many possibilities that it was impossible to spin them all out. Yet Cassava seemed to be trying all the same.

Cassava put on her black clothes with a quiet dedication. She had learned a lot in her time as a Black Sin; she had learned to be stealthy, to slip among people like a snake, to strike from the sky like a hawk, and to never let anyone know she was coming. She had learned things beyond the mere skills of fighting and survival however. She had learned to trust herself and her judgment. She had learned how to wield power and also how to bow to it. She had been someone else's instrument and learned how to see the world through her own eyes as well as someone else's. She had learned how to stand on her own two legs after great tragedy and push on, gain higher heights, and settle into the after of heartbreak. She had gained confidence in herself and trust in her fellows. Now she would lean on all those skills.

Cassava did her hair up in a tight wind of braid that circled around her skull until what was left ponied out in the center. She had not worn makeup in some time, but today she fished out an old bottle of mascara and made her eyes pop. Normally, Cassava didn't want anyone looking at her and her ruined face, but today she would command attention.

Cassava looked herself over in the mirror. She had not done this in a very long time, ashamed of the marks on her face. But this time when she looked at the scarred visage she did not see a broken girl; she saw a broken system that had cast her like a cow and worthy of little more thought. Today the marks symbolized what she had been through—what they had all been through—and there was power in that. Because Cassava had learned from Veran that she was not worthless, and her mother had shown her those old ties were not necessarily broken. They may in fact be stronger now than they ever had been.

Beneath those marks, in spite of them, maybe even because of them, Cassava was beautiful. She was not one to be presented to some foreign prince as his lovely companion by any means, but her face was roughly symmetrical, her eyes appealingly almond, and her nose faint but pert.

She made her way to Ferran's home as the morning light was attempting to trickle in, stymied by dark clouds that clung to the air and kept it dim despite the rising hour. She rapped impatiently at the door, her body somewhat warm at the prospect of the day.

"Ferran!"

It was some time before the door opened, and when it did it revealed a recessed version of her friend. He looked unspeakably tired, his hair was disheveled, and his clothes were ill fitting and unmatched.

"Ferran, get dressed. We've got to get going."

"Going where?" Ferran asked, rubbing his eyes. "I thought it was back to my little hovel never to be seen again."

"No," Cassava said. "I'm going to do something very reckless and terrifying and I want you to come with me."

Ferran pulled his arms around himself. "I've been involved in enough of your harebrained plots, Cassava, and while I do appreciate you saving my life, I think I'd like to leave it at that."

"This could be so good though," Cassava said. "I promise I'll get you out. Me and Henequen will make it happen."

"Where are we going?" Ferran asked. He left the door open as he walked inside the house, pulling out new clothes.

"The Asylum."

Ferran set down the shirt he had just picked up. "Are you crazy? The Priests will kill me if they find me back there! Veran said himself he's an outlier."

Cassava put her hand out. "Just trust me?"

Ferran shook his head for a moment before taking her hand in his. "Okay, Cassava, but this better be spectacular."

"It will be," Cassava promised.

The gloomy day had broken now, and large wisps of cloud floated in front of the sun like a continual parade, weakening its gaze. As Cassava led Ferran up to the Asylum, she noticed the streets were unusually clear, and the docks, normally in full bloom at this time of day, creaked with abandonment. Cassava's palms were sweaty. Apparently, Henequen had tipped off the right people.

"Where is everyone?" Ferran asked.

Cassava put her key to the lock and turned it. "Somewhere safe, I hope," she said.

"Barli…"

"Ferran." Cassava grinned. "I promise I'm not setting anything on fire."

"Small comfort," Ferran muttered. But he followed her inside.

The foyer was quiet; there was no one to greet them, just as Cassava had expected. She knew—just down the hall in the auditorium that doubled as a recreation room when the Priests weren't using it for the masses—there would be an influx of Priests from all eight Asylums meeting to debate the fate of the children Veran had brought from the Trikingdom.

Cassava took Ferran to the main gate that led to the courtyard. Ferran looked around anxiously. "Are you sure about this?"

"Yes." Cassava had been surer of few things.

The courtyard was full of people, despite the weather. Cassava saw the familiar faces of her Black Sins, as well as several of the local regular Sins. They turned toward Cassava and Ferran as she entered. Cassava smiled widely at them and waved.

"Cassava, what's going on?" Arablest asked.

"I'm glad you asked. I'm just waiting for a few guests, but I suppose we should gather everyone else up."

"This isn't how it works," Arablest said. "Black Sins don't call meetings; Priests do."

"One of many things I want to change," Cassava replied. "One of many things."

"Well, I'm curious enough about your time in the Trikingdom. It sounds fascinating. I suppose you're worth listening to, if only to see what trouble you're stirring up. You young people are like that."

"It doesn't have to be just young people," Cassava replied. "I mean for a lot of trouble."

"The demon is strong with you."

Behind her, the gate opened again. It was Henequen, bringing with him Xiben, Chail, and two of the other older children. Behind them, with wide eyes and stepping as though each motion might trip a landmine, was Cassava's mother.

Cassava sensed a shift in the clearing. There were murmurs and whispers, people staring at the people who had just come through the gate. Cassava wasn't sure who they were more curious about.

It was time to get this show on the road.

Cassava walked over to one of the large barrels in the center of the courtyard that kept a supply of water. She remembered watching Henequen sit atop one of the barrels, making intricate designs with a long stick. She had been afraid of Henequen then, and Henequen was still someone to be cautious of now, but he was also one of her best friends. They had come a long way.

Now she would test that bond, and her bond with everyone else here. Cassava hefted herself onto the barrel and stood up. "Attention, all! Black Sins and residents alike!"

They turned toward her, some faster than others; some kept their gaze on the other new entrants. Cassava put her hands on her hips, trying to feel the power she needed to get this done. It would take everything she had, and plenty from others, but she didn't think she was insane. It would work, wouldn't it?

"What's with the meeting?" Danil called out. He was one of the older Black Sins, and generally took a commanding presence among their number.

"I have something to say. I think it's worthwhile. I think what you have to say is worthwhile too, but I'm going to go first and then we can hash it out."

Cassava bit her lip for a second, floundering on where to start. She had thought about all the pieces she wanted to put together but not exactly how to do it.

She caught sight of her mother's eye, and then she began speaking. "When I was a kid, I thought Sins were evil. I thought the way some people were born, the things that happened to them, left a mark on their soul that couldn't be shaken. I know a lot of you thought that. I know a lot of you were taught that, just like I was. But that's not the case. It's a lie that's been taught to us by people who were afraid of difference, by people who wanted power, by people who didn't care who got hurt as long as their life was idyllic. Yes, I'm talking about the Priests. But I'm also talking about the people that spout their rhetoric, who would never want to touch one of us for fear our misfortune might rub off on them. Black Sins, I know you've met their kind."

Cassava took a deep breath. "I didn't know I was sick for a long time. I grew up thinking I was just like every other kid on the block. But then things began to happen to me. I began to have racing thoughts, and bursts of insane amount of energy. I also started noticing people. Girls. I thought everyone else must feel this way, for a while. But then things started to get worse. I would stay up for days, I would get furious at people and blow up, or I would spend weeks so depressed I could barely get out of bed. I became infatuated with a girl, and I had such strong feelings for her I began to realize this all couldn't be normal."

"But instead of trying to seek help, instead of letting the people I cared about in, I shut down and closed off. I did my best to hide from them, because if I didn't hide, I was afraid of what would happen. But hiding didn't help. It didn't make those feelings go away. Instead, I was constantly plagued by them within my own head, constantly racing against some clock I couldn't see to try to beat the unbeatable. I believed the only way I could keep living was by living a lie. I was terrified that one day people would wake up and see the truth about me, and then…well, I wasn't sure what would happen then, only that it seemed like the end of the world. Of course, it did. I didn't know any of you, I didn't know people could carry on their lives in the ward, I didn't know I could find some of the best people, some of the most meaningful relationships, in a place like this. I was taught it was pure evil, a place where the demon was barely contained, where people were dangerous and frightening. And I was scared. I was scared I was dangerous and frightening. But the fear of that all beat it out, so I kept living my life."

Cassava took a deep breath. "But that couldn't go on forever. The hiding things was poisoning everything—my relationship with my parents, with my friend, with my crush. I needed more, and they needed things from me, things I wasn't giving them because I was hiding. It wasn't the illness that was holding me back. It was the secrecy, the fear, the stigma, that built it into something terrible and horrifying. And I couldn't stand it.

"So one day, I lost it. It had been a long time coming, but everything built up on top of each other until the weight was just too great for my sick self to handle. I don't think I did wrong, I don't think I could have been expected to do anything else in those circumstances. I shouldn't have been in those circumstances." Cassava swallowed.

"So I tried to kill myself. I was so unbearably unhappy, and my illness was just insurmountable with the pressure I felt to stay normal and keep up appearances. And, as I'm sure you've deduced, it didn't work. I woke up tied to an Asylum bed and felt like the world had ended and I had moved into some dystopian afterlife.

"It took me a while to adjust, anyone who saw me then could tell you. I was lying to myself again, just to make it bearable. But I found friends, and good company, and mentors. The people I met weren't frightening. They were kind and resourceful. Sometimes rude and prickly; you get all kinds. But no one was evil. And coming from the world I had grown up in, that seemed flatly wrong. I was always waiting for the other shoe to drop, for the scary side to come out and get me. But the only time I witnessed cruelty was when it was forced by the Priests. The Priests put together a contest that pitted people against each other; the Priests dictated that the only way to get a taste of freedom was to become a murderer. So I did. And I do have regrets. I'm glad I have the skills I do, and I know they've been used for good. But I don't know that that's always been the case.

"I believe you know what I'm talking about. We aren't

here because we're stupid. We have important thoughts and feelings—senses. And even the Priests rely on them, at least where Henequen is concerned, and they wouldn't do that unless they believed we were capable of independent thought. Looking back at your kill list, of all the people you've murdered for the Priests, can you really tell me there hasn't been one that gave you pause? That made you question your mission? That made you think about going rogue?

"Well, I had those thoughts, and so did Quen. And we did something about it." Cassava leaned down and tugged a startled Ferran over to her. His eyes were white. "This is Ferran. The Priests decided to have him killed six months ago. Six months ago I helped Ferran fake his own death. He's been living on his own since then, and the world hasn't exploded, evil hasn't gone unchecked, and everybody is safe in their beds. I've touched him, numerous times, for considerable length, and had no ill effects." Cassava reached out and touched Ferran there in front of all of them.

"The Priests are lying to us. They've concocted a scheme that works for them and supports and keeps them in power. But we aren't evil. We're not destroying the world. We don't have to believe what they're telling us. We have independent minds.

"Has anyone's illness ever spread beyond a cold and a fever? Have you ever lost an arm because someone else did? We don't need to be kept from people. We don't need this wall." Cassava waved her hand over the massive stonework keeping them contained.

"I know it seems crazy, but I've seen it. And my friends

from the Trikingdom have lived it." She pointed to Xiben and Chail. "There are other places in this world that don't live like we do. Their injured, their deviants, their infirm live side by side with them. Now, sometimes that's cruel, and I'm not suggesting we do things like the Trikingdom. But it's possible for us to live without these barriers. I didn't see my mother for a year. The Priests told her I was dead, and she mourned, and tried to recover. But I saw her. I met her. I touched her. And she's here now, to support me, because she still loves me and she's not afraid. I believe you have families too—I know many of you do—that you miss dearly. I missed mine too, only I could hardly think it because I couldn't accept the fact that they might be gone forever. But we don't have to live that way. There are people you love who think you are worth looking after, who believe they can be around you and still be whole."

Cassava was silent for a moment, and looked out over the crowd, trying to gauge how they were feeling. "I brought my friends here as evidence of all the things I've said—my mother, these Triking children, my best friend Ferran. Question them as you like. But I'm here asking for your help.

"Right now, Priests from all over Filoli are gathered. They are going to decide whether a bunch of kids who haven't done anything to anyone, except maybe by accident, should be locked up, or not even given harbor and shipped back to the Trikingdom where they will be locked up and possibly killed because of something beyond their control.

"I know it's a novel idea, but it isn't everywhere. I don't believe people are born wrong. I don't think we are doomed from the moment we are born, and I don't think the things that happen to us make us evil either. I think we have a choice about whether the wrong in our lives spreads, and that's a choice every person makes, not just a Sin. We've all known people in the outer world who did bad things— someone who lied, or cheated, or made someone else feel small. It's not unique to Sins. We're not unique. And I believe that means we should live like everyone else, free in this world. Cared for, in the ways we can't take care of ourselves, but free to come and go and make choices. I believe these gates should be open."

Cassava jumped off the barrel, landing lightly on her feet. Cassava watched the silent faces that stared back at her, moving away as she moved toward them, as though she was afflicted by some disease that would catch. Cassava watched them all part, and began to feel the silence in her bones, unsure what would happen next, terrified that this would all come crashing down on her head.

Cassava reached the iron bars and slid her fingers around them. The cold metal stung her fingers. She felt it in every digit, they burned with the cold ice of separation. "There's a world out there," Cassava said, "and I think we all deserve to be a part of it."

She took the keys from her pocket and slid them into the gate. Cassava turned the key slowly, feeling the tumblers roll. It clicked, louder than she would have felt possible. Cassava pushed the gate. It was heavy, and normally she never had to move it very far, but now it whined under her protestations. Cassava ignored the weight and pushed harder. At once, the burden became lighter, and the gate began to move more quickly.

Cassava looked to the side and saw her mother on one side of her, pushing with her. Cassava grinned. She sensed a presence on her other side and saw Anelace there, also pushing.

Cassava stepped back. The gates were wide now, an invitation instead of a demand. She felt as though she could feel wind and light, precious rays of sun, coming in from far off places, a hint of what might come.

Kazini stepped toward her, an unreadable expression on her face. She came nearer and nearer, her face serious and drawn. For a moment, Cassava was terrified she was about to kill her. It would be what the Priests would want; the proper response to one pleading for revolution.

But Kazini instead grasped Cassava's hand and thrust it into the air with her own. "Freedom!" she called. Around them, the cry was picked up by others. Cassava saw members of the Asylum, in small packs, begin to shuffle toward the open doors. There was much they would not be able to do still, but venturing out past the gates was a symbolic first step.

Cassava watched as a pair reached the threshold; they were old and Cassava knew they had been inside the walls for at least fifteen years, if not significantly more. Now they glanced around, looking to the Black Sins as though one of them might lance a knife through their heart if they went any further.

But none came, and the man and woman took hands and gently stepped into the horizon. As they did, a few droplets began to fall from the sky. Cassava imagined them washing away the horrors of the past.

Cassava watched as several more groupings took sight of the gates and spilled out, and before long half the Asylum was in the streets, making its way out into the world.

Ferran stared open mouthed at Cassava. "Are you insane?" he asked finally.

Cassava lifted her chin. "I am, indeed, as you well know."

"Clearly. The Priests and the people—they won't stand for this. They've led us apart for ages; they're not going to change track because of some speech."

"No, they're not," Kazini agreed, "which is why we'll have to do something about it." Kazini looked out at the other Black Sins.

Cassava had not expected, of all people, for Kazini to be the one who took to her side. She looked at the others. Anelace was nodding, Arablest stood with her arms crossed and a stern look on her face. Cassava couldn't tell what she was thinking. She looked at Henequen.

Henequen was shaking slightly, his gaze fixed on a spot in the distance, vibrating like a humming bird.

Cassava approached him gently. "What do you think, Quen? I know I've said all this—done all this…but it won't matter unless enforcement turns my way. I need you. All of you." She looked around at each of them, meeting their eyes one at a time.

Henequen didn't say anything.

Celeruit and Jin glanced at each other, and Jin took Celeruit's hand. "It would be a dream to be a couple like anyone else, able to go on strolls, restaurants...to have a home for the two of us? Don't you think, Cel?"

Celeruit kissed his hand. "What if something goes wrong?" he asked. "I can't be taken away from you."

Kazini put her hand on her hips. "If we all go in, there's nothing to go wrong. What are the Priests supposed to do without us? What can they do? We run everything," Kazini said. "We are what people fear. We're the ones who take people in. We murder those who can't be trusted. We are everything."

Henequen shook his head. "No. You're wrong. The Priests do a lot. If we get rid of them, how will we take care of ourselves?"

"I can take care of myself just fine," Kazini said.

"Maybe you can. But others can't," Dani said. He was the oldest of the Black Sins, and had his arms crossed and a frown on his face. "Yes, we upkeep the Asylum, but we don't pay for anything. The Priests collect taxes, teach people to read, and run a bunch of administrative duties. They take care of us in the Asylum, and not everyone has supportive family on the outside who would help us if we made this change. We can't take the Asylums away. People still need them, and they run with Priests."

Cassava thought about it—thought about the homeless magical children who wouldn't have a home without the Asylums. She thought about Veran, how well-intentioned he was, how he treated them well, how he knew things about Filoli's history that nobody else did. "We don't have to destroy them," Cassava said. "We need to reinvent them. Keep them around to do the paperwork, teach classes, run the money…all those things we don't know how to do. But with us on top instead of them."

Kazini scowled. "If we must. But us…we are enough. I believe we can figure out this stuff, put them in cages until they comply, just like they've always done to us. They deserve it."

Cassava wasn't sure she shared Kazini's vindictive streak, but the idea of keeping the crew together was attractive. Although having to rely on Kazini was uncomfortable. She wasn't sure she wanted to give Kazini that power. Kazini was scary on her good days.

Celeruit frowned. "Maybe. What, a council?"

"Yes, the Black Council," Arablest suggested.

Dani shook his head slowly. "It's not that easy. Do you think the Priests aren't busy? Do you think they don't have plenty to do? Are you sure you want to sign up for that? Looking after a nation?"

"We already do. We keep people in line, and we get none of the glory for it. There are insane people in the world—leaders in other places have huge palaces built, and spend heaps of money on making things look nice. We don't have to do that performative stuff; we're used to life like this. Yes, we'll be busy, but we're busy now. And the Priests will still run most things, we'll just have to look after the big scale things, not the little details."

Henequen looked at all of them. His hand went to his belt, running along the length of his rope. "It sounds as if we're decided."

"What about us?" Chail asked.

Everyone turned and looked at him.

"They're deciding our fate right now. I believe we deserve some place to be safe, just like the rest of you. But if you're going to cast us out, I don't know if we can let it stand."

Jin looked Chail up and down. "You have magic?"

"Yes."

"You mean anyone any harm?" Jin asked.

"No."

Jin shrugged. "I don't have a problem with it, as long as you don't cause problems. Just like anyone else."

Kazini nodded. "Besides, I feel like it would be a good thing to have people with particular skills around, especially since no one else on the island seems to have these powers. It puts us nationally at a disadvantage."

Cassava hadn't thought about that, but she also knew the problem perhaps wasn't as far from them as it seemed, if Xiben's hunch about Henequen was true. Perhaps there was some magic hidden in others on the islands too. "I think we should support them. They're outcasts like us."

"Well, let's take a vote as the first act of the Black Council," Anelace said. "All in favor?" Everyone raised their hand. "Great," Anelace said. "Motion carried. Now, let's stop that meeting."

Chapter Seventeen

Cassava glanced over at Arablest. The extremely short and stocky woman smiled grimly at her. "So, how long were you planning that speech?"

"Oh, that?" Cassava said with a little smile. "I don't know, it was taking a while. I mean, it's been a long time coming. But it was seeing my mom that pushed it over the edge."

"She seems like quite the woman," Arablest said. "I doubt things will change much for me, but I suppose if it's better for others, it's worth it, right?"

Cassava looked at her sadly. "I hope that's not true. I want us to not be seen as outcasts—any of us. I know it's easy for me to pass as able-bodied, but in the Trikingdom I saw all kinds of people treated just as people, and their eccentricities were accepted. Now, that wasn't true of everything, but if it's true of one thing, can't it be true for something else too? I know it's hard to imagine it now, and maybe it will come through fear first, but I hope someday people will look up to you as a leader, no matter how big you actually are."

"Thanks, Cassava. You know, you kids are really

something. I wasn't taking on the government at your age. I was stuck in a rut of hating myself for everything I was."

"That's what I want to change, you know? All these kids growing up thinking they're broken? It's heartbreaking. And I didn't grow up that way, and I saw Ferran grow up like that, and I don't want to see anyone else grow up like that."

Arablest smiled softly. "You're a hero, Cassava."

"It doesn't feel that way. I feel like I'm just pushed by circumstances and this thrill in my bones to do, do, do. And I just happen to have big things to do," Cassava said. "It's actually exhausting. I just need to sit down and sleep after this, but things keep piling up, and I can't sleep anyway. I have this drive that I can't set down and I feel like I'm pulled in a hundred directions at once. I'm glad I'm not alone anymore. I need you, and all the others too."

The rain had started to come down harder, but Cassava and Arablest were in the hallway, waiting for the signal. Dani, as the eldest and most accomplished Black Sin, had taken the lead on this particular plan. Cassava was more than happy to delegate.

Cassava checked her knives again, making sure they were free of any of her normal poisons. This was a somewhat atypical mission for the Black Sins; their goal wasn't to murder anyone unless strictly necessary. "How long have you been a Black Sin, Arablest?"

"Sixteen years," Arablest said. "It'll be quite a time shifting gears to governance. I don't even know that I have the head for such things."

Cassava thought about all the boring meetings she had

sat in on and not been listening to a bit. She hoped actual governance was better than that mess. She wondered if Henequen had understood it at all, and whether he would have a head for politics. "Are we really doing the right thing?" she asked.

"It will be hard," Arablest replied, "and we'll make many mistakes, but in the end I think it will be worth it."

And for the moment, Cassava decided to believe her.

At that moment, Cassava heard a loud bang. Arablest nodded and they threw the door open.

The Priest's meeting room was a large gymnasium-type room, with long tables pulled up into a huge lopsided rectangle verging on circle. It had several doors; two that led to the courtyard and two on either short side. Cassava and Arablest burst through the far end at the same time the others unlocked and pushed into the room from the other entrances. As far as secure meeting locations went, this was far from ideal.

The mass of Priests were in mixed positions; most were still seated where they had been debating their current theory. There were nearly thirty of them, a representative from each Island at least, and then those who regularly attended and taught the growing populace on the larger Islands and the younger Priests. It was clear that no one had ever attempted to interrupt their meetings before; no one had dared. There were cries of shock and one of the main Priests had his hands raised as though trying to count down rowdy five-year-olds who didn't want to pay attention. Dani, big, broad, and powerful did not stop in his confident stride.

The Black Sins swarmed into the room. The Priest's cacophony was growing, as was their confusion at the swarm of what should have been their servants, their tools. Dani kicked over the main table with one hefty stomp. "Enough!" he roared.

The Black Sins followed suit, doing their best to move in cohesion, despite never having actually worked together on anything before. It was not the most graceful takeover ever, but it was still intimidating. The varied Black Sins brandished their signature weapons: Kazini with a long thin blade, Jin with his mace, Celurit his, well, celurit, Dani with a mace, Henequen his garrote, Arablest with her crossbow, and Anelace with their twin daggers. Cassava had her special knives, but she had replaced her normal poisons with a paralytic. In fact, most of the weapons out were drenched in the same paralytic, courtesy of Ferran's garden. No one was used to not killing; they had been trained for one purpose. If there were accidents, the Priests had only themselves to blame.

Cassava wrapped her arm around the nearest Priest, a middle-aged woman called Goba. She pressed her knife gently to the fabric of her shirt, just neatly nicking her flesh. She watched as the Sins assaulted their own targets, pulling about a third of the members of the room into compromised positions.

Priest Feyru rose to his feet, his hands out. "What is the meaning of this?" His voice boomed over the mid-sized room. "Dani? Anelace?" He looked around at them. "Have you lost your minds?"

"No," Arablest said, "we're finding them. We've been

under your thumb for years—some of us our whole lives—but it's not going to be like that anymore."

"We talked, and we decided things are going to change around here," Dani said. He moved into the center of the room, jumping over the downed table with ease.

"I don't think you have a say in that, Sin."

"That's the first thing," Jin said. "We won't be called Sins anymore. No one is a Sin. No one is born wrong. We're people. Just like anyone else. We deserve the same rights and privileges as anyone else."

"This is preposterous. Where are all these silly ideas coming from? Dani, you've worked with me for twenty years, and now something truly evil has come over you."

"The only true evil I see here are all of you," Kazini said. "We know there are places unlike here. Places we could be free."

"Ah. So it was our sea-faring voyager's return. Did they tell you how destitute the populace is? Did they mention the disease and death that awaits such supposed freedom?" Feyru replied. "Henequen, I know you can sense we only mean the best for you."

"Some of you, perhaps," Henequen replied. "But there are other solutions to the problems you describe."

"I suppose you think you can do better?"

"Yes," Kazini said sharply. "We do."

"You? Be in charge?" Feyru scoffed. "I would find it funny if it wasn't for the doom that would most certainly follow for our little nation. Do you even know how to read, Kazini? Do figures? Arablest, the public would only laugh at you. And, Anelace, you think anyone would have the patience to deal with your lip-reading? Will you do as well when a crowd of angry citizens is shouting all manner of things at you? And how will you respond? Henequen, you can hardly keep yourself in a presentable manner, I shudder to think what the nation would look like with you at its head. Cassava, the pressures of the job would surely have to take your own life before a single life was improved." Feyru spoke imperiously. "No, and beyond that, there is not a single one among you that the people would follow. It is not enough to take power, you must have the power of the people behind you. And none of them would follow any of you, Black Sins, known murderers, who are poisoned and only inspire fear. Is that the nation you wish to run?"

There was silence in the hall following his speech. Cassava wet her lips. They were broken people. They had become Black Sins for a reason. How could they think they could lead? All they had ever done was take orders. No one would listen to them, and if they did it would be out of fear. Feyru was right.

But he wasn't right. Cassava knew. She was stronger than he thought. So she had doubted herself before, so she had struggled in the past? She had grown since then, she had learned. They would all learn. They would adapt. Cassava was accommodated by her friends, burdens taken off her when it became too much, and now she had the support of so many others.

"That's not true," Cassava said. "Together, as a team, we're more than competent. So I can't handle everything; Jin will help. Anelace doesn't have to be in front of people, and if they do, we'll have a translator. These are challenges, yes, but we were born from challenge. We'll be plenty welcome to take on some more. We're equipped. We've worked hard to get to where we are, harder than any of you, who had your lives handed to you in a basket. We'll work hard again. We'll work together and get through it."

Henequen gave Cassava a little nod. "It won't be fear," he said. "Maybe at first, that's how it will start, but you Priests raise fear—fear of us—once you're no longer holding the reins, people will see us differently. They'll see us put their families back together, keep them from being ripped apart, and they'll be grateful."

"You are fools, all of you. You won't get a thing done without us."

"We know," Arablest said, "that's why you're not going anywhere."

"What—"

The Black Sins moved in unison, marking their targets and stepping to the side. "What you feel is a prick of something you can't quite name; it's called Orinder Root, and it provides a powerful paralytic. I'm afraid you'll be quite unable to move until we've got you right where we want you," Cassava said brightly. "And when you wake up, you'll be lucky not to have a brand on your face. You'll be contained, carefully under supervision till we can be sure of your motives, and then we'll put you to work, doing numbers and figures, levying taxes...all these things that you might find us lacking in. I'm sure some of you will accept the work, the way we accepted your work. You will find yours far less odorous, not a moral quandary as ours is."

The Black Sins stood each in their own space, letting their victims drop sideways as the paralytic took root.

"If any of you feel ready right now to aid us, you can avoid this fate," Dani said. He stared Feyru down. "Otherwise, you'll soon find yourselves treated the way you've always treated us. I hope you like it."

"Henequen, this is your last chance," Feyru said. "I know you're the best of all of these fools. You have something to you, some substance that no one else does, a gift from the light, a gift of an angel inside a demon, a saving grace."

Henequen stood up and walked several steps toward Feyru. "Is that what you think? This sense of mine is an angel's influence?" he asked, coming closer.

"Yes, my boy, you are the chosen Sin. The Sin to bring light out of its deepest darkness."

Henequen closed his eyes, standing at the center of the room. At that moment a loud clap of thunder shook the room. Henequen's eyes flashed open and there was a burst of pure white light.

As the burst faded, and Cassava, temporarily blinded, sought to place herself again, she saw most of the others were similarly staggered. However, now in the center of the ring stood four children: Xiben, Chail, and two others, roughly where Henequen had been. She looked a moment longer and saw Henequen was now standing on the overturned table's lip, his garrote wrapped around Feyru's neck.

"It's magic," he said, "the light is magic." He tightened the rope around Feyru's neck and the man's eyes bulged slightly. "All this time you've been profiting off another darkness. But maybe it isn't darkness. Maybe it is light. In that case, it's high time they ruled together, don't you think?"

"Henequen. Don't do this. I saved you as a child. You were a murderer before you were seven years old. You should have died a long time ago. You owe me. You owe us all. Don't turn your back on the only ones who would ever give you a home."

"I'm not alone anymore," Henequen said, "and I know what it's like to have people who truly care about you. I don't owe you anything. I can see your mind. I can feel your fear, and most of all the fear that you've lost. You're not worried about the country, or our lives, or the consequences, you're worried about yourself. Now I see it—all the people who have met their end because of your order. I'm the hired killer, but you, you were the trigger. And now you've triggered something else." He tightened the string slowly, and Cassava and everyone else in the room seemed to still and hold their breath as the life was slowly strained out of Feyru. When he was done, he placed the rope inside the folds of his robes and looked at the others. "All of you are guilty, but we will be merciful. If you help us, you can live out your life with dignity, see your families again, and make a better world. If not..." Henequen shrugged. "You may meet the same fate."

Cassava found Veran in the room. He was looking between them all, aghast, his hand on the shoulder of a paralyzed fellow Priest. The sea of blue was staggered with the black cloaks of the Sins, and in the center the Trikingdom's bright colors shown like a bright mast.

Cassava sheathed her knife and slipped over the table into the circle. She held her hands open as she approached Veran—not a threat, as Henequen had been, but open and trusting. "Veran, I know you don't believe in everything that's happened. I know there are many of you here who've had doubts. Well, we're asking you now to stretch yourself. Try to think about things differently, live in our shoes, live in the shoes of family you once knew, family you still know. Remember all that's been done to us, what we've done, and ask if it was justified. I'm asking you to put your beliefs aside for a moment and just think about us as people. Think about whether we have put in the effort, whether we've been good—whether we truly deserve the life we lead? Forget about the Sin nature of things, and just ask yourselves, if we're humans just like you, that fate turned a little cruel, that chance made suffer, do we really deserve to be locked away from the rest of society, doomed to be our own sad little society?

"Veran, I know you've seen us, truly seen us as people. People with unfortunate pasts, unfortunate futures, people who have taken whatever steps they can to gain some amount of freedom. And we've done well with it. Now take the leap of faith. Perhaps this hasn't been the plan at all, perhaps the Demon has been laughing at us this whole time—perhaps we're supposed to work to heal the wrongs, make them nothing, instead of making them as huge as it possibly could be. Perhaps we're meant to try to set things right."

Veran glanced around at his fellow Priests before he looked Cassava square in the eye. There was a set to his chin, a determination Cassava had seen a few times before. "It is quite the leap of faith," Veran said at long length. He swallowed. "I should like to see it."

Cassava held back an excited grin. It would have been quite improper to do as she wished and take Veran into a deep hug. Instead, she gave him a quiet nod. Inside, her heart was racing. For the first time she thought this really would go through. Veran truly was a friend; even as often as they were at opposites. Their purposes now would be aligned, and she would actually be allowed to treat him as a friend instead of imperial foe.

There was a general gasp of surprise and feeling of unease that permeated the room. Henequen brandished his rope. "Thank you, Veran. Your assistance will be much appreciated."

Cassava looked around the rest of the room. The Priests who remained in full functionality were staring at Veran with a mixture of expressions. Many seemed shocked and angered by Veran's betrayal, but others regarded him with a closer look of concern. Cassava held her breath, waiting for the next to speak.

Finally, a young Priest named Jambi stood up. "I agree with Veran," she said. "They're right. We treat them terribly. Even if the Demon is fully realized, perhaps that's the price to pay. We can't hurt them to make the demon pay. In a way, that causes the demon to win."

"You all are fools. Give in to all the ideals we taught

you as children! Of course, you youngster wouldn't understand," Feyru demanded.

"They are not alone," a rough voice said. They all turned to look at a Priest who spoke from the corner of the room. He was older, with white hair and a long beard. Cassava did not think she had ever seen him before, but the other Priests bowed their heads and averted their eyes as he spoke, suggesting his importance.

"Orantu—you can't be serious."

"I am. These children have taken a bold step, and with us by their side to guide us, I believe they can succeed. I have long looked deep into the annals, and I believe we have misconstrued our mission in this world. We have clearly failed these fine Sins, and if they believe they can do a better job, I believe we should let them try."

"Blasphemy!"

"Perhaps. But I do not seem to be stricken by sudden illness, so perhaps not," Orantu replied. He nodded to the Black Sins. "I will help you. The rest of you make your choice."

They did so, and though there were mostly younger Priests who offered quietly to add their strength to the Black Sin's number, a couple older Priests did as well. The rest refused whole-heartedly, though Cassava had a hunch their minds would change after enough time locked up in a room by themselves. But they had enough to get on with, and that is what mattered.

Cassava felt heartened by the support, as grudging as it might have come from some. They were left with about nine Priests out of nearly thirty. There were still some Priests that would need to be accounted for, those who were not present at the large meeting, particularly the staff of young Priests ranging from ten to twenty years.

The Black Sins made quick work of the dissenters, paralyzing the rest of them without much ceremony. Cassava felt a hint of regret to treat them so, but it was all that could be done and it would be best.

Together they heaved the many bodies into the Asylum's locked ward until it was full, and then they took the rest into a cart to take them down to the docks where they would be transported to some of the other Asylums.

That work was quite exhausting. Cassava was not used to carrying so much weight, even with many hands to make the work quicker. The rain continued through the day, though the worst of the storm had abated.

In the dark of the day, they cast their boats off and made for their diverse Asylums, keys jangling in their pockets as they looked to unlock still more gates, until all the Asylums were free.

It was very late that night when Cassava finally laid down in her bed. They would deal with the public the next day, the Black Sins had decided to send the Priests out with the information of the coup, followed by the Black Sins making an appearance on each of their respective islands.

Cassava had a hard time falling asleep. In her head, she kept playing the image of the gate opening wide over and over again, and the flash of light would come, like a lightning bolt to blot out everything, and then when her vision came back, she would see Nimmory and Visea standing together, staring at her. She couldn't tell what they were thinking, and as none of it was real anyway, it didn't really matter. Finally, some piece of her gave up the ghost and she managed to fall asleep.

Chapter Eighteen

The next several weeks were a trial the likes of which Cassava had never encountered before. The people had met the Black Sin's declaration with a show of fear and unease, but given the situation, there was little they could do but accept it. The people were not fighters, and they had always cowed to the needs of the Black Sins, so accepting them as their leaders now was, while mentally an anguish they felt quite frightened of, also rather natural.

Cassava hoped in time things would change. Already there were small differences for others. The Sins themselves went to market, buying their own food for the dinners they were to make for one another. And the open gates had encouraged some to come in to the Asylum and witness the Sins in their home environment. Children saw parents that had been taken from them long ago, and there were even a few timid touches between them by the time the meeting had come to a close.

The Black Sins still locked the gates at night; not because they were afraid the former Sins would escape, but because they were afraid that some person on the outside would, in their fear, take up arms against one of the Asylum members while they slept. This fear was not wholly unfounded; Arablest had intervened one afternoon when a crazed man had come into the Asylum brandishing a butcher's knife and declaring they all deserved death. He had met his fate, and the Black Sins made certain the details were clear and spilled out to the populace in order to dissuade any similar repetitions.

The shopkeepers soon began not to fear the former Sins as they feared the Black Sins. Some members of the Asylum were not treated to the same courtesy. This was especially true of those who were slower to respond and could not communicate as well; a woman unable to communicate like typical people was not seen as the same level of fright as a Black Sin, and they began to deny entry. When the Black Sins heard news of this, they made a visit to the offending establishment themselves and set things right. It was a tiresome duty, managing the integration, but Cassava did find the work to be rewarding.

The Triking citizens did their best to settle in, finding homes within the Asylum walls. They were slowly adopted by the mothers or would-be mothers of the Asylum, who longed for children of their own to care for, and under their administrations began to set some order and expectations for them. The structure proved useful, as without it the children had begun to cause some amount of chaos. Some had a more difficult time settling into life in a foreign land than others. Some had quite the trauma from their experience, and the Black Sins were not infrequently dispatched to contain a child whose outburst had become too much for whoever was watching the children that day.

But despite the trials and tribulations, life settled into a pattern and was not too roughly disturbed. The next matter of business Cassava had was integrating the Asylum members into everyday society, instead of as a rare sight on occasional trips, or taking time at the docks. With the world open to them, Cassava found that the former Sins complained assiduously about feeling they were taking advantage of others, and that they wanted to have some place in society. Ferran spearheaded these efforts; his time was spent learning more about cooking and talking to just about every chef in the whole of the Islands about perhaps working for them; but so far they had all rejected him, saying that no one would eat at their restaurants if they knew a Sin was working there—and those were the kind ones.

Cassava wasn't sure what to do about that problem; she supposed if enough people got involved it would become impossible to avoid, but getting to that point at the current time seemed rather impossible. It was a matter she planned to discuss with Veran. The Priest was very wise and had been instrumental in aiding them in the transition.

She was sitting now with Ferran, laughing in a moment of downtime, about Ferran's last trip with a crew of disabled individuals to the sea.

"Did she really just jump in?" Cassava asked, laughing.

"She saw everyone else doing it and plum forgot she couldn't swim. It's fortunate I've learned and was able to assist."

"Water's a sight tricky if you've never experienced it."

"Yes, I remember," Ferran said, taking a sobering breath. "Have I thanked you recently, for saving my life?"

"Not too recently, no," Cassava teased with a smile. "And you and Henequen? How's that?" she asked.

Ferran blushed. "It's good," he said shortly. "Although he gets in his head about it sometimes—the whole seeing into my head bit. It doesn't bother me, but he sometimes decides he must run off to give my brain some space. Sometimes I worry there's something about my head that turns him off. Maybe my thoughts aren't good ones," Ferran said with a sigh.

"I wouldn't think so much about it," Cassava said. "Quen has always been a bit lost in his own head, perhaps he's just getting his thoughts straight from yours. It must be confusing to hear a voice saying I love you, and trying to decipher whether it's something he's thinking, something he's hearing, or something *your* thinking."

Ferran bit his lip. "You're probably right."

"Of course, I am. I'm very wise at all, being a member of the Black Council."

"You've got to find some other name for yourselves," Ferran said, "and another name for us as well."

"Yes, especially since I don't have to actually wear black all the time now. What a relief!" And it was—though Cassava still donned her cape when she went on official duty, she had taken to wearing red. There was something comforting about its sharp crimson color that made her feel vibrant and alive. Today she wore a dark blue top with a deep red skirt that came down just below her knees. It was a Triking fashion, one Xiben had let her borrow until she could trade for one of her own. It gave her pride to dress herself again, to get to take care in her appearance. There was nothing that could be done about her facial scars, but Cassava was looking forward to getting some of the eye shadow from the Trikingdom to take away from the scars and bring interest to her eyes and other unmarred parts of her face. Cassava was still working on accepting the damage done to her face. She wondered if Ferran felt the same way, but recalled that he had hardly known what he looked like until a very short time ago. He would have never seen himself unmarred; and his scars were older, lighter, and less obvious in many ways.

"Cassava?"

Cassava turned to see Xiben in the doorway. "Yes?"

"There's someone here to see you."

Cassava heaved a sigh. No doubt someone else come to complain about being mistreated. At least they were reporting it, she reflected. Some people, she knew, were not. They perhaps thought they deserved the poor treatment, and Cassava could only do so much to dissuade it. "The work never ends," she said with a sigh. "We'll catch up later."

Ferran gave her a hug. "I'm proud of you, Cassava."

Cassava smiled. "Thanks, Ferran. You're doing pretty well yourself." She got up and followed Xiben down the hall to the gates.

In the foyer, she saw the back of a young woman with long black hair and a moderately sized figure. She didn't recognize her as one of the former Sins who had come to her before, but she had not met everyone. Still, on this

Island she rather thought she would have noticed a woman like that. "Yes? How can I help you…" As Cassava spoke, the woman turned and Cassava was affronted by vivid flashes of memory and wholly reabsorbed into a heartache she thought she had quashed. There, in the halls of the Asylum, stood Visea Alrenti.

"Hi, Barli."

Cassava took a deep steadying breath. Visea was as beautiful as she remembered; a healthy figure, with weight to tug on and a good set of breasts, teeth straighter than the average person, a particularly long nose—for a Rhimeon at least—and almond eyes with just a touch of another color to them, one that could not be named but seemed inherent in their depths. She remembered touching that face with a gentle tracing hand, feeling her breath on her neck, the anticipatory moments when it had seemed they were about to kiss but hadn't…the heat of her skin, the softness of her eye, the strength of her arms that had held her when she cried. "W-what are you doing here?" Cassava asked, her voice shaking slightly.

"I wanted to see you," Visea said. "I heard you were here; a Black Sin now. Some people say all this madness is your doing."

"I played a role," Cassava said uncertainly. She wasn't sure how to react; Visea being here was nothing she had ever planned for. Once, Cassava had been desperate to leave this place just for the chance to see Visea again. But when she had finally had the opportunity to leave, Cassava hadn't taken it. She had been badly wounded by Visea, and even now seeing her made Cassava's arms itch where she had taken a knife to her body in an attempt not to think about Visea ever again because it was too painful. Now she was right there in front of her face.

A moment of panic seized her, and she stepped back from Visea, breathing hard and fast. She remembered Visea; she remembered how beautiful they had been together; she remembered all the pain her betrayal had caused her. Nimmory and her had shared no promises, had made no vows to each other. She and Visea had, and Visea had broken them. Visea could not be trusted.

"It's incredible, truly. I didn't think such a thing was possible," Visea said.

Cassava was having trouble focusing on what she was saying; it all sounded like gibberish, and none of it seemed to matter at all. Her chest was tight and she tried to take deeper breaths, to steady herself, but the room suddenly felt as though it was spinning. "What are you doing here?" Cassava asked again, fighting for her words.

"Barli? Are you okay?" Visea asked, taking several steps closer to her.

Cassava backed to a wall and tried to take comfort from its solid firmness, its structural integrity lent her some strength she desperately needed now. "I-I can't do this," she said.

Visea reached out and touched her, but Cassava recoiled like a snake. She reached out her hand and caught Visea's fingers. The touch seemed to burn. "Barli, please, let me help—"

"You-you can't help me," Cassava said through breaths that were quickly becoming fast and shallow. "You did this."

Visea pulled her hand back to her chest. "Barli, I only left you because I didn't want to lose you. I didn't want to lose you forever. I didn't know...I didn't know you'd end up there anyway."

"You knew I wasn't normal," Cassava said. "Didn't you know you were keeping me sane?"

Visea took a shuddering breath. "Maybe I did," she admitted, "maybe that's why I did it. I couldn't handle it anymore—being everything to you. It was one thing when we were friends, there was some distance between us, but then...I knew you were feeling more and—"

"You felt more too! Or do you deny it?"

Visea looked shocked for a moment before she bowed her head. "Yes, I felt it too, encouraged you when I shouldn't have. Suddenly, we were not only best friends, but secretly something more and you...you needed me so badly and I wasn't sure...I wasn't sure I could handle all that. But I didn't know how to back off a little, not the way you were. I thought a clean break would be better."

"You were wrong." Cassava said in between tense breaths. Her heart was racing in her chest, she felt it would fly out of her and she would drop dead the next moment.

Visea had a tear in her eye that she pushed away with her hand, her gesture hard and rushed. "Maybe I was. No, I was, I can see that now. I'm sorry. I wanted to take it back, but when I went to your parents they told me you were dead." Visea sniffled. "Please, Barli, let me help you."

This time when she moved closer, Cassava did not swat her away. Her hand on her shoulder felt like the sun's most direct ray, burning into her shoulder, but after the initial pain it dulled to a pained ache until it was almost healing, like a muscle that had been strained in exercise being treated by heat. Cassava began to cry in earnest then, unable to hold back her tears. Now that the worst of the fear had passed, her emotions bled through and dropped hot and heavy from her eyes.

"I'm so sorry, Barli. I am. I've been horrible, I know." Visea said. She took her other arm and pulled Cassava into her side. Cassava smelled Visea's perfume—a soft violet—remembering it before. The scent triggered many memories: Cassava crying on Visea when her father's ship had not been heard from in several days, Cassava massaging Visea's back after the two of them had been on a run together, Visea squashing a mosquito on Cassava's shoulder and then kissing it better. A warmth Cassava had forgotten radiated from her insides, and Cassava shuddered under their weight and import. Despite all she had done to get over Visea, a touch from her and the feelings and attachments were back.

"You left me," Cassava said. "You left and I needed you."

"I'm sorry," Visea replied. "I'll say it as many times as you need and hope one day you'll forgive me."

Cassava held Visea, and remembered all the times she had done so before. Visea had put on weight since she had known her, and Cassava had to readjust her somatic memory of how Visea felt to match this new but familiar person. "You hurt me. And I know, it wasn't all you, it's this thing in my head but...but it still feels an awful lot like you."

Visea kissed her forehead. "It may be too much for you

now. I'm sorry. I've been thinking about this moment for a while—a few days before I mustered up the courage to come here. It's not like I expected everything to be perfect. I just...wanted you to know that I'm here, and I'm proud, and I'd like to try again, if you're willing."

Cassava pulled back, drying her tears and looking Visea over again. Her hands were at her sides, willing and open, her stance tense but quiet. "I need some time," Cassava said.

"I'm still the same place, when you're ready," Visea said.

"You didn't settle down with some boy?"

"It made me sick to even try. After I thought I lost you...I wasn't much of someone to be around," Visea said.

"Cassava?" Xiben's voice came from surprisingly close; Cassava had not noticed the teen's approach. "It's time to shut the gate."

Cassava wiped her hands on her skirt and nodded, wishing she had something to blow her nose on. "Thank you for coming, Visea. Perhaps I'll see you again."

"I hope so," Visea said. "I really do hope we can be friends again."

Cassava nodded, though she was too disorganized in her feeling to have a particular feeling on that issue. "You have to go now," she said.

Visea nodded. She came in for one more quick but firm hug, before turning away. "I want to help," she said, "whatever you need."

"Thank you," Cassava said. She swung the gates closed slowly. It took her several tries to fit the key into the lock, but finally she did it and the gates clicked shut. Cassava collapsed to the ground in the aftermath and cried for some time, with Xiben awkwardly patting her shoulder.

After Cassava had recovered herself some, she made her way to her bedroom where she could puzzle without the prying and ever curious eyes of the Asylum's other residents. Cassava wasn't sure what she wanted, and that made it difficult to know what to do next.

Visea had betrayed her, betrayed her trust, taken away a support that Cassava had admittedly leaned very hard on. But she had never heard Visea's side of it before—how Visea had felt daunted by the prospect of being Cassava's one and only. And maybe Cassava had been unfair; she had laid a bigger burden on Visea than she had ever done to Ferran. They kept a healthy distance from each other, supported but did not live in the other's misery. That, Cassava thought, was the difference. She had been struggling even before Visea had called it quits—something she remembered now that Visea had spoken to her. Cassava had forgotten in all that had come after, how terrible she had felt...but it hadn't been Visea. Not in the beginning. It had been Cassava's illness, an illness neither she nor Visea could comprehend. Cassava was overwhelmed by it to the point of death; was it so shocking that to hold someone that close, they would feel it too?

Cassava could not decide if she was balancing things out properly; for a long time she had pined for Visea, not cared about her, and then, when she had recovered some, she had blamed Visea and vilified her. Now, Cassava began to try to strike some common ground. It would be a lengthy process, she thought, but perhaps it was possible.

Everything had felt so right taking Visea back into her arms, but it had stung at the same time and Cassava felt strongly that she would pay for a simple return to the way things were. Clearly, it hadn't been working.

Cassava was up late that night, thinking about Visea, how things had been, how they were now, and how they might be in the future. Nimmory had occasionally crossed her mind as well—Nimmory who had taken to her quickly like a fish to water, and who had vanished just as suddenly and completely. Would she come here, with their gift of freedom once the news reached her? And how would Cassava receive her? Nimmory had been her first girlfriend, her first real kiss with a girl, steps down the bases that had never quite materialized.

The next morning the Black Sins gathered for another meeting. Orantu gave his report on how collection was going, and mentioned an old tradition from before the institution of the Demon and the Priesthood that had once dazzled the Islands.

"What is this...circus?" Anelace asked, stumbling over the word in their unfamiliarity. New words were hard when you were profoundly deaf, but the others all had the same question and there was no judgment among the Black Sins.

"It was a gathering of spectacle—it was performed on boats brought near the docks, so that people could watch it from a distance and it was easy to carry between one Island and the next; it would tour between the Islands to present itself to each one in turn."

"What kind of spectacle?"

"Feats and talents of all sorts, entertainments of varying

kinds. Some showed their strength by lifting heavy things, others flexibility, others arts such as great paintings done, or plays put on."

"What's a play?" Henequen asked.

"It's where certain people portray a story for entertainment."

"Like a book?"

"Yes, but acted out, so it as if the people are doing the thing," Orantu said. "I have never seen one myself, but there are copies of very old plays in the library, and I think I have a sense of such things."

"I fail to see how this will bring everyone together," Dani said. "It sounds like a lot of fancifulness without any practicality."

"Yes, indeed. The point is to have a good time, and if people realize they can have a good time under these new circumstances, I believe it will improve relations as a whole."

Cassava could see the logic. "It's like dancing at a bar," she said, "when people do it together, good feeling just sort of radiates and everything seems like it will be alright."

Dani looked doubtful, but Arablest nodded her head slowly. "I could see it," she said, "we can show that we are more than killers. People will see we are not just instruments of the Priesthood gone rogue."

They voted to approve the circus, to begin in two weeks. They decided that the acts should be done by members of the Asylum, in a show of strength and humanization of the demonized. Word was promptly put out, and at once began different groups studying for their act; Anelace would throw knives, Dani and Arablest determined to do a strength act, and Jin declared he was writing and reciting a poem for Celeruit. Orantu made available these plays to the populace and took it upon himself to direct one or two shorter pieces for those interested. The members of the Asylum generally were a multi-talented crew, and Cassava anticipated a good show with them around to watch.

Cassava thought for some time about what she wanted to do. She had considered joining Anelace, but her knife work had never been as good, and Cassava wished to show something else about herself. Finally, she determined what she wanted to do. Now, all she needed was a partner.

Chapter Nineteen

Cassava woke up late the day of the circus. She had been up late last night practicing, and talking to Ferran. The two of them had been close to each other since they had gotten over their rocky road to friendship. Now that Ferran was able to be a full human being, their relationship had gotten even deeper. Cassava could talk to him about so many more things now that he understood things that had been beyond him before—friendships, relationships, purpose in life. These were all things he had been lacking.

Cassava had gotten clothes from the Trikingdom in the last shipment, and today she was wearing a rather slinky red dress. Sometimes she didn't want to be a Black Sin; she'd rather be bright and vibrant without a cloak and hood to hide her face. Cassava got ready slowly, applying blush to her cheeks and color to her eyes, blacking them with mascara and pulling the focus to their brown depths. She had to go to a special room in order to find a mirror that gave her the full view of her new purchase.

The dress was fitted at the top, just off the shoulder, and bunched at the side with a gold accent. Cassava gave herself another glance over in the mirror. She looked good, which wasn't something she had thought she would ever say again. But now she didn't hate the creature staring back at her in the mirror. She had been through a lot, and grown because of it. Some of it had been ugly, but that didn't mean Cassava had to be left behind that way.

There was a knock on her door. "Ready to go, Barli?"

Cassava opened the door to Henequen and Ferran. They were dressed both in neat tunics. Henequen had taken the black of the Sins and decked it out with blue accents. Ferran was dressed fully in blue, a well fit tunic that showed off his chest. Cassava smiled. It felt like they were headed somewhere truly fabulous, as honored guests, and it felt so good.

"Wow, Cassava. That's a different look," Henequen said.

"Thank you," she said, "but you haven't seen the Rabians yet. They are going all out."

They exited the Asylum together and walked together down the main street. Cassava felt occasional eyes on them, but most people were already down by the dock in order to get the best view. Those who remained were no doubt the most wary and would be hard pressed to change their minds over a single show. Still, Cassava had hope for the rest of the islanders.

They took long boats to the barge. Not a normal ship for the area, it was the only one in the Islands, and the Black Sins had commandeered it for this performance.

Cassava found her way back stage where many of her comrades were sitting. The color and energy was a sight to behold, and the former Sins, cheering and ragging on each other as they prepared to show themselves to the world, warmed Cassava's heart.

Finally, and at once too soon, the drums beat and it was time for the show to begin. Cassava looked about anxiously, but did not see her partner.

The show began with dramatics—Dani and Anelace began with a deadly show of force, just in case someone didn't believe the Black Sins were capable of great feats of danger. This was followed by a simply beautiful song sung by Arel. Cassava saw the shadows of the acts, cheering as Henequen and Ferran took the stage. Henequen announced himself as a magician, and proceeded to read people's minds to general amazement and a little bit of fear. Ferran meanwhile did sketches of the audience members who participated and gave them the pictures as souvenirs.

A small hand touched Cassava's shoulder and she turned. "Hey. Sorry I'm late. I broke a string right before I had to leave," Visea said, sitting down beside her.

Cassava smiled. "The best is yet to come," she said. Visea sat about a foot away from Cassava, but as the acts wore on the distance somehow closed until they were knee to knee. Then the gong sounded again and Cassava got to her feet. "It's time," she said.

Cassava stepped out into the stage. There were still cheers from the last act, and they buoyed Cassava as she faced the crowd. Cassava had never done this before—put herself so vulnerable before so many others. Her stomach felt tight in a way she hadn't felt in a long time, since she was a small child. Cassava had never been given overly to nerves, but for a moment they held her enraptured. Then the familiar chords strummed and Cassava was taken by the music.

She began to move; her feet knew the steps and they moved without her needing to think about it. Cassava thought about the majesty of this moment: the Islands turned out to watch a nobody like Cassava dance. The wonder gave her power and she felt herself grow stronger in her steps, her arms as she swept became more bold and strong.

All too soon it was over and Cassava could hear only the claps and cheers of the crowd. Exhilarated, Cassava swept into a bow and then pointed toward Visea standing there with her violin, who also took a little bow.

At the intermission, Cassava took a boat back to the mainland with Visea and they hunted for a good spot to see the show. Finding none, Cassava promptly broke into a warehouse and climbed to its loft, pulling Visea with her. As they settled together, Cassava did not relinquish Visea's hand and they sat side by side as the Rabians had their turn.

It is hard to describe a magic show that utilizes actual magic. People flew through the air in graceful leaps in time to music, objects floated up along with them and streamers flew from their hands and up into the sky. At the finale, bursts of color took the stage, and fired up over their heads, raining down showers of color.

The crowd was on their feet below them, cheering and clapping in a great chorus. And it seemed then as if everything would be alright.

About Jacyn Gormish

Jacyn Gormish (they/them) lives in Minnesota with their wife, dog, cat, and a whole lot of fish. They are disabled, neurodivergent, non-binary, and still growing into and learning all those identities. They are dedicated to providing more queer and disabled main characters to their genres of choice. They don't tend to be very active on social media, but you can sign up for updates @jacyngormish on instagram.

Books by Jacyn Gormish
The Mark of Ravage and Ruin
The Mark of Silence and Secrets

Also from Deep Hearts YA

Stone Feather Fang
A.G. Rodriguez

The gods—the cemi—have left the world of Ke', and their lush and verdant Andolin Islands are now inhabited by impious followers.

Teenage priestess Hildy Rios is tasked with saving her religion. In a special ritual called the Telling, she must somehow reawaken her people's love of the gods. Her effort is the last hope of her people: after this Telling, there will be no more chances, as the cemi will vanish into the past, their power forever lost to the world of Ke'.

The weight of her world on her shoulders, Hildy rewrites the Telling's story—and her own. She weaves a tale of her distant ancestor, a boy named Jenaro, blessed with the ability to see and speak to the cemi; a boy who, though long past, becomes as much a part of the present by way of the Telling's power.

For three days, Hildy brings to life the tale of Jenaro and his yearning for adventure, how he is haunted by the cemi of death, and who—like her—is fighting against the shackles of his family and society. For three days, Jenaro becomes real, and the power of the cemi to reach across time should be enough to convince Ke's people, but their impiety runs so deep…

Hildy and Jenaro. Two people joined by cursed blood, but separated by centuries of time. Only the cemi know how their tales will end.

Available now in ebook and paperback

Also from Deep Hearts YA

Cage of Nightingales
Elizabeth Hopkinson

Two boys. One meek, one rebellious. Both discover a power that will set them free…or sever them.

In a highly structured eighteenth-century society, the city-state of Angelio is known for two things: its music and its guardian, the Archangel Michael.

At Angelio's music school—nicknamed the Cage of Nightingales—castrato singer Carlo is destined for fame at the opera…at the price of his freedom. Charity pupil Tammo hates the school and the restrictive future it offers, dreaming instead of escaping to live in the woods to charm birds with his flute.

When Tammo meets Carlo, their lives change forever. With the Archangel's help, they are granted the power to fulfil each other's deepest desires—but every gift demands a price.

As music opens doors to a glittering world beyond the Cage, the bond between them is tested by ambition, longing, and the fragile promises they have made. And their choices will shape not just their futures, but that of Celestina—a young aristocrat who will become entwined in their lives in ways neither of them can foresee.

Cage of Nightingales is a story of found family, and queer identity—featuring a tender portrayal of an asexual, nonbinary eunuch at its heart.

Available now in ebook and paperback

www.ingramcontent.com/pod-product-compliance
Lightning Source LLC
Chambersburg PA
CBHW030126010826
48973CB00002B/439